20 OCT 1997

The Hangman

Gavin Newman

PIATKUS

This one for Lisa Roberts

Copyright © 1994 by Gavin Newman

First published in Great Britain in 1994 by
Judy Piatkus (Publishers) Ltd of
5 Windmill Street, London W1

**The moral right of the author
has been asserted**

*A catalogue record for this book is available
from the British Library*

ISBN 0 7499 0238 8

Phototypeset in 11/12pt Compugraphic Times by
Action Typesetting Limited, Gloucester
Printed and bound in Great Britain by
Bookcraft (Bath) Ltd.

'Dislocation of the neck is the ideal to be aimed at.'

Handbook on Hanging
by Charles Duff (Andrew Melrose, 1928).

'The threat of capital punishment is often sufficient of a deterrent to persuade even the most hardened evil-doer that he would do well to consider mending his ways lest the full majesty of the law fall upon him with dreadful power.'

Spare the Noose and Other Essays
by Trevor St John Newhey (Northern Authors, 1897).

'I know but one truth about the hemp collar. No man I hanged ever came back to harm another soul.'

Tom Hoyle – Frontier Hangman
(privately printed in New Rochdale, Nova Scotia, 1906).

Prologue

'Lawrence, *do* hurry up and clear your things away, Daddy will be home for his lunch soon, and you know how cross he gets if the place is in a mess!'

Emily Prendergast peered round the door into the spacious dining room where her eight-year-old son had happily busied himself throughout this atrociously wet morning. A combination of lead toy soldiers and cowboys and indians littered the floor and cardboard boxes had been arranged to represent a shanty town in a game which embodied both system and imagination. An open comic book lay nearby; it obviously had some influence on the game-playing.

'Just another five minutes, *please*!' The youngster looked up, his blue eyes pleading. His brown hair had a short back and sides cut and he wore a grey flannel suit with short trousers and matching knee-length socks: this was his preparatory school uniform and school was where he should have been today if he hadn't been sick at half-past eight precisely, just as Emily was about to back the car out of the garage to take him.

She'd heard the upstairs toilet flush, shouted to him from the foot of the stairs to get a move on or else he'd be late for school. Then he had appeared on the landing, retching and crying. His performance hadn't seemed wholly convincing, any other time she would have insisted that he went to school. But today just happened to be an exception. She didn't fancy the drive into the city in this torrential rain, which probably wouldn't let up all day. Lawrence didn't look very ill, but you could never be sure with children.

A single day at home today might save a whole week off school.

Bill wouldn't approve. He thought that one should overcome all maladies by grit and determination, stick it out unless you were practically dying. She had only known her husband be off work once in fifteen years and that was when he had had an impacted wisdom tooth extracted and they had kept him in hospital overnight. Even then he had threatened to discharge himself. He certainly would not be pleased to discover Lawrence at home, even less so to find him playing with his toys.

'Lawrence ... I think perhaps you ought to go up to your bedroom.'

'Oh, *no*, Mummy!'

'Just while your father has his lunch. He has to be back at the bank by two o'clock, so you can come downstairs again then.'

'*Please*, Mummy!'

'Oh, all right. But get these toys put away as fast as you can. You know that Daddy's always in a bad mood when he comes home at lunchtime.'

Reluctantly, petulantly, the boy began to toss lead models into one of the boxes. 'I hate Daddy.' His mutterings were barely audible but she heard them nonetheless. 'He doesn't like me playing with *anything*.'

Emily was tense; she always was at this time of day. It had been the same since the day they had returned from their honeymoon. Every morning Bill awoke in a bad temper, performed his ablutions and ate his cooked English breakfast in silence whilst she hovered around him, pandering to his every whim, however outrageous or unreasonable. After the slamming of the front door as he left for work, came the welcome relief of a few hours' respite until he returned for lunch.

After lunch his mood seemed to change and he became almost tolerable. In the evenings he was fine – most evenings, anyway. Possibly the daytime irritability had something to do with the tensions of his job, the responsibilities of running a bank. A disciplinarian at both home and office, he was disliked, even feared, by his staff.

At least Glenn, their elder son, was well out of it now, Emily thought, spending nine months of the year at boarding school. Initially, she had worried about him leaving home but he had settled in right from the first day. He had probably been glad to get away. But there would be further problems when Glenn finished his schooling. William was determined that both his sons would follow him into banking and already Glenn was resisting the idea. It all made life so stressful, so worrying.

'Lawrence, do hurry up. What on earth are you doing?'

She popped her head round the door again. Most of the toys were in the box but Lawrence was engrossed under the dining table where a number of mounted models were arrayed in a circle. One of the lead figures had a length of string attached to its neck, swung from a supporting strut.

'I won't be a minute, Mummy. This is the killer, the bank robber. He's got to be lynched.'

'Lawrence, how dreadful! Come along, now, Daddy will be here any minute!'

The child had some unhealthy preoccupation with hanging; every game he played seemed to end with one. That dreadful sideshow at the church garden fete had obviously preyed on his mind: pay tuppence and watch a model of Hitler swing from the gallows. Most of the children had taken one appalled look and wandered away, but Lawrence had insisted on watching the morbid ritual, time after time. Finally Bill had decided he'd spent enough money and had dragged his protesting son away. Moments later, the vicar, accompanied by a group of outraged parents, had come bustling along to close the sideshow down. Of course, he should never have allowed such a disgraceful peepshow to take place at all. Emily had been horrified when Bill brought the contraption home a few weeks later, having been given it by the fellow running the sideshow. When the opportunity presented itself, she had secretly put it in the dustbin.

'That's it! He's dead!' A cry of infant exultation, a clapping of hands. 'Now I'll pack everything away.'

'Too late!' Emily strode across to the window, saw a beige Morris Oxford pulling into the driveway. 'Daddy's already here.'

The front door banged and she heard her husband in the hallway, hanging his coat and hat on the stand. Then the dining room door was flung wide and William Prendergast stood there, his cheeks flushed, lips a tight line.

He was an older, grimmer version of his son, his hair shorn back and sides, the remainder brushed austerely back, shiny with Brylcreem. He was slightly overweight, his menacing bulk suited to the heavy tweed suit which he wore like a skin. His gaze alighted on Lawrence crawling from beneath the table.

'What on earth's that boy doing here, Emily? Why isn't he at school? And what's he doing under the table?'

Emily took a deep breath, her clasped hands trembling slightly. 'He was sick just as I was getting ready to take him to school.'

'He probably shoved his finger down his throat and you fell for it! He looks perfectly all right to me. If he's ill, then he should be in bed. Are you ill, Lawrence?'

The boy gulped. 'I still feel sick.'

'Well in that case you won't be wanting any lunch. You can sit up at the table and watch us eat.'

Emily never protested; it never achieved anything, only serving to make the situation worse.

'Lawrence, go through and wash your hands, then come back and sit at the table like your father says.'

Lawrence ran to obey without question. William laid his daily newspaper on the table, lifted the chequered cloth and bent to peer beneath it.

'Cowboys and indians, eh! And one of them is a victim of a necktie party by the look of it!' He let the cloth fall back, straightened up. His features were even redder.

'It's unhealthy.' Emily turned back from the doorway; the lamb chops smelled ready and she didn't want them to burn.

'It demonstrates a respect for law and order, a fitting sense of justice,' William Prendergast answered, shuffling round to take his place at the head of the table. 'I hope lunch is ready. I've got an appointment at two.'

Lunch was always a silent and solemn affair, whether Emily and her husband ate on their own or both boys were home. You didn't speak unless William spoke to you: to break that rule was inviting trouble. He did not like his concentration broken whilst he read his paper, demanding also absolute attention when he commented upon some item of news.

Lawrence sat up straight in his chair, hands folded in his lap, staring at the place mat in front of him. He was starving, but his mother would rectify that once his father had gone back to the bank.

Emily picked at her small portion. She was on edge, glancing from Lawrence to the newspaper propped up against the vegetable dishes behind which her husband devoured his food ravenously whilst he read. Any second his head might appear over the top of the printed page to glower disapprovingly at either of them.

'Anything interesting in the paper, dear?' She was mistress of the diplomatic approach. It might lure Bill into a civil conversation or he would just grunt. She didn't really mind which.

'John Christie has been found guilty of murder.' William Prendergast's head appeared over the top of the newspaper, his expression smug, almost gloating. Sentenced to hang!'

Emily winced, glanced protectively at Lawrence but her son appeared to have overcome his nervousness. There was an eagerness about him that was disconcerting.

'They're going to hang somebody, Daddy?'

His father smirked, folded his newspaper and pushed it to one side. 'A murderer! The trial has been going on for some time. Everybody knew that he was guilty, but a jury's verdict is always unpredictable. Thank God they saw sense in this instance. The man had killed several women – you're far too young to know why – but he will pay the supreme penalty for his crimes. His hanging will act as a deterrent to others. Without the rope, none of us would be safe.'

'How do they hang somebody, Daddy?'

'Lawrence!' Emily's voice was shrill. 'It's not something that a boy of your age should know anything about.'

'On the contrary.' William Prendergast fixed his wife with a stony stare. 'It should be part of a child's education. They should be made to realise at an early age that the law says a life for a life, that if they kill another human being when they grow up, they will be deprived of their own.'

'How *do* they hang people, Daddy?'

'In much the same way that your toy cowboy is hanging under the table right now! Except that it is far more terrible than simply being caught and crudely strung up, as used to happen in the Wild West. In this country, once the murderer is found guilty, he is taken to the death cell. Oh, he knows full well what his fate will be! Sometimes he has to wait weeks for the execution. That's all part of the punishment process – it puts the fear of God into him, makes him realise what a dreadful thing he has done.'

'I'll go and fetch the pudding.' Emily left the table hurriedly but her husband was too engrossed in his lecture on execution even to notice.

'Then comes the fateful day. The condemned man is awoken early, allowed to choose what he wants for breakfast. The hangman has already visited him, measured and weighed him: a good hanging hinges on that, because the executioner must know exactly what thickness of rope to use and how far to drop him. A prison padre then comes to the cell and tries to comfort him, prays to God that He will forgive him. But I wouldn't think even He would forgive a murderer. Would you?'

Lawrence shook his head, wide-eyed.

'Some call it the 'Eight O'clock Walk' – the slow procession of warders, hangman, padre and, of course, the condemned man from the cell to the gallows. They put a hood over the man's head. Then he's made to stand on the trapdoor over the drop, and the executioner slips the noose around his neck. The hangman pulls a lever which opens the trapdoor and' – Prendergast clapped his hands loudly with a resounding crack – 'that's it. The murderer plunges downwards and his neck snaps.'

'What do they do with the body afterwards?'

Emily appeared in the doorway, carrying a dessert bowl in each hand. She shuddered; one of the bowls almost slipped from her fingers but she just made it to the table in time.

'Bill, don't you think this is rather morbid? Lawrence will be having nightmares.'

'I won't!' Lawrence banged his fists on the table gleefully, rattling plates and cutlery. 'I may dream about it, but I won't have nightmares!'

'It's barbaric.' Emily Prendergast seated herself but made no move to pick up her spoon. 'Treacle tart, Bill – your favourite.'

'Wonderful!' He spooned some greedily into his mouth. 'Now, where did we get to, Lawrence?' Emily watched, sickened, as his powerful jaws masticated the tart.

'What do they do with the body afterwards, Daddy?'

'Ah, good question. I like somebody who asks intelligent questions! They don't bury it in a churchyard like you might suppose. What self-respecting person wants to be buried in a cemetery next to a murderer? They dig a grave, usually on unconsecrated land, and drop the hanged body in. Then they tip quicklime over it – '

'What's quicklime, Daddy?'

'Much like the lime I use on the garden – it might even be the same, for all I know. Anyway, it makes the corpse rot down that much quicker, gets rid of it. The grave remains unmarked, of course. And that's about all there is to it.'

'I'll start the washing up.' Emily stacked plates, put her untouched bowl of treacle tart on the top. If Lawrence had some kind of stomach virus that had made him sick that morning then maybe he'd passed it on to her. She felt decidedly queasy.

William glanced at the clock on the mantle shelf. 'Good Lord, it's ten to two already, I'll have to get a move on. Lawrence,' he looked back into the dining room as he shrugged on his overcoat, 'just remember what I said – no more of this dodging school. You'll go in the morning whether you're sick or not, understand?'

Lawrence nodded. He didn't like his father, but he was glad that he had stayed off school. He had learned a lot of interesting things today that his teachers would never have told him.

Emily finished washing the dishes, dried them and hung the cloth on the rail over the open range. She had not realised previously just how obsessed her husband was with the death penalty. Hanging was something that she accepted as an unpleasant truth; she certainly did not wish to know the gory details. But William had revelled in explaining an execution to their son – and Lawrence had hung on to his every word with a fascination quite inappropriate to a child.

She opened the oven door. The third lamb chop looked a bit dried up, but maybe he would eat it.

'Lawrence? Do you want some lunch now?'

There was no answer.

'Lawrence? Are you all right?' Perhaps he really hadn't been well this morning.

There was still no reply from the dining room. Could he have fallen asleep? She had better check.

'Lawrence ...' She flung the dining room door wide, then stood and stared in horrified amazement. The boy had dragged his toy boxes out from under the table; the boxes contained a mixture of lead models and wooden bricks that he had used since infancy. Sometimes the bricks were built up into stockades for the cowboys to defend against a circle of attacking indians. Right now, though, he was using the blocks for an entirely different purpose.

Lawrence had constructed a platform and gallows with a drop beneath it. A cork beer mat was the trapdoor, a battered and scratched model of a tin soldier, standing to attention, with a string noose around its neck, stood upon it.

'Lawrence! No!'

Too late. The length of string was taut, twisting; the model soldier had disappeared down into the well beneath.

Lawrence was oblivious of his mother's presence. He laughed loudly, clapped his hands the way his father had done, and hauled the dangling soldier back up for a repeat performance.

Emily hated her husband right then, more than she had ever dared to do in the past. And she was frightened: not simply of William but of what he had done to their son.

Chapter One

'I am the resurrection and the life, saith the Lord: he that believeth in me, though he were dead, yet shall he live: and whosoever liveth and believeth in me shall never die.'

The congregation in the packed village church rose to their feet as though by numbers from the front, as if prodded by an invisible hand. For most of them it was a social occasion: they had meticulously spelt out their names to the local press reporter on their arrival, repeated it so that he got it right. That was most important, that they were known to have paid their last respects to the recently departed. When the deceased was your former bank manager, you wanted his successor to know that your loyalty did not end with his retirement.

In a small community such things mattered.

All eyes glanced sideways at the bier, wondered what William Prendergast looked like now: frail, insignificant in his shroud, no longer any use to anybody. He had retired twenty years ago, but had continued to make his dominating presence felt, until the onset of his first stroke two years ago. His widow, Emily, bore the stamp of his last long illness, the months of tending him, the tolerance of his return to childhood, his ramblings and incontinence. Her slim figure was stooped and she wept behind her veil, clutching the arm of her elder son.

Glenn's expression was stoic, camouflaged by his bushy black beard. Of indeterminable age, some suspected that he disguised the grey flecks in his hair; but those who remembered him as a boy, scrumping apples from the church orchard, knew he was around forty. Powerfully built, he seemed out of context in the dark suit which he kept just for funerals: a farmer who wore working clothes seven days a week never adapted to formal wear.

His wife attracted some curious gazes; she wasn't from these parts; small and attractive, she was an 'outsider' and nothing could excuse her from that. Her solemn expression seemed a well-rehearsed act; she wasn't grieving. She had nothing to mourn.

The younger son, Lawrence, was bigger than any of them, his late father's suit strained at the seams. Tall and grossly overweight, he must have weighed at least seventeen stones. His unkempt brown hair had been combed as an afterthought in the funeral car, but the strong December wind had nullified his efforts. His shoes were dull and unpolished, the heels trapping the turn-ups of his trousers at every other step; his stomach bulged over his waistband. His tie was askew; there were food stains on his ill-matching blue shirt.

Although only five or six years younger than his brother, Lawrence's fleshy features aged him beyond his years. Slouching, reminiscent of a spoiled child compelled to go on an outing with his parents against his wishes, he scowled; but there were no tears in his narrowed eyes. William Prendergast had enjoyed some limited success with Lawrence: unquestioning, the younger son had followed his father into the banking profession, although Lawrence Prendergast would never aspire to managerial status. No, he would remain amongst the faceless ones. It was best that way.

Lawrence fidgeted in his pew, wiping a shoe on the back of his rumpled trousers under the seat: a public school habit, dating back to the time when chapel prefects had checked footwear for cleanliness after the service, meting out punishments for dirty shoes.

Emily leaned against Glenn. She wouldn't faint: she was made of sterner stuff. Her overwhelming feeling was one of relief at the blessing of her release from nursing an imbecile to his grave. Her husband's retirement had been an ordeal lasting two decades for her; it would take time to come to terms with freedom. There were rumours in the village of how he had cut off her promising literary career in its prime, forbidden her to attend writers' circles; rumours too of his skill at emotional blackmail, feigning the symptoms of a heart attack, sitting with closed eyes and a hand pressed to his chest whenever any of the family dared to argue with him.

They were only rumours, though. But they were remembered at a time like this.

'Man that is born of woman hath but a short time to live ...'

Lawrence had not bowed his head. Instead his thick neck was thrust forward, as he stared at the coffin, draped with a masonic flag. None could see his expression.

He felt decidedly strange. Everything seemed unreal, like the sensation which preceded a bout of influenza: a feverishness, a distortion of vision. There were whisperings all around from the congregation.

'*They hanged him, you know.*'
'*Who?*'
'*William Prendergast.*'

Lawrence experienced a surge of excitement, a sensation that bordered on the orgasmic. *Hanged*!

It was ridiculous, of course; he had been told that his father's death had been the result of the lengthy disintegration of mind and body. But they *had* taken William Prendergast away a few weeks ago ... They said it was to the hospital, because Emily Prendergast was no longer able to nurse her husband.

They *said* ...

Realisation had Lawrence's pulses racing, his heartbeat quickening. He didn't want to know what his father had been guilty of; that was irrelevant. Suffice it to say that he somehow knew they had taken William Prendergast away and hanged him.

Lawrence trembled violently with excitement. He wished that he'd been there to watch the execution. He envisaged William Prendergast being supported on the gallows by the outstretched arms of prison warders who took care to stand clear of the trapdoor. His father would have been unrecognisable as the man who had dominated his childhood, his once bulky body now frail and wasted, his features hidden behind a black hood.

A padre muttered from a prayer book, gabbling the words, rushing to proceed to the important part. The hangman stood motionless in his dark suit and matching homburg, his features were in shadow.

Lawrence clutched at the pew. Just a fantasy ... How he prayed that it might be real! He held his breath, feeling dizzy, his vision fogged so that he was unable to see. He heard a clang as the trapdoor dropped, swung and hit the side of the well – a crack like the dislocation of a neck.

For God's sake, let me see! Now, as his vision cleared, he stared searchingly at the coffin on the bier before the altar. He had stopped shaking, his excitement replaced by a feeling of disappointment. He had made a determined effort to convince himself that this funeral was a charade and he had failed.

Lawrence bitterly regretted the abolition of the death penalty. He had often dreamed of becoming an executioner, a hangman, in the same way that some young boys longed to become engine drivers. He still thought about it in idle moments, particularly when, from time to time, there was a public outcry over some especially brutal murder. If there was a referendum, the rope would be brought back without any shadow of a doubt. It was all these do-gooders in parliament who voted against it, because they were frightened of death. Frightened that one day they too might swing.

If hanging was returned, Lawrence would apply for the job of hangman: he promised himself that. He might well get it, too, because folks were squeamish when it came to killing. They demanded a life for a life but they weren't prepared to do the job themselves. Like those who ate meat so long as it came ready dressed and packaged from the supermarket.

Lawrence felt mentally and physically drained. It was as much as he could do to rise to his feet as the congregation stood and began to file through the doors at the back of the church. Outside there was a hint of sleet in the rain; the punters were confident of a white Christmas.

The church walkway was crowded right down to the

lychgates; beyond, a single-file procession fought against the elements. The cemetery was beyond the line of Scots pines and the freshly-dug grave lay ready just inside the gate. There was room for about another two dozen graves before the graveyard was full; William Prendergast had timed his death to ensure him a place in the original nineteenth-century burial ground. Some were walking away towards the car park, glancing furtively back; a graveside procession was not worth the reward of tea and sandwiches back at the big house afterwards. Nobody would notice their absence.

'We therefore commit his body to the ground, earth to earth, ashes to ashes, dust to dust.'

Emily dropped a red rose into the gaping oblong hole, might have fallen if Glenn had not been holding her firmly. He threw his flower with his left hand; the wind took it and it hit the side of the excavation and dropped down.

Lawrence moved surreptitiously away from his mother and her elder son, away from the vicar. He leaned over the grave awkwardly, his left hand cupped to shield his face from the onlookers.

He spat directly upon the coffin.

Emily Prendergast made a brave effort to celebrate Christmas that year, for the sake of her grandchildren. If she wept, then it was alone; but the prospect of January and February, the bleakest of the winter months, was daunting. Selfishly, she was glad that Lawrence had never married. At least he would be returning home from his job at a bank in the city each evening. And there were always Glenn's fortnightly visits to look forward to. He never failed to make the trip over from his small farm, battling through in the Land Rover if the weather was bad. Most of the time he was here was spent doing odd jobs; gardening, mainly. Lawrence never did any odd jobs, never had. It wasn't his nature and he wasn't going to change at thirty-four.

Neither of the boys had been close to their father, but that had been William's fault. Banking was his life and he had wanted both his sons to follow in his profession; Glenn had tried it, given it a few years and then opted for a sparse hill farm. He had made a go of it, too, capitalised on the trend towards organic growing, but his father resented his independence and success. Lawrence, however, for so many years the shy, overweight failure, had pleased his father by somehow sticking to banking against all odds. But even then William Prendergast wasn't satisfied. The boy should have been looking towards promotion, not wasting a promising career in a large city branch, lost amidst a large staff, hiding his shortcomings in a crowd. And Emily was painfully aware that her younger son was a social misfit, an introvert who immersed himself in amateur photography and fantasised about owning a high street studio. It would never happen, of course; Lawrence simply didn't have the confidence.

For so many years Emily had pandered to William's every whim, forced herself to believe that he was right. It *would* have been selfish of her to persevere with her writing against her husband's wishes. He was the master of the house, he had given her status, provided for her. You accepted that in your marriage vows: to love, honour and obey. She had done just that, and had sacrificed her younger son for it.

But now William was dead, she refused to admit defeat. She wasn't going to sell up as several of her widowed friends had done. The house was large, in its own grounds on the edge of the village overlooking rolling countryside. It would have fetched a high price; she could have banked a few thousand and bought a luxury bungalow. But at sixty-six she still had a lot of living to do. William had left her well provided for; she would travel, visit exotic places ... The last time they had been on holiday was that fortnight they'd had at Lyme Regis when Lawrence was fourteen. Two weeks of cloudless skies, blue sea and golden beaches, and William had made it a misery for all of them.

But Emily would stay put for the time being. She had to get over her husband's death, and that would take time. She still woke up in the night, thinking that she heard him calling for her – Dr Marsh said that happened to most bereaved women. She thought about writing that book she had drafted out thirty years ago, set in Ancient Greece; she would try to pick up the threads again. There was an awful lot she could find to do. William was gone; and in his place she had her freedom.

Lawrence should have started back at the bank on the day after Boxing Day. Emily had slept late that day, hadn't awoken until after nine; there was nothing to get up for, it had snowed overnight and she wouldn't risk taking the car into the city.

It wasn't until midday that she heard her son moving about upstairs. It puzzled her a little; but perhaps he had a day off, some holiday due to him.

'Are you all right, Larry?' She had taken to calling him Larry ever since William had had his stroke, it created an artificial closeness, a maternal intimacy which she badly needed.

'I'm okay.' He appeared at the top of the stairs, clad in a torn pullover and faded jeans. He obviously wasn't going to the bank. There was defiance in his posture, his tone of voice: *Try making me go, Mother.*

'Oh ... That's fine, then. I just wondered ...'

'No need to.' His reply was abrupt. 'Like I said, I'm okay.' He turned back onto the landing and she heard the click of the spare bedroom door; Larry had been using it as a darkroom for some time. Obviously he intended to spend the day messing about with his photographs.

Lawrence stayed at home on the following day, too. Still Emily was not unduly concerned; somehow her son had managed to wangle a longer Christmas break than usual. Anyway, he was better off in the warm this weather.

The following day was Saturday and Lawrence spent most of it in his photographic retreat: Sunday, too. He had prepared his own food since his father's death; in the beginning that had been hurtful, a kind of rejection of her maternal duties, but she had come to accept it. Yet although he didn't appear to over-eat, he was still putting on weight, and that was worrying.

She barely saw him over the weekend. On Monday morning he still didn't get his car out of the garage to go to work. The snow had melted, so there was no reason for him to stay at home; unless he were ill, of course. Could he be grieving secretly for his father? She had to find out what was the matter.

'Larry?' She stood on the landing. 'Larry, aren't you going to work today? It's Monday.' Perhaps he had forgotten which day of the week it was.

She heard the bedsprings creak as his heavy body turned over, listened for the sound of bare feet padding on the frayed carpet, the rustle of hastily donned clothes. But there was only silence.

She remembered the difficulty she had had getting him up every morning when he was at school. Sometimes she had had to plead with him, threatening to call his father; that had usually worked. But it wouldn't work now.

She moved towards his bedroom door, noticing that it was wedged open with a book, enabling her to see inside. He had changed the position of the bed; it now stood in the centre of the room with the back of the headboard towards the doorway. That in itself created the effect of chaos, not to mention the general untidiness of the rest of the room. The curtains remained closed.

Emily cleared her throat. Without actually going inside it was impossible to see whether or not her son was still in bed.

'Larry?' Her voice was timid. 'Larry, you'd better get up. It's time to go to work.'

The bed creaked; she heard a guttural grunt.

'Mind you don't go back to sleep.'

'Just leave me in peace, will you?'

'It's Monday morning, Larry.'

'I know what fucking day it is!'

She gasped. He had never spoken to her like that before. 'Larry!'

'Just leave me alone!' the bedsprings creaked again but he made no move to get up.

'Aren't you going into the bank today?' She found that she had stepped back involuntarily, her voice a whisper. Perhaps she had not heard right.

'No, I'm not!'

'But why?'

'Go *away*!'

Her breathing was constricted; she felt a little faint. 'Larry, *please!*'

It must be a reaction from his father's death. Even though there had been no love lost between them, he must have been affected by it.

She had to bear with him.

'Have you got some holiday due to you?'

'No. Why?'

'Well ... The bank might ring up to see where you've got to.' *And to ask why you weren't in last week, either.*

'If they do, tell 'em to mind their own bloody business.'

'Larry, I can't do that. You know I can't.'

'Then don't answer the phone.'

Suppose William had been alive to hear! Emily began to tremble. Turning, she made her way shakily downstairs. Just as she reached the hallway the telephone began to ring: harsh and shrill, demanding to be answered. She found herself cowering from it, backing into the kitchen.

It had to be the bank calling to know why Lawrence had not been into work, why he hadn't phoned. She could have lied, told them he was ill — but she couldn't go on lying indefinitely.

She knew then that he would never be going to work again.

Chapter Two

'Are you quite sure you're all right, Emily?'

Joyce Barron smoothed her hands along her bulky thighs, a subconscious attempt to push her tight-fitting tweed skirt down to hide her fat legs. She always did that when she crossed one leg over the other. Then she adjusted her rimless spectacles, checked the grey bun of hair on the back of her head. A smile that was no more than a stretching of the lips designed to put the other at ease. *Come on, tell me what's going on here. I'm dying to know.*

'I'm fine. Really, I am.' Emily lifted the lid of the teapot, hoping the tea might have run out so that she would have an excuse to go through to the kitchen to boil the kettle. A diversion, but it wouldn't be any good because the Reverend Ken Barron's widow would follow her, keep up that incessant chatter, open cupboards and look inside drawers. Fifty years on she was no different from when Emily had first known her, an insatiable curiosity that transcended etiquette.

'But the place is in such a *mess*!' Joyce waved a hand in the direction of the piles of magazines and books which were stacked untidily along the skirting boards; and when floor space had run out the journals had been piled on every chair except the two which she and Emily occupied. Rolls of camera film were heaped on the sideboard; the pile of photographic equipment on the table had been pushed to one side to make way for the tea tray. 'Goodness, doesn't your cleaning lady ever tidy up?'

'I don't have Mrs Clifford any longer.' The hand which

poured the tea trembled slightly, so that liquid splashed the saucer. 'She left just after Bill died – she was over seventy then.'

'But surely there's somebody else who could come and do for you?' Incredulity that was in itself a remonstration. 'I mean, you can't be expected to cope on your own in a house this size!'

'I don't want anybody else. I can't be bothered with somebody coming in.'

'Which is why the place is like it is! Goodness me, doesn't Lawrence do any housework?'

'He's too busy.' This was all leading round to Larry. Everybody was asking what Larry did these days.

'I think he was very foolish to leave the bank.' It was as though her late husband was speaking: *You should never have allowed the boy to leave the bank, Emily.* 'I mean, a nine till five job in convivial surroundings, a good salary and a pension at the end of it. I just wish Ken had worked in a bank – I'd be a lot better off now than I am. So what's Lawrence doing these days?'

'Photography.' Emily passed a cup and a saucer across the table, did not elaborate. She would try to side-step the barrage of questions one at a time.

'Oh, what sort? Portraits? Where's his studio?'

'He works from home, does quite a lot for picture libraries. Mostly magazine covers – views and the like.'

'How nice,' Joyce's eyes were unblinking behind her lenses. 'I suppose the whole house is taken over by it, that's why it's in such a mess. If I were you dear, I'd make him clear it all up, get himself *organised.* Better still, make him rent some premises somewhere. Homes aren't made to be turned into workplaces. Now that Ken's passed on, I spend a lot of time in the reading room at our local library. They get most of the magazines in there, but I don't think I've ever seen one with a cover photograph by Lawrence.'

'Well – er – sometimes they don't give credits. And when they do it's often in small print on the inside.' Emily bitterly resented Joyce's intrusion; she pried into everybody's private life. She regretted letting the late vicar's widow call round.

It had been just the same when the Reverend Barron had been alive: Joyce had upset all the parishioners, offended the Mothers' Union and the Women's Institute and made herself thoroughly unpopular; but she was too brazen and conceited to believe that anybody could possibly really dislike her. When her husband had been offered a large parish up north, the villagers had urged him to take promotion, feigned sadness at his departure. But they hadn't got rid of Ken and Joyce. Oh, no. Every few months the pair had returned to the village, planned their itinerary of calls so that they were assured of two meals a day and afternoon tea in between. Of course, it wasn't scrounging because everybody missed them, was delighted to see them. And Mrs Smithson was only too pleased to put them up at short notice; except that the elderly widow's arthritis was beginning to take its toll and she couldn't cope any longer. Which meant that Joyce needed fresh accommodation for future visits.

'I could have a good go at tidying this place up for.' Joyce Barron's eyes roved the room. 'No trouble at all! I'd have it shipshape and dusted in a few days. And all that rubbish could go to the tip!'

'Larry needs it for his work.' Emily loyally came to the defence of her son.

'Nonsense! It's just been allowed to accumulate. And if he really does need it, then he can find somewhere appropriate to store it. What about that shed of yours, the one that Bill begged from the bank when they gave up having a branch at the cattle market?'

'It's full of gardening tools.'

'Well, what about that old air-raid shelter? Didn't Bill have that converted into a proper nuclear fall-out shelter in the sixties after the Cuban missile crisis?'

'It's too damp, Joyce, And full of rubbish.'

'Then order a skip and get Lawrence to clear it out so that he can put his stuff in it. I'm sure you could deal with the damp. Why don't we take a walk down the garden and have a look at it?'

'I really don't feel like going in there today.' Emily glanced at the clock, wondered what time Joyce was moving on to the Ravenscrofts'. Probably not till seven, and it wasn't five-thirty yet. 'Honestly, Joyce, I'm quite comfortable here. Lawrence looks after me, and that more than compensates for all his stuff.'

'If you say so.' Joyce Barron drained her cup, clinked it in her saucer. 'Where is he, by the way? His car's in the drive.'

'Probably developing some films. Once he goes into his darkroom he can't come out until he's finished. Sometimes he's in there for most of the day.'

Joyce snorted disapprovingly, then stood up. 'Now, I must just pop upstairs to the loo.'

'Use the downstairs one, Joyce.' Emily's hopes that her guest was on the point of leaving were dashed. 'Save yourself the traipse upstairs.'

'I can go up and down stairs all day long.' Joyce was piqued at the doubt cast on her agility. 'After all, I *am* a few years younger than you, don't forget.'

I'm eighty next birthday, Emily calculated, and I know darned well you were seventy-six last June. I'm thin and arthritic and you're fat and wheezy. And you're going upstairs come hell or high water to see if the house is in as much of a mess up there as it is down here. And to make sure that you haven't missed anything since your last visit!

Emily had been too slow to think up an instant excuse when Joyce had phoned. *I'm awfully sorry, Joyce, but it's my writing class this afternoon. Or, I've got a touch of 'flu and I'd hate to pass it on to you.* Mrs Smithson usually phoned a warning when Joyce Barron was in the area. The Ravenscrofts might have had the decency to tip her off, too ... But it was too late now, she was here and she wouldn't be leaving just yet.

Emily hoped that Lawrence didn't suddenly emerge from his bedroom. He had a habit of walking across the landing in just his underwear with his capacious stomach flopping in front of him. Or else he dressed in filthy jeans and a ragged sweater, the soles of his worn-out trainers flapping as he walked. Surely, Joyce wouldn't have the cheek to look into Larry's bedroom because that was surely where her son was, sleeping off an all-night video viewing session. Please God that she doesn't have the neck to poke her nose in *there*.

Lawrence hadn't done a day's work since his father's funeral fifteen years ago; well, Emily thought, you couldn't really call the odd trip out with a camera *work*. Yet Lawrence was a talented photographer; he sold a few superb pictures for a pittance and then didn't bother to take any more for months. Emily didn't begrudge him his keep — her son was all she had. She didn't mind him not doing anything, didn't mind the fact that he was moody, always in a bad temper for several hours after he got up, whatever time of the day that happened to be, didn't mind his foul language. No, she could forgive him all that. Companionship was all that she asked. Even if he did spend the night hours watching videos and most of the day sleeping, he was around, and that meant a lot.

She heard Joyce coming back downstairs and braced herself for the next interrogation.

'He's in *bed*!' Joyce Barron announced from the doorway.

'Larry was complaining of a headache earlier,' Emily tried her best to make it sound convincing. 'I think he must have a migraine — he gets them occasionally.'

'And no wonder, sleeping in a room in that state! It's filthy — it can't have been cleaned for months — and it's damp. Emily, have you been in there lately?'

'Look, Joyce ...' Emily was seldom angered but this was becoming one of those rare occasions. There was a roaring in her ears and her fingernails gouged her palms.

'It's a pigsty, Emily. Worse — pigs would refuse to live in there. My goodness, I've never seen anything like it. Or smelled anything like it!' She gave an exaggerated wrinkle of her nose.

'You've no business poking your nose into any rooms in my house, Joyce!' Emily's voice shook. She clenched a fist and her arthritis began to send pulses of pain through the whitened knuckles.

'Oh, yes, I have!' Joyce Barron was shouting now. 'You need somebody to look after you, Emily, and I'm going to do just that. No doubt you'll protest — all old people do when somebody does something for their own good and they don't see it that way. I was very annoyed with you when you wrote last year and ticked me off for taking that tatty old wreath off Bill's grave. It should have been thrown away weeks before. Well, this afternoon I went up to the cemetery and cut down all that hypericum on his grave. It was like a jungle. You see, you *need* somebody to do all those kind of things for you. It seems to me that those boys of yours are neglecting you.'

Emily's features drained of their colour. 'How dare you? Glenn will be furious. He planted that hypericum — he takes a pride in looking after the grave.'

'Well, he's not making a very good job of it,' the other sneered. 'Anyway, it doesn't matter what Glenn thinks. From now on —'

'Oh yes, it does,' Emily's hands gripped the arms of her chair as she made a concerted effort to get to her feet.

'I'm not going to argue with you, Emily. Jobs will just be done and I don't care what you, or Glenn — or Lawrence — have to say about it. Between the lot of you, you've let everything slide and consequently you're living like vagrants. I'm used to looking after people, I was a nurse before I met Ken, I know just when to step in. I know when people are crying out for help. Tidying up Bill's grave was just the start. That hypericum will grow again and then I'll cut it back each autumn. Next I'll start on the house. I'm going to fill as many dustbin liners as I can find with all this rubbish,' she waved a hand in the direction of the piles of magazines, 'and after that I'm going to wash all the walls down. And when I've done that I'm going to get that lazy good-for-nothing son of yours out of his bed. I'm going to impose myself upon you for the rest of my stay here and get you habitable again.' Joyce paused, breathless; her cheeks were flushed.

Emily managed to get to her feet and stood unsteadily, holding on to the chair for support. 'Please leave, Joyce. In spite of her anger she maintained her dignity. 'This very minute. You are not going to interfere with this house and I must ask you never to touch Bill's grave again. Now, please, will you go?'

'I will not.' The other stood her ground, hands on hips. 'I'm doing all this for your own good, Emily. Afterwards you'll see sesnse. Now sit down. Stay right where you are and let me get on with what I have to do.'

Emily was determined not to obey, but her legs were weakening, starting to shake; they would not be able to support her frail body for many more seconds. She thought she might faint and lowered herself back down into the chair. She gasped her anger and frustration aloud. If only Bill were alive, he would soon have sorted out Joyce Barron. She would have been shown the front door. But Bill had been dead for fifteen years and as an added insult this woman had been pruning his grave flowers to *her* liking!

'There, that's better, I knew you'd see sense,' Joyce's bulky frame towered above Emily like a leering female colossus. 'You sit right there and don't move. Now, just tell me where you keep the cleaning materials and the bin liners. I'll bring you a cup of tea shortly. Perhaps you'd like to watch the television whilst I get on?'

Emily was trembling with helpless rage. If she could have got to the phone she would have called Glenn – or even the police. But the last thing she wanted was to involve Lawrence in this. She struggled to speak. Then without warning, the door burst open, banging back against the wall.

'What the hell's going on in here?'

Lawrence's huge figure filled the doorway. An obese giant clad only in a pair of Y-fronts, his jowled features were dark with rage. His wobbling flesh gave the illusion of a cartoonist's caricature that was stepping out of its frame.

Joyce Barron uttered a shrill cry and turned her head away, her flabby fingers splayed across her eyes. 'Emily, this is disgusting!' Her shout bordered on a scream. '*Do something!*'

Emily stared, managed a cracked whisper. 'Larry ... please ...'

'Get out!' Lawrence padded into the room, his stomach spilling in a roll of fat over the elastic of his briefs. He thrust his face close to Joyce's, jerked a thunb in the direction of the hallway. 'Right now. And don't ever come back.'

'I won't stand for this!' Joyce's feature were suffused with crimson. 'Your behaviour is intolerable, Lawrence. Whatever would your father have said?'

'He can't say much, can he? He's dead. Now, get out or I'll bloody well throw you out, and you'll get a kick up your fat arse to go with it.'

'Larry ...' Emily's voice was pleading, pathetic.

Lawrence picked up Joyce's coat, thrust it into their visitor's hands.

'Don't you dare to touch me, Lawrence.' But she was already shambling hurriedly out into the hall, clumsily knocking over a pile of magazines as she went. 'You'll hear more about this, I can promise you.'

Lawrence herded her as he might have done a farm animal, pushing her towards the front door, leaning across her to flick the yale latch. Her final protest was cut short by the slamming of the door.

'Larry, you shouldn't have – ' Emily tried to get up out of the chair but didn't have the strength.

'She looked into my bedroom!' His stomach quivered with the rage that seethed inside him. 'Well, she won't ever be coming here again, Mother, that I can promise you.'

'I could've got rid of her by myself, Larry. After all, Joyce and Ken were friends of ours when your father was at the bank. Ken conducted your father's funeral – surely you remember?'

'Mother', Lawrence sighed, 'if somebody slit your throat and left you to die, you'd still see some good in them. Joyce Barron is an evil, interfering old bitch.'

'Well, like you say, I don't suppose we'll see her again.' Emily was close to tears. 'She means well, it's just her way. She'll doubtless open her big mouth all round the village, tell people what a dreadful pigsty this house is, and by this time tomorrow everybody will know.' She gave way to a sob.

'What's wrong with this place?' Lawrence was incredulous, spreading his hands wide. 'Come on, tell me – I'd like to know.'

Emily closed her eyes. Oh, God, she didn't want to go into all that again.

'Come on!'

'Well, it's a bit untidy. It could do with a good clean, Lawrence.'

'Don't worry, I'm going to see to all that,' he snapped.

He had been going to "see to it" for the last fifteen years; he still hadn't made a start. 'I know, Larry. I know you'll get round to it one of these days.'

'A lot of *your* stuff could be thrown out, Mother.' He became petulant at the slightest hint of criticism.

'I'll see to it.' She had long learned not to argue with her son when he was in one of these moods, just as she would never have argued with her husband. Over the years, Emily had learned to remain silent; in due course the issue would be forgotten.

'Oh, by the way, Lawrence, my bedside light's gone again.' She seized upon an opportunity to change the subject.

'I'll fix it.'

'We really should get an electrician in, Larry.'

'They rip you off. I said I'll fix it.'

Emily nodded. Her greatest fear was the condition of the wiring throughout the house. Glenn was worried, too; he had begged her to have the whole place re-wired. She would have done so had it not been for Lawrence, who refused to have workmen in the house. He even wanted to dispense with Arthur, the jobbing gardener, who came fortnightly from April until October. 'Let's have a *natural* garden, Mother.' Which meant a forest of weeds; he would like the garden in the same state as he kept his room. But Larry had an answer of some sort for everything.

When Emily went upstairs to bed that evening she saw that Lawrence had 'fixed' her bedroom electrics, trailing an extension lead across the landing from the small bedroom. The two-way switch from the hall below had ceased to function a couple of weeks ago; he had 'made it safe' by taping a length of elastoplast across it. The landing itself was lighted by one of his photographic lamps – a second extension flex snaked from beneath the door of his makeshift dark room.

He had definitely been getting more peculiar these last few months, there was no doubt about that. For years she had told herself that his problem was simply laziness – he was bone idle and that was all there was to it. She had almost come to believe it. Now she was unable to convince herself any longer. There was definitely something wrong with Larry. Something — Emily hesitated before using the word — something psychological. Just as there had been with William to a lesser degree. It could be hereditary. Bill's father had been like that too, from the day she met him until the day he died.

Lawrence lived in the past, had been doing so for a long time. His memories weren't happy ones, though; his remembering seemed fuelled by a kind of vindictive nostalgia. His schooldays had been a nightmare; it had been a mistake to send him to a strict preparatory school. That devilish headmaster, Wilson, had ruled like a sadistic dictator, almost worshipping the cane. It was called discipline then; today it would be perversion. Emily recalled the weals she had seen on Larry's buttocks in the bath that time, how he had begged her not to tell his father — Bill, though so fond of the idea of punishment wouldn't have stood for that.

Lawrence still hated the headmaster. On occasions she had heard him muttering Wilson's name. It was all so pointless — Prebendary Wilson had probably died years ago. If he was still alive, then he had to be a very old man.

Putting Larry in the bank had been another mistake. A big one. He had been a square peg in a round hole. But Bill could never accept that his son was unhappy, that he loathed the profession. How could anyone dislike banking — the profession which had made William Prendergast the man he was?

Deane, the sub-manager at the small branch where Larry was posted in his twenties, had added to the boy's misery with a vindictiveness spawned in a feud with Bill when Deane had been a clerk under Mr Prendergast senior. Deane had seen a means of exacting revenge for old wounds: venting his rage on the son, treating him as he had never been able to treat the father. That was when the rot had really set in; the bullying, the emotional traumas, leaving their invisible, painful scars. Wilson began it; Deane finished the job.

Oh, my poor boy.

Maybe Janice Peters could have been Larry's saviour — but it was no good blaming Janice. By the time he met his first and only girlfriend, Larry was already too far gone down the roads of eccentricity and embitterment. Janice had been a lovely girl — so gentle and understanding — but no woman would have put up with the likes of Larry for long. Emily would willingly have consigned herself to a life of loneliness and solitude to have seen Larry happily married.

Or simply happy. Anything but *this*.

He was bitter towards Janice, too. Blamed her for walking out on him. All that had been before William's death and Larry's mental state had worsened considerably since. He had been the victim of circumstances, all his life. Circumstances had moulded him into what he was now.

Emily climbed stiffly into bed, her gnarled feet going in search of the old metal bed warmer. Ironically, it had been a wedding present from the Barrons; maybe she ought to throw it out, buy a more modern one, something plastic and easily cleanable. But she was grateful for the warmth. At times like this she could forgive Larry his Heath Robinson electrics. And if she never saw Joyce Barron again it didn't matter one jot.

Emily did not put the light out; sometimes she left it on all night. It gave her some comfort. This house in which she had lived for the past half-century had lately become a forbidding, frightening place. It was as if it had picked up Larry's moods; the house, like her son, brooded malevolently.

It wasn't just the eccentric electrical arrangements which worried her. No, they were only part of it ... The windows, upstairs and downstairs, had all been screwed shut. Larry's home-made double glazing — polythene pinned to the insides of the frames — was both an eyesore and ineffective. Last summer he had refused to remove it; he was always going to do it 'tomorrow'. It was still there.

He liked the curtains kept closed, too. She opened them before he got up, trying to let light and air into the fusty rooms, but she quickly closed them again when she heard him moving around. Last summer a rumour had spread in the village that she had died, but Larry still objected to having the curtains open. It was as if he were consciously shutting himself away from the world.

His untidiness increased daily, adding to the fire risk. And there were mice in the house; in the stillness of night Emily could hear them scurrying and gnawing. She suspected they were in the mountain of cardboard boxes and newspapers which filled the stair cupboard, but was afraid to look, fearing that if she opened the door she would be buried beneath an avalanche of yellowed, decaying paper.

The house smelled musty, old, the wallpaper peeling and the paintwork faded. The whole interior needed redecorating, but that was a vain hope; a decorator would never be permitted to cross the threshold. Joyce had been right, Emily grudgingly admitted to herself. She *had* let things go. But Larry was more important than a little shabbiness. If she upset him he might leave home; he had threatened to on more than one occasion. Not that he had any money to find a room elsewhere; he was entirely dependent upon her. Until after she was gone ... But he was stubborn enough to walk out on a foolish impulse, and she dreaded to think what might happen to him then.

Yes, Larry was brooding over his schooldays, his failed banking career and his one, lost love. That was why he stayed shut away in his dirty, stinking room, surrounded by dust-coated and cobweb-draped stacks of paperback books which he added to almost every time that he went out. She doubted if he even read them; more likely he just hoarded them, like he did everything else.

Except the war books. Emily shuddered. She had seen him poring over novels of Nazi death camps, torture, the holocaust: books about human evil in its grimmest form.

Maybe she should speak to Glenn about it. He'd know what to do. And a little discreet cleaning might help; dispose of the clutter a bagful at a time so that Larry wouldn't notice. That way at least one of the rooms might be made habitable.

It was the early hours of the morning before Emily finally drifted off to sleep. When she awoke at ten o'clock the curtained room was in darkness. Lawrence's improvised electrics had failed again.

Chapter Three

Frank Coleman had bought the red-bricked house adjoining the Prendergasts' in 1950. It was one of three utility dwellings erected on the field that lay between the pine forest and the main road. The builder had somehow managed to obtain planning permission for a trio where previously only two had been designated – which meant small houses with narrow gardens. By 1960 twelve others had been built, using all available space right down as far as the church orchard. At least, Frank consoled his uncertain-tempered wife, Mary, they wouldn't possibly be able to build any more.

Frank was small and thin, seldom seen dressed in anything other than a pair of faded blue dungarees and a checked cap. He rarely smiled and mumbled when he spoke, largely due the eternal cigarette which smouldered in the centre of his mouth, dislodging its ash at frequent intervals. A man who did not believe in waste, he lit the next one with the soggy butt of the last.

His solemn expression was a monument to the profession from which he had retired. It was with no small amount of agonising that he had sold the family undertaking business to a large concern. In the end the very generous purchase price had eroded his stubbornness and more than compensated for the guilt over what his long-dead father might have thought. The day of the craftsman, of hand-made caskets of carefully chosen and lovingly polished oak, was long gone. Nowadays the wood was imported and the coffins machine-made in a factory. The art of mourning was left to the bereaved; the undertaker provided only the basics.

But there was no way either Frank or his wife were going to be buried in ignominy. For years he had worked meticulously in his garden workshop constructing a pair of perfect coffins. The big one was for Mary – he had persuaded her to be measured, to get the proportions exactly right – and the smaller one for himself. It was a task to be savoured. In fact, he had invited Glanville, the new manager of the business, round for a sneak preview; so impressed was he that he had asked if Frank could possibly make the odd hand-crafted coffin for the firm: just occasionally, when a wealthy client demanded old-fashioned quality for their departed loved one.

So Frank continued with the trade which he had learned in his youth. His small workshop was more than adequate; he had all the necessary tools. His instinctive furtiveness, the jealousy of a master tradesman, returned. He worked quietly and unobtrusively, not wishing to draw the neighbours' attention to his backyard business. The deal with Glanville was for hard cash and Frank had no intention of having any of it appropriated by the Inland Revenue.

He had no time for the Prendergasts. Just because they lived in a big house and had a banking background they thought they were a cut above the rest. Frank hadn't been on speaking terms with William for several years before the latter's death; the final insult had been when Emily had asked Sharps in the city to make the funeral arrangements. 'Sharp by name, sharp by nature' was an old quip of Frank's, and it was as true today as it had been when old Albert Sharp had set up in competition to Frank's father. They tried to pass themselves off as a family business but the only family touch was in the sharing out of their ill-gotten proceeds. They hadn't made their own coffins even back in the good old days; instead, they had contracted the work out to Johnsons, the cabinet makers. Joe Johnson might have made reasonable furniture, but when it came to coffins he thought it was just a box with a lid. Once they'd got the measurements wrong and rumour had it that old Sharp had got them off the hook by folding the corpse's legs. Word got around when you were a bodger.

Mary had nagged her husband for years to get the hedge

which separated them from the Prendergasts' cut down by at least three feet. The thick privet reaching a height of nine feet, was so dense that she had to have the light on in the kitchen all day. But William Prendergast had steadfastly refused to hack down his boundary hedge to a height whereby his neighbour could look over it. Neither was he prepared to cut down the line of larches beyond the old air raid shelter, insisting that they were most unlikely to be uprooted in a gale and smash Frank's workshop, and even if they did then household insurance would make provision for any damage.

After William's death, Frank thought that perhaps Emily would concede to her next-door neighbour's wishes. He was wrong. She didn't argue; she listened patiently to his rantings about restricted daylight and danger from falling trees, smiled sweetly and said that she would prefer to leave things as they were when her husband was alive: Bill had liked his privacy.

Perhaps, Arthur, the gardener, could be bribed. He wasn't the brightest of men; surely he could 'make a mistake' at autumn hedge-cutting time? Frank proffered a couple of quid, then, in desperation, a fiver; but, money didn't enter into it, it seemed. Arthur had a regular, well-paid job and he wasn't prepared to risk it. So the offending hedge continued to be trimmed at its original height.

To placate an irate Mary, Frank compromised. Instead of clipping their own side the way he usually did, priding himself on his straight eye and steady hand, he used long-handled secateurs to hack at the branches reducing the bushy foliage to a skeletal thinness that was an eyesore to behold. In places you could see right through into the Prendergasts' garden. He anticipated a protest; but there was none. Possibly Emily and that layabout son of hers hadn't even noticed. Frank decided that, if nothing was said during the following twelve months, he might risk a discreet levelling at the top. Maybe take a couple of feet off to start with. And so far, so good.

Frank had not seen Lawrence all winter. Occasionally he'd heard the car going out and coming back again, often in the early hours of the morning. The boy was up to no good. Nobody stayed out that late for legitimate purposes.

He'd probably got a woman somewhere, more than likely somebody else's wife. He should get married and settle down like most men did long before they reached his age. It was the old girl who was keeping him at home to look after her, no doubt about that.

Much to his surprise one sunny April morning, as Frank was busy in his shed working on a rush job for Glanville, he heard Lawrence coming down the path on the other side of the hedge. Dragging footsteps, laboured breathing: either the boy was asthmatic or he was doing something strenuously physical, which seemed a remote possibility. Frank stepped outside his workshop to peer through the mutilated hedge, which was only just beginning to sprout its greenery.

Lawrence was bowed down under a heavy length of timber, freshly cut so that with keen senses you could smell the sawdust. What the devil was he up to? Surely the Prendergasts weren't going to erect a fence now that the privet had been thinned.

'Morning.' Frank showered cigarette ash down his front and parted an obstructing branch.

Lawrence started. The wood he was carrying slipped and one end thudded on to the grassy path. He staggered and almost fell, grunting with pain as a splinter embedded itself in his fleshy palm.

'Making summat?' Frank's grey eyes noted guilt as well as surprise in the other's expression.

'I beg your pardon?' Lawrence let his burden go, examining his hand for the offending sliver of pine.

Frank Coleman cleared his throat. 'I said, it looks like you're going to make summat.'

'Oh, yes.' Lawrence fumbled a grubby handkerchief out of the pocket of his baggy jeans, dabbed at a speck of blood. He hesitated, dropping his gaze. 'I'm ... I'm thinking of building myself a new darkroom.'

'A what?'

'A darkroom. For developing photographs.'

'Oh, I see. You need planning permission for outbuildings, you know. That old shed of yours counts as your entitlement.'

'Oh, I'm not going to *build* anything.' Lawrence spat

on his wound, rubbed at it. 'I'm going to convert the old shelter.'

'What, that old thing! Surely it's damp. Probably holds the water after a rainstorm.'

'I'm going to renovate it.'

'Best of luck. How's your mother?'

'Not good. Arthritis, you know. She's pretty much housebound — manages to use the car to get to her writing classes but that's about the only time she goes out.'

'I wonder if you could do us a favour?'

Lawrence examined his hand even more closely. 'What's that?'

'Get that gardener chap to take a few feet off this bloody hedge. It obstructs the light. Makes our kitchen like the Black Hole of Calcutta.'

'I'll have to ask Mother.'

'Go and ask her now.'

'I can't. She's not up yet.'

'Well, ask her when she gets up. I'll be out here all day today.'

'Still making those coffins, eh?' Lawrence had been told about the his-and-hers coffins when he was a boy; it had taken Frank that long to complete them.

'That's right.' Frank wasn't going to reveal that he did a bit of work for Glanville.

Lawrence lifted up his length of timber carefully, decided to drag it. 'I must get on — I've got a lot to do.'

And no way was he going to lower that hedge. There were certain things which Lawrence didn't want his neighbours to see at any price.

'Whatever have you been doing, Larry?'

Emily had dozed off in the armchair after lunch; she had not woken until nearly four and only then because her son had brought her a cup of tea. He looked even more dishevelled than usual; there was a smudge of dirt on his cheek and a length of cobweb clung to his hair. He seemed tired, dragging his feet and leaning against the table for support.

'I told you I was going to make a start tidying this place up, Mother.' His tone was smug, self-congratulatory.

Emily managed to stop herself from exclaiming out loud. Somehow she kept her composure. 'That's marvellous.' Then came a nagging fear that he might have made a start with her own belongings. 'Where have you made a start Larry?' She held her breath, fearful of his answer.

'The air-raid shelter.'

'Oh. I see.' Trust Larry to get things back to front! If he had embarked upon a clear out, then the shelter was the last place she would have suggested he begin. The underground shelter had been a convenient resting place for all sorts of unwanted items: not any more, it seemed.

'I've put out quite a few bags for the dust cart on Monday,' Larry continued.

'And – again she hardly dared ask – 'what are you going to do with the shelter when you've cleared it?'

'I'm going to renovate it. Turn it into a darkroom.'

'That's a marvellous idea!' Emily wondered if by any chance she was still asleep and dreaming. 'That means we can use your present darkroom as a bedroom again!'

'No!' His tone was suddenly abrupt, angry. 'The new darkroom is in addition to the other.'

Emily's hopes were dashed. Still, it wouldn't really make any difference to her what Larry did out there. 'Do you really *need* a second darkroom, Larry?'

'Yes.' He tensed, ready to stand his ground. 'I want to build up a good business, ready for when I move into proper premises.'

'I am not lending you money to rent a shop, Larry!' That was the one issue she had stood firm on throughout. 'For one thing, you wouldn't be up early enough to open it – and then there would be rates, heating, lighting ...'

'Don't let's go into all that again!' He stood over her, almost threatening. 'Mother, I'm not asking you for money. I shall work from home and save up to buy a shop out of what I earn.'

'That's fair enough, then.' She humoured his fantasy. At least it would be something to occupy his mind and he would make most of his mess outside the house. 'I think it's an excellent idea.'

He relaxed again. 'It will take time. I've bought some

timber, I've got to build a structure for the studio lights. And whilst I think of it,' walking across to the window, lifting a curtain and peering out, 'we must make sure that old Coleman doesn't snip at that hedge behind our backs. He wants the privet slashed right back. I'm not going to stand for that – he'll be nosing over all the time, minding our business.'

'He'd better not cut it!' she snapped. She wouldn't permit it; Bill would never have given their neighbour leave to cut the hedge and she still liked to think that she was pandering to her husband's whims. 'If he tries anything on the sly I shall telephone my solicitor.'

'By which time it will be too late.' Lawrence sighed. 'I'll just have to watch him carefully. Anyway, as I'll be spending most of my time in the shelter I'll be able to hear if he gets snipping with the shears.'

'That shelter was quite smart once,' Emily reminisced. 'In the sixties, when your father had it converted into a nuclear shelter – before that it was pretty grotty. I can remember sitting in there at night in the forties with you clutched in my arms, listening to the German bombers going over. I'll never forget the night they bombed Coventry. The vibration was so strong in the shelter that we thought it might fall in and bury us. It was pretty solid, though. Originally, when it was dug out below ground, it was bricked in and reinforced with steel girders and the soil out of the dug-out was used to strengthen the roof in case of a direct hit. The old hump looks quite attractive now, with all those shrubs growing on it. It's the site of the old dumbwell, you know.'

'The what?'

'The old cesspit. Before we were put on to main sewage. After that it became disused. Then, after the Cuban missiles crisis and all the fuss about World War Three, your father converted it to a nuclear fall-out shelter. It was the only one in the neighbourhood – quite a status symbol. He really went to town on that shelter – made me think at one stage that he was planning to move out and live in there! Strip-lighting, water supply, foodstore: you name it, it's there. All wasted, as it turned out. Still, if you can make good use of it, good luck to you. It's bound to be rather cold and damp – you'll have to take the oil-heater out there with you. I don't want you catching pneumonia.'

'It's already out there, drying out the damp.' Lawrence seemed relieved that his mother had raised no serious objection; all things considered, it was easier to have her approval.

Emily smiled fondly. 'I think your father would have been pleased to think that you were taking his shelter over.'

'I couldn't give a damn whether he would have been pleased or not!' Lawrence kicked petulantly at the table leg.

'Larry, he loved you.'

'So he sent me to a hellhole of a school then put me to work in a bank, where I was utterly miserable?'

'He was only trying to do his best for you, Larry. The village school was really rough ...'

'He just wanted to boast that he had his sons at private schools and that they were going to be bank managers like him!' Lawrence clenched his fists. 'It was nothing but snobbery. He never even asked if I was happy, if it was what I wanted!'

'Larry, it's all over now. It's in the past and you don't have anything to worry about. You're quite safe here.' If she could have reached him she would have put her arms around him. She was close to tears.

'That doesn't alter what that bastard Wilson did to me!' His cheeks were flushed, his eyes bulging in their sockets like bubbles about to burst.

'He was a tyrant in an age when it was permissible.'

'He was as bad as bloody Hitler!'

'I expect he's dead now.'

'He's not!' There was obsession in his voice; it frightened her. 'I looked him up in *Crockford's*. He's eighty-nine, lives about seventy miles from here.'

'Larry, does it really matter?'

'To me, it does.' He let out a sigh. 'Sometimes it seems like yesterday. I still dream about him. Not dreams – nightmares.'

Oh, God, Bill, whatever have you done to your son?

Suddenly Lawrence's eyes narrowed. 'By the way Glenn

wasn't messing about in the garage last week, was he?'

Emily swallowed. There had to come a point where her elder son's surreptitious clearing up was going to be noticed. 'I don't know what you mean.'

'All my bits and pieces have gone. My cartons, my pile of cardboard and my boxes of jars – they've all disappeared.'

'Come to think of it, he did mention that Jill was going to make some jam. And he did ask me if I'd got any spare cardboard – apparently they use it for mulching in their vegetable patch.' Her lies sounded ludicrous; she wondered if he would believe her.

'Well, he might have asked me first.'

Emily was only too familiar with Lawrence's sulky, offended tone. Now he wouldn't be speaking to her for days.

'I don't suppose he gave it a thought. I'm sure he never dreamed that you would have any use for empty jars and easte cardboard.'

'I don't want him interfering – it's none of his business.'

'I'll tell him when he visits again.'

'And when's that going to be?' The question was urgent, peremptory.

'I suppose it will be Friday week, as usual. He'll maybe come here first, then he'll go on into town and meet me for lunch after my writing class, like he usually does.'

'Why's he got to come here first?' Insistent, demanding an answer.

'I suppose he likes to see his old home.'

'Well, he's not to come when I'm not around. Tell him that next time you speak to him.'

'I'll tell him, Larry.'

'Now, shall we have boiled eggs for tea?' She attempted to change the subject, lighten the atmosphere.

'I'll do one for you.' He moved towards the door. 'I'm dieting. Remember?'

She nodded wearily. Larry was one big facade. For a long time now he had not eaten with her; he always claimed to be "dieting". Glenn had confirmed her worst suspicions when he cleared all the rubbish out of the garage: the fish and chip papers stuffed in the cartons, the pile of pizza boxes. Lawrence was clearly a compulsive eater; worse, he ate in secret, going out late at night to fetch takeaways, junk food, cramming it down where no one could see him. And there was no doubt about it: he had put on a lot of weight recently.

Perhaps, she consoled herself, the exercise involved in clearing out the shelter and converting it into a darkroom would help him to slim a little.

Not only did he have an unhealthy body; Emily was also uncomfortably aware that he had an increasingly unhealthy mind. But she could not face the thought of not having him around. Which was why she would tolerate his phobias, help him to hide from the world which he feared. She would protect him. Even from Glenn.

Chapter Four

Glenn arrived at the family home an hour earlier than usual. His mother had warned him last week that Larry's suspicions were aroused. 'I think we'll have to abandon the spring-cleaning, Glenn.' It was a plea, an excuse for emotional blackmail. She had added, diplomatically, 'For the time being, anyway.'

Glenn had not argued. He seldom argued with his mother; instead, he decided upon a compromise.

It was a beautiful spring morning; his son Gary was eighteen now and could be trusted to tend the livestock on his own. So Glenn had left early. The traffic was sparse and he had made good time.

He parked his Subaru at the bottom of the drive, noticing that his mother's garage was empty. She must have already left for her writing class. Lawrence's rusting Mini stood, as always, forlornly on the tarmac.

Glenn had the feeling that he was somehow intruding, trespassing; he found himself moving stealthily, like a burglar stepping on to the grass so that his feet would make no noise. He looked up; every curtain at the front of the house was closed. But that meant nothing — they always were, whether Lawrence was up and about or still in bed. A tiny shiver trickled down his spine. It was eerie: as though somebody had died.

He let himself in, closed the front door quietly behind him and stood there in the gloom of the hallway, listening. There was silence except for the ticking of the clock in the kitchen and the whirr of the windmill ventilator in the window over the sink. A handwritten sign propped up by the telephone caught his eye.

DANGER – GAS LEAK!

Larry had really lost his marbles. This latest ploy – presumably to deter house-breakers, Glenn had no way of knowing – merely confirmed that his brother showed no sign of a return to sanity.

Glenn crept upstairs, testing each step before putting his full weight upon it. He stumbled against a pile of magazines in the darkness of the first landing; they scattered like a pack of cards, pages fluttering. He stopped, held his breath; but nothing moved.

He peered over the top bannister, waiting whilst his eyesight adjusted to the gloom. Lawrence's bedroom door was half-open as usual and another cardboard sign hung from the door handle. He squinted, making out the crude felt pen lettering with difficulty.

DO NOT DISTURB. NIGHT WORKER ASLEEP.

Glenn listened until he could detect Lawrence's rhythmic breathing. He was tense, trembling; he could smell his own sweat. Relief that he had not woken Larry made him feel weak.

But there was work to be done.

Glenn crept back downstairs. The shed key was kept in a bag on the hallstand; he was relieved to find it had not been hidden some place else. The back door key was also where he had expected it to be, under the oven grill; Larry must be slipping. He usually changed the hiding places every week.

Glenn went outside, disturbing a pair of grey squirrels feeding on waste bread beneath a couple of huge dead branches which had been stuck in the soil outside the kitchen window. Perhaps his brother planned to take some wildlife photographs.

During the previous weeks Glenn had finished slowly tidying the garage and the covered patio. There was just the shed left to do – and the stair cupboard, of course, but he would have to leave that for the time being. Certainly Larry would have hidden the key in some obscure place.

He shook out a dustbin liner, eyeing the untidy array of margarine tubs that littered the rose garden. Some were filled with stagnant water, coated with green slime; others were empty and had been overturned by the wind. Presumably they were originally intended for the birds, although the concrete bird bath had clearly not held water for some time. Glenn picked the tubs up and dropped them into the polythene bag. The trail of litter led down past the conifers; the last tub was entangled in the shrubs on the hump of the old air-raid shelter. And something that his mother had said on the phone last week flashed into his mind: *Larry was clearing out the shelter, turning it into a darkroom.*

Glenn was curious. The steps down to the underground room seemed to beckon. He remembered the last time he had looked in there: the place had been piled with mouldering and rotting junk, soggy cardboard cartons that had disintegrated, spilling their rubbish. He'd just take a quick peep today, see how much of it his brother had shifted. A wheelbarrow stood close by − Larry had obviously been using it to ferry his rubbish away. He'd have a heart attack if he wasn't careful. He was in poor shape and he wasn't used to physical labour.

Glenn glanced about him guiltily. The rear windows of the house were all firmly closed and the back door was shut. Bees hummed on the aubretia flowers; a dove cooed in the topmost branches of the larch trees. So peaceful.

So sinister.

He found himself shying away from the steps of the shelter, finding frantic excuses for going no further. If Larry wanted a new den, for whatever purpose − maybe to consume his secret stocks of junk food − well, that was his business. It clearly didn't worry Mother.

But it worried Glenn.

He found himself tip-toeing, looking behind him furtively. The stone steps were slippery with moss. He remembered that the original door used to hang by one hinge, with a hook and eye to close it. Then Dad had had a new, stout version fitted, with well-oiled hinges and a spring handle. To Glenn's knowledge, it had never been kept locked.

It was now.

Glenn twisted the handle, pushed, but his efforts were

useless. He supposed it was only to be expected: Larry's long standing fear of burglars had evidently spread as far as the shelter. He would have the key carefully hidden in some unlikely place. Maybe under his pillow ...

In spite of the sunshine, Glenn shuddered. He realised that he was relieved that access had been denied him: whatever lay behind that door, he did not want to see it.

'Morning, Glenn.'

Glenn started. Turning he saw the melancholic features of Frank Coleman regarding him through the mutilated privet branches, a cigarette smouldering between his lips.

'Oh ... morning, Frank.' Glenn was shaking, as if he had been caught red-handed in some nefarious act. 'I didn't see you there.' Coleman moved about with an habitual furtiveness; as a boy, playing in this garden, Glenn had always had the feeling that Frank was watching him.

'That brother of yours has turned over a new leaf, hasn't he?'

'Oh? Why's that?' Glenn sensed an interrogation was about to begin.

'Clearing out the rubbish from that shelter, taking it away. Barrowload after barrowload. Bringing in a lot of timber, too, like he's making summat in there. I told him he might need planning permission if he's making living accomodation. Reckon maybe your dad ought to have had permission for that shelter in the first place. Got away with it because nobody knew about it — except me and the missus.'

'Well, it's not hurting anybody.' Glenn resented Frank's insinuation. 'All you can see is a bank of shrubs, and you wouldn't be able to see that if you hadn't decimated the hedge.'

'Maybe you'd have a word with your mother for me, Glenn.'

'She's not too well at present, Frank.'

'She was well enough to go out this morning. I heard her car going down the drive.'

'It's her only means of mobility outside the house.'

'This hedge needs lowering a bit.' Only the obstructing branches prevented Coleman from thrusting his face closer to Glenn's; he spoke in a sibilant whisper that was barely audible through his cigarette. A length of ash dropped; he sucked on the sodden stub. 'It's making our house very dark.'

'I'll mention it, but I don't think she'll be amenable. She likes her privacy.' He added, before the other could protest, 'Still making coffins on the quiet, are you, Frank?'

'The odd 'un, now and then.' His pride was tempered by caution, suspicion. 'Why?'

'Well, it might be better from your point of view to keep the hedge high, let it thicken again. Mother's thinking of selling up, moving somewhere smaller, and you never know what sort of neighbours you might get in here. Could be the nosey sort who are always looking for trouble. They could shop you to the council for running a business in a residential area. Might even tip off the taxman.'

Frank grunted and shuffled back into his shed. That Glenn Prendergast had always been a smart arse, right from when he was a boy, and he hadn't changed any.

Glenn scraped back the warped door of the dilapidated shed and stared at the pile of rubbish heaped inside. It looked as if Larry had taken the easy way out, dumping the contents of the shelter in here: a mulch of damp and mouldy cartons; rotted garments that were out of fashion a decade ago; a broken umbrella; a pile of bent aluminium curtain rails.

He fetched another handful of bin liners and with difficulty located a shovel at the back of the shed. God, the stuff stank; he wished he'd brought a pair of gloves with him.

He tied the bags as he filled them, then carried them down to the car. He prayed that Larry would sleep late as usual. Another half hour and he'd be finished.

'What the hell's going on?'

The patio door opened and Lawrence emerged wearing only a pair of filthy jeans, his stomach bulging over the waistband. His face was red with anger, his eyes bulging. Bare-footed, toenails uncut and engrained with dirt, he shambled into the garden, wobbling and enraged.

'I'm just giving you a hand.' Glenn dropped another

shovelful of rubbish into the bag. 'I'll take some of this stuff away for you.'

'Leave it where it is!' Lawrence pushed past him and grabbed the curtain rails; a couple fell, clattering onto the concrete slabs. 'These things cost a fortune nowadays!'

'Not those.' Glenn tensed, a trickle of sweat stinging his eyes. 'They're all bent.'

'I'll take them up to my room.'

'Whatever for?'

'Because I need them!'

Lawrence turned away, clutching the rails.

'Please yourself, then.' Glenn picked up the bag.

'Where're you going with that?'

'To the tip.'

The curtain rails were hurled down as Lawrence grabbed for the bag. 'Leave me alone, Glenn!'

Glenn walked away. He heard bare feet padding in his wake; but he was fitter, slimmer than his brother, and could move faster.

He unlocked the door of the Subaru and slid in behind the wheel. It was stifling hot inside; the smell from the sacks was repellent. The engine fired as Lawrence reached the car and banged on the window. He'd seen the bulging dustbin liners in the back and his enraged features were smudged on the glass.

'Wait a minute! That's my stuff you're stealing!'

But Glenn had already let in the clutch and was pulling out on to the road. In the rear view mirror he glimpsed his brother, a lump of obesity shaking with rage and frustration; a multitude of obsessions that had gone beyond the boundaries of sanity, reached the point of no return.

And Glenn's fear now was for his aged mother, her life dominated by an escalating madness in that house where the curtains were never opened. He remembered that door, leading into the stinking depths of a dark dungeon, and he cursed his father for having built it.

Chapter Five

'*Oh, my God!*'

Emily stared aghast at Lawrence's considerable bulk, slumped in the ornate Victorian chair by the telephone. His torn pullover was blood-soaked and a handkerchief, drenched *in* crimson, was held to his nose. Head back, eyes closed, he was groaning.

'Larry! What's happened?' She had been on her way to bed; her son had gone out earlier, but she refused to believe Glenn's accusations of visits to the chip shop or the pizza parlour. 'Have you been mugged? I'd better call the doctor.'

'No.' His eyes opened, his hand covering the phone by his side. 'I'm *not* having the doctor. If it doesn't stop in a minute, I'll drive myself down to Casualty.'

'What happened, Larry?' She stared at his blood-smeared face.

'A nose bleed,' he grunted. 'Came on just as I opened the door. It'll stop soon.'

But it didn't. Five minutes later he accepted the towel which his mother had brought from the kitchen, the sodden handkerchief splatted on to the floor. His nostrils poured bright red twin rivulets.

'Let me drive you to the hospital.' It was a brave offer; Emily had difficulty coping with daytime traffic and at night oncoming headlights rendered her nearly blind. But she would risk it. She would risk anything for her son.

'I'll manage.' He lumbered to his feet, face hidden in the

brown and white striped towel which was steadily turning a shade of claret. 'I'll be back shortly.'

'At least let me come with you!'

'No!' He opened the door. 'We can't leave the house unoccupied. Not at this time of night. By the time we got back everything might be gone! You can't trust anyone nowadays.'

Emily stood in the hallway, listening to the Mini driving slowly away. Suppose he fainted at the wheel! She wrung her hands together helplessly, puzzled for a moment by the unfamiliar odour which assailed her nostrils. Then she saw the package on the chair which Larry had vacated, smears of blood on the greaseproof paper. So Larry *had* been to the chip shop! Still it was probably only an occasional treat; he deserved it. After all, he had next to nothing to eat most of the time. Everybody should be allowed to indulge once in a while. She picked up the fish and chips and took them through to the kitchen. Larry would probably be hungry after his ordeal and she could heat them up in the microwave.

Nosebleeds were always frightening – not just because of the sight of the blood, but because the cause was more worrying than the symptom. Emily recalled how heavily her mother's nose had once bled, just like Larry's. Old Dr Parker had had to come out in the middle of the night. He'd said it was a near thing – if the pressure hadn't eased that way then she would probably have had a seizure. In the event, she'd lived to more than eighty.

Larry wasn't an old man, but his health was poor. In the days when he had still been prepared to visit the surgery, Dr Clark had been concerned about his blood pressure and had ordered him to diet. Poor Larry had nearly starved himself – but he was the type who just couldn't lose weight, no matter how hard he tried. Well, they'd surely put him right at the hospital.

She struggled to fill a bucket and a cloth. Larry would be in no fit state to clean up when he got back. As she worked, wiping down the carved oak before the blood soaked into the chair and dried, she kept glancing at the phone, praying that it would not ring. *Please, Glenn – don't phone me tonight.*

Glenn hadn't done Larry any good, upsetting him like that the other week. In fact, Larry had complained of chest pains afterwards. Emily was really cross with her elder son — she'd told him to stop the clearing out but he had gone on with it, regardless. He was indirectly responsible for Larry's nosebleed! Pray God that it didn't lead to anything serious.

And all this physical work was too much for Larry — she'd told him that. He's spent a whole week cleaning up the old shelter, then he'd been working in there virtually all the time, getting his darkroom ready. He'd told her that he'd already converted the bathroom area; the big room was going to be his studio. She would have loved to view his handiwork, but those steps underground were just too much for her. Larry had really put his heart into it; and at least he would no longer pester her to invest money into a high street premises. That was a relief!

Emily had thought that once Larry had got his studio and darkroom how he wanted them he'd take it easy for a day or so. He looked so tired, bless him. But no — the following day he'd come up with another project.

'You know, Mother' — he was certainly much more affable these days — 'I've been thinking how nice a pond would look by the shelter. Shrubs overhanging it, lilies floating on the surface. maybe a few goldfish in it ...'

'It would be absolutely splendid!' she agreed. 'The idea occurred to me once, but I thought that with me not being able to go down the garden a great deal and you — with other interests, it would be a waste of money.'

'It won't cost much at all.'

'Someone would have to dig it out.'

'*I'm* going to dig it out,' he announced. 'I'm going to make a start tomorrow morning.'

'Larry, no!' She was shocked. 'You've no idea of the work involved! You'd never ...' She had not liked to continue, fearing he might be offended.

But the next day Lawrence had commenced his excavations. Emily stood at the patio door, listening to the clink of the spade on stones and soil. She was worried about her son. He wasn't cut out for labouring; it would be a strain on his heart, especially in this hot weather.

Lawrence staggered into the kitchen every evening, drained a glass of diet lemonade, then went straight up to his room. No longer did he sleep in until mid-day; he was back out in the garden again soon after nine. Day after day of toil: and only this afternoon he had announced proudly that the digging was finished.

She was curious. 'Maybe I could have a look.'

'I'll help you.' He had not objected and that was a surprise; in fact he seemed eager that she should admire his work. He took her arm and steadied her all the way down, past the rose garden and the small orchard, to the edge of the pond.

'Larry!' She stared aghast at the jagged hole, ten or twelve feet in diameter, which went down to a depth of at least six feet. 'Larry, surely you didn't have to go that deep?' Just looking down made Emily dizzy.

'I wanted a really big pool,' he said. 'Eventually, I'll get a roll of heavy duty polythene to line it. The rain will fill it.'

'Are you sure you feel all right, Larry?' He looked tired and haggard, the arm that supported her trembling from his exertions.

'I'm fine!'

But he obviously wasn't. Within six hours he had had a monster of a nosebleed. Arthur could finish the pool – she would insist on that.

The kitchen clock gobbled the hours; no sooner was it midnight than it was one. Then two. Emily sat huddled by the storage heater, frantic with worry. At two-thirty she heard Lawrence's car turn into the drive and park by the front door. She rushed out to meet him in the hall.

Lawrence looked pale, exhausted; there were plugs of cotton wool in his nostrils and his blood-stained pullover gave the impression that somebody had blasted him at close range with a shotgun.

'Larry!' She clasped him to her, fighting back tears of anxiety and exhaustion. 'Are you all right?'

'They stopped the bleeding eventually.' He steered her

back into the kitchen and slumped on to the old settee. 'They say my blood pressure is dangerously high.' His voice shook. Evidently he too was shocked by the experience.

'Have they given you anything for it?'

'They told me to go to the surgery in the morning.'

'Yes. Dr Bilton will give you some tablets.'

'I'm not going to Bilton!' He was stubborn.

'But you'll have to see *somebody*.'

'I'll be all right.'

'Larry, please!' She knew it was futile to plead. Her son was long overdue a dentist's appointment to have a temporary crown removed and a permanent one put on one of his back teeth; only nights of agony had driven him to Mr Stanforth six months ago. The dental surgeon had treated him and made another appointment, but Larry had cancelled six since. He would not go until chronic toothache drove him back. In the case of his blood pressure, he might not get a second chance.

'I'll be fine. I'm going to rest for a few days.'

'That's not the answer.'

'I'll lose some weight, too.'

'You know that even when you starve yourself, it makes no difference. *It's all in your make-up.* If you're destined to be big, you'll be big. The important thing is to get some tablets to bring down your blood pressure.'

He struggled to his feet, swayed. 'Right now I'm going to bed.'

'Larry – your fish and chips are in the microwave.'

There was a fleeting expression of guilt in his eyes. 'I bought them for you, actually,' he said.

'You know I can't eat anything fatty, Larry. But it was a kind thought.'

'Maybe I'll have them tomorrow.' He made for the stairs. 'Or I could put them out on the bird table for the squirrels! I'd be sure to get a good photograph that way.'

'You go and get some sleep,' she called after him, listening to his footsteps dragging up the stairs. She heard a thud, followed by a muttered curse, as he stumbled on the landing.

Emily thought she would ring Dr Bilton early in the

morning, before Larry got up. She could ask for a home visit; say that her son wasn't well enough to get to the surgery. She sighed heavily.

It wasn't altogether fair to blame Glenn for Larry's condition. He could have done without the additional distress, but it had been all the digging that had brought this on. She couldn't for the life of her think what had possessed him to make a pool, especially one as big as that. He'd never shown the slightest interest in the garden previously; only weeks ago he was wanting her to dispense with Arthur and let the garden grow wild.

It was all so puzzling, so disconcerting. It was all so frightening.

Chapter Six

Lawrence awoke with a splitting headache. He closed his eyes again, tried to shut out the half-light of the permanently curtained room – but there was something wrong. His breathing was obstructed, as if he had snuggled down into the grimy blankets on a freezing winter's night and run out of air. Instinctively his fingers went up to his nostrils and he jerked away the wads of cotton wool. Only then did he remember.

Heedless of the pain in his head, he scrutinised the plugs, relieved when he saw only dried bloodstains. At least his nose had stopped bleeding. He lay back, pulling the sheet up over his face; but even in darkness he found no relief.

His entire body ached. every nerve quivered, every muscle throbbed. He never wanted to see another spade again as long as he lived. With hindsight he should have taken his time, dug out a few barrowloads each day, but then the task would have taken weeks – and there was always the fear that time might run out for him, that twenty-five years of bitterness would be wasted. If all went smoothly, the effort would be well worth it. Less than six weeks ago he had hit on the plan ... But he didn't want to dwell on that now. Even his mental energy was sapped.

Suffice it to say that he was ready.

'Larry? How are you feeling this morning?' His mother had crept out on to the landing; he sensed that she was peering in through the partly-open bedroom door. She never ventured inside these days. She liked to pretend that this room was exactly as it had been when he was a boy, neat and tidy, the furniture dusted and the carpet hoovered twice a week. For Emily nowadays, everything was a game of Let's Pretend.

But not for Lawrence. For Lawrence Prendergast, reality was about to begin.

'I'm all right.'

'Can I get you anything, Larry? A cup of tea?'

'I'll be down shortly.'

'I think you should stay in bed today. If you want anything I'll bring it up to you.'

'I said, I'm going to get up!'

She didn't argue. Earlier she had phoned the health centre, spoken to Dr Bilton, but had been taken aback by his abruptness.

'Look, Mrs Prendergast,' he was brusque to the point of rudeness, 'I'm fully aware that your son has high blood pressure and I'm not prepared to discuss it with you. I have to respect the confidentiality of the patient. A home visit isn't necessary. If you would like to make an appointment for him to come and see me, I'd be happy to do that, but the decision must be his. He's a grown man, not a child.'

Emily said she'd call back. She wouldn't of course; it was pointless. Only unendurable pain would force Larry to seek the advice of any medical practitioner.

She made her way downstairs to the kitchen, where she opened the curtains to let the morning sunlight in. As soon as she heard Larry moving about she would quickly close them again.

Outside the window, on the crudely-made bird table, a grey squirrel sat expectantly, waiting for Larry to throw out some food. Emily remembered the fish and chips in the microwave, but decided to leave them for Larry. She couldn't imagine that anyone would eat day-old, greasy fish and chips, but with Larry one never knew.

Some time later she heard the toilet flushing, followed by the sound of footsteps coming downstairs. She tensed, hardly daring to look up as Larry entered the kitchen.

'I'm fine now,' he said quickly before she could ask. 'Nothing to worry about.'

He looked dreadfully pale, his tattered clothes and

uncombed hair doing nothing to enhance his jaded appearance. She watched him put the kettle on. She would have loved to bustle round giving him a hand, making him comfortable; but Larry liked to make his own drinks.

'It was just one of those things,' he went on. 'A one-off. It probably won't ever happen again.'

'I do hope not.'

He squeezed the teabag and placed it on the draining board; he never ever put anything in the waste bin, refused to regard anything as rubbish. 'Mother – Glenn won't be coming again for a while, will he?'

'He'll probably be here on Friday week, as usual. Why?'

'Whilst you've gone to your writing class?'

'I expect so.'

'I don't want him to come when you're not here!'

'Whatever are you talking about, Larry?'

'I'm scared of him, Mother. Terrified, in fact.'

'Larry – I ... I don't believe it!' Emily stared at her son. It was true; Lawrence's expression looked desperate, wild-eyed.

'Well, it's true. I don't sleep for nights beforehand and I'm really scared when you've gone to your class.'

'That's nonsense!'

'No, it isn't. He's evil, Mother. He's intent on clearing out all my belongings because he hates me. It's a way of getting at me – it's almost as if I don't exist.'

Emily was aghast. 'Glenn wouldn't do anything like that! He's your brother.'

'That's why he's doing it. He's hated me since we were children. Don't you remember how he used to bully me? That time he threw my breakfast out of the window?'

'Oh, Larry, you were both boys then. You'd be about eight, Glenn'd be fourteen. All boys do those sort of things. I know I used to get worried about you two always fighting and quarrelling, but everybody I spoke to who had boys said exactly the same thing. Girls bicker, boys fight – it's only natural.'

'Glenn meant it.'

'I'm quite sure he didn't. I expect he's forgotten all about it. He's got his hands full with Gary and Andrew. Teenagers can be terribly hard work. Anyway I've told him to stop the tidying-up.'

'He still does it, though, snooping around ... I shudder to think what he's chucked out.'

'Well, I'll make sure he doesn't do any more.'

'I'm going to lock all the doors from the inside in future.'

'That's silly, Larry.' As silly as keeping all the curtains closed ...'

'Is there any post?' He changed the subject; he had made a decision and did not want any further argument. Just as his father used to conclude a disagreement.

'It's on the mantelshelf. Just one letter – an electoral register thing by the look of it. I'll fill it in later.'

Lawrence grabbed for the buff-coloured envelope, slopping his mug of tea in his haste. He tore clumsily at the flap and extracted a single sheet of paper.

'*I'll* fill it in. I don't live here. Get it?'

'Larry, we could get prosecuted ...'

'They'll never know. I don't draw the dole' – I'm not sponging off them. I ask nothing from them – why should they ask anything from me?'

'But it's against the law to –'

'*I just don't want them to know about me!*'

Emily sighed. It had been the same ever since Bill had died. It was as though Larry wanted to lose his identity, become a non-person. Was it a kind of phobia, a fear of bureaucracy, of being part of the system? He would only qualify for a small state pension when he reached retirement age because he had stopped her paying his contributions – for the same reason. Now he was going to make false statements on the electoral register!

Larry found a ballpoint and began filling in the questionnaire, pressing hard with the point, angry with whoever had pryed into his privacy. 'There.' He folded the sheet, pushing it back into the torn envelope so that the return address showed in the window, and scrabbled on the heaped sideboard for some sellotape. 'That's told them all they need to know!'

Now it was Emily's turn to create a diversion, turn Larry from his rage. 'I haven't seen the *Mercury* for two weeks now, Larry. If you're going into town, call at the newsagents and ask them why they haven't delivered it.'

'I cancelled it.' He didn't look up.

'You *what*?'

'Well, you don't read it properly! It's just a waste of twenty-five pence.'

'Larry, I like my *Mercury*. Nobody reads a local paper from cover to cover. If I don't have it, I won't know what's going on locally, will I?'

'It's better not to know.'

'Larry, I *want* to know –' Emily's usually placid nature was seriously ruffled.

'All right, all right.' He shrugged. 'When I go into town I'll re-order it.'

She would phone the newsagent when Larry wasn't within earshot. Because she knew her son would not ask for the paper to be delivered again. It was yet another contact with the outside world which he had attempted to sever.

'I should take it easy today, Larry. Have a sit down in the armchair, watch a video.'

'I've got a lot of work to do and I'm off to a late start already.' He stood up, drained his mug.

'What have you planned for today, then?' She was taken aback; she had never known her son to show an eagerness for work.

'I've still got a lot to do in the new darkroom. I'll be out there for some time, so don't worry about me. And if anybody phones, you've no idea where I am. Right?'

'Very well.'

'Good.' He shuffled out of the kitchen. She heard the patio door open and close.

Some time later the sound of muffled hammering reached her. She thought at first that it might have been Frank Coleman making coffins but he never used nails, he'd made a point of telling her that he only worked with best-quality brass screws. It had to be Larry, then, working in the old shelter. And he really wasn't in a fit state to do carpentry. Perhaps he was only knocking one or two nails in to finish off that special wooden structure he'd told her about, the one to support his lighting.

But the banging continued for most of the afternoon, only ceasing shortly after five o'clock. Emily waited apprehensively for her son to return to the house. Several hours later there was still no sign of him.

'Larry, are you all right?'

Emily had negotiated the moss-covered steps down to the shelter door with some difficulty, supporting herself with one hand on the brick wall, and using the other to hold the small torch. The beam flickered dimly: it needed a new battery.

She had not anticipated encountering a locked door. The key had always been kept on the ledge just inside but even in Bill's day it had never been used because there was not anything worth stealing. Of course, Larry had valuable equipment in there, but why on earth did he want to lock himself in? She sighed. Doubtless, he would pin some ludicrous notice on the door – HIGH EXPLOSIVES or something like that.

'Larry, can you hear me?'

'What's the matter, Mother?' His voice seemed a long way away, muffled by the double-thickness walls.

'Are you coming in, Larry? It's dark now, you can't possibly see in there.'

'I've got *lights*, Mother. What d'you think I've been spending all this time rigging up?'

'Oh, I see.' He always made her feel foolish when he spoke to her in that tone of voice. 'Anyway, can't you pack up for the day?'

'In a bit.'

'I'd love to see what you've done to the old shelter.'

'Another time, maybe.'

Awkwardly, she turned around to retrace her steps. At least her son was all right even if he was going to stop in there half the night.

Lawrence was exhausted. He sat on an old straight-backed chair, leaning against the blue brick wall. He tried to relax

– he had earned it after all the hard work, the weeks of manual labour.

The lighting worked well off the two car batteries; he must remember to put them both on charge before he locked up for the night. The old oil heater in the corner smelled a bit in the confined space but that didn't matter. He would clear the old ventilation shaft to counter that problem. Apart from one or two minor finishing touches, he had achieved his goal. Phase One, the hard work, was completed. Phase Two would be much more interesting.

He was entitled to a feeling of smugness, an hour or two in which to survey his domain, his very own kingdom, the one place on this earth in which he wielded absolute power. Back in the house, in the garden even, Mother was queen: she dictated what was to be and what was not to be. And if he tried to bully her then she phoned Glenn. Lawrence was outnumbered. But not in here.

The big room was some fifteen feet long by ten feet wide, with plain brick walls. On the right a door led into a small cubicle which housed a basic lavatory and a tiny wash basin. With considerable difficulty he had fitted a heavy-duty security lock. A crude job but it was sufficient. As was his primitive lighting system: better than being pitch dark in there when the door was closed and locked.

The scarcity of furniture in the room did not concern him. The array of shelving along the wall might come in useful at some stage, and he had kept the table and chair – they were too good to throw out.

But his real energy had been directed elsewhere – to his own special furnishings. The steel cesspit cover had been removed and replaced by a wooden trapdoor – rough sawn planks held together with two diagonal crosspieces. Hinged, it fell inwards to reveal a drop of eight feet to where the outlet pipe lay. It had not been used for forty years, not since the Prendergasts were put on the main sewage.

Lawrence's tired gaze followed the wooden uprights all the way up to the reinforced ceiling above, eight-foot lengths of four by four wedged securely between floor and ceiling. Crosspieces connected and held them parallel, one flush with the ceiling, the other sloped and nailed securely at both ends.

As firm as the proverbial rock. He had tested them and was satisfied that there was no play in them.

The rope dangling from the upper beam was of the finest woven hemp – pristine, not a frayed fibre to be seen. He'd found it lying in the road at the bottom of the driveway; it had probably fallen off a haulage vehicle. He had bought the brass eyelet to hold the noose from an antique shop in the city. The lever was held by a steel bolt, and the taut chain was fixed to a ring on the trapdoor. A sharp downward tug on the handle jerked out the bolt, released the steel linkage, and the trapdoor shot downwards. He had tested it with a leftover bag of cement. It worked perfectly.

Lawrence was satisfied that his gallows was as stout and professional as any that had existed in HM prisons prior to the abolishment of capital punishment.

Chapter Seven

Lawrence shivered. He was covered in goosepimples. Not because he was cold. Because he was frightened.

Ahead and behind him stretched a queue of silent boys, their ages ranging from eight to thirteen. Tall ones, short ones; thin ones, plump ones. Apart from their grey shirts and corduroy shorts, some washed until they had faded to an off-white, the only other common denominator was their facial expressions: solemnity that bordered on fear. Like his own. Dry tongues; lips that trembled. Tomkinson, the new dayboy, was beginning to sob quietly. Before long, Clegg, the red-haired duty prefect, would whisper hoarsley to him to 'shaddup'.

Up ahead the corridor turned sharply at right angles. It was when you got as far as that that you really began to shake. Beyond the corner, a few yards down on the right, was that heavy oak-panelled door with a shiny brass knob. You hoped you'd never get there, that there would be some diversion. A fire, perhaps, or, maybe the headmaster would be taken ill. You wouldn't cry if he died. Anything rather than this.

Thwack ... thwack. Lawrence listened, counted. It was a kind of Chinese torture, waiting for the next *thwack*. You learned from experience to discriminate whether the unfortunate pupil in that study was being caned with his trousers up or down. If it was bare buttocks, for a more serious offence, the sound of bamboo on flesh was crisper, made you wince because you knew how it stung. He would be bent over the arm of the couch, shorts ignominiously around his ankles. You never knew how many strokes Prebendary Wilson had assigned you until he ordered you to 'stand up, pull your trousers up'.

Lawrence heard the door open and close, the sound of somebody crying. He didn't know who it was. Once you had been punished you left by the door at the other end and went directly to assembly.

The routine began again with another victim. The sound of knuckles rapping timidly on heavy wood. A long pause, then a 'come in'. The door opened, closed. You waited and listened. The wait was part of the headmaster's system, exquisitely timed to play on your nerves. A one-man judge, jury and executioner. By the time he'd consulted his notes and read the accusation, you'd already confessed to get it over as quickly as possible. He'd cane you whether you were guilty or not. If you were innocent, then by a twisted logic, the punishment was a safeguard against you doing whatever you were supposed to have done. He never spared the rod – it made a man of you.

'Move along there!' Clegg pushed a boy at the back, and the line of boys bunched up like dominoes. Cattle being driven to the slaughter. Pupils huddled, pseudo psychological safety in numbers. 'Form a straight line; stand up properly.'

Lawrence counted a 'six' and a 'four'. Always even numbers, never more than six. Tolson, the fourth-former, had been caught cheating in the end of term examinations. He had got off lightly – the expected six, but he'd been allowed to keep his trousers on. He didn't cry until he got to the far door, hurrying along because he didn't want the juniors to see him blubbing.

'*Next*!' Wilson was impatient. He hadn't heard the small boy's light tap on the door.

Lawrence tried not to listen this time. Usher-Evans was only eight. He was having problems with homesickness in his first term. The last thing he needed was a caning, whatever he'd done. He'd probably been late for breakfast because he was a slow dresser. Here, nothing was taken into account; no allowances were made.

Usher-Evans received two with his shorts on. He was crying when he came out.

The bastard!

Suddenly, Lawrence realised that he was next. He heard the boy who had gone in before him receiving four on his bare bum. You were permitted to cry out − the head liked that. It was Griffiths Junior, his eyes watering, biting on his lower lip as he closed the door behind him.

Lawrence lifted his clenched fist, struck as firmly as he could; the woodwork hurt his knuckles.

'Come in.'

Wilson was never seen without his long black cassock and white clerical collar. Just as you never saw him without his long-stemmed rustic black pipe. A heavy smoker, he left a trail of pungent Latakia tobacco smoke in his wake wherever he went; the old deanery, which was now part of the cathedral preparatory school, was impregnated with it.

He smoked his pipe now, leaning back in the swivel chair behind his leather-topped desk, iron grey hair unbrushed, an expression of early-morning bad temper rather than severity on his thin features. Slowly he wiped his glasses with a handkerchief − all part of the procedure of intimidation.

He held his spectacles up to the window, squinted through them, put them back on. Then he reached behind him and picked up something from the floor. A pair of muddied football boots, real leather with the studs nailed to the soles. He held them at arm's length, affecting disdain with a wrinkling of his nostrils.

'These are yours, Prendergast. Don't deny it, your name is inside them.'

'Yes, sir.' Lawrence stood how he was expected to, with his hands clasped behind his back.

'They were left outside the changing room yesterday afternoon. Inge brought them to me. Have you not read the notice I pinned up on the changing room board instructing that *all* items of wear *must* be put away before tea?'

'Yes, sir.' Damn Inge − he went round looking to shop anybody he could for whatever he could.

'Why didn't you put them away, then, Prendergast? Why did you deliberately disobey my orders?'

'Because, sir', Lawrence swallowed − telling the truth was often more difficult than inventing a lie, 'I ... er, that is, the school were playing a home match against Ripley, sir. They were in the changing rooms when we got back from football practice. We're not allowed in when visiting teams are in there. The bell went for tea, and I'd've been punished if I'd been late for tea.'

'And you're going to be punished for not putting your boots away, instead.' Gloating now, lighting his pipe. 'At least you could have gone back after tea and put them away.'

'I went back, sir, but they were gone.' Lawrence couldn't suppress the suggestion of a whine in his voice.

'Because Inge had already found them. You made the school look like a litter dump, Prendergast, on the very day when we had a prestigious school visiting us to play a football match.'

'Yes, sir.'

'Come here, Prendergast.'

Lawrence shuffled forward until he stood right up against the desk. Wilson rose to his feet, wincing at a twinge of sciatica. The boots thudded back on the floor, then his long white fingers stretched out and fastened on the boy's ear, pinching it firmly.

'What are you, Prendergast?'

'I'm ... forgetful, sir.' Lawrence gasped as his ear was tweaked sharply, stretched and held, his head pulled to one side.

'Yes, and what else?'

'Ouch! Careless, sir.'

'And what *else*?'

'I ... don't ... know, sir.'

'Then, I'll tell you, Prendergast.' The ear was being screwed into a ball, suffused with blood. 'You're a fool, Prendergast.'

'Yes, sir.'

'What are you, Prendergast?'

'I'm a ... fool, sir.'

Lawrence hoped that the admission would spare him further agony. He was mistaken. The cruel fingers released their hold, but seconds later they had grasped a handful of hair, and tugged hard. He couldn't hold back a cry of pain.

'Dayboys are fools, Prendergast.' Lawrence felt his head being dragged down until his forehead rested on the shiny leather of the desk-top. 'What are they?'

'Fools, sir.'

'Fools and mummy's darlings.' Vindictively, Wilson banged Lawrence's forehead hard on the surface, three soft thuds, one after the other. 'You'll never make a *man*, Prendergast, you'll be a cissy until the day you die.'

'Yes, sir.'

'What are you, and what will you always be?'

'A cissy, sir.'

'Right, drop your shorts and bend over the arm of the couch. Quickly, boy!'

Lawrence hastened to do as he was ordered, casting a sideways, blurred glance at his tormentor. Edward Wilson had turned away and was carefully surveying his array of bamboo canes that were propped up prominently in the corner by his desk; all sizes, eight-foot beanpoles down to three-foot pea canes. He chose one of the latter, and wiped it affectionately, using the same handkerchief with which he had cleaned his glasses. He held it, bowed it, tested its flexibility.

'This is going to hurt, Prendergast.'

Lawrence closed his eyes, leaning over the shiny leather arm.

'I said, this is going to hurt, Prendergast.'

'Yes, sir.' Of course, he was right. There was no way the caning wasn't going to hurt.

'Four, I think, Prendergast. Next time it will be six.'

'Yes, sir.'

Lawrence jerked at the first stinging blow, felt the pain before he heard the crack of bamboo on soft flesh. A pause, three seconds, maybe four. The second hurt more than the first. The third a lot more. The fourth brought a cry to his lips.

'I said it would hurt, Prendergast.'

'Yes, sir.'

'Pull your trousers back up, boy, and don't start blubbing.'

'No, sir.' It wasn't easy not to cry when your arse

felt as if it had had a red-hot poker dragged across it.

'You're getting fat, Prendergast.'

'Yes, sir.'

'Because Mummy give her little darling stodgy food. If you were a boarder you would eat a carefully balanced school diet.'

'Yes, sir.'

'Go on, off with you!'

Lawrence didn't start to cry until he reached assembly. A group of pupils who had not had the misfortune to be caned that morning were laughing at him. Dayboys were an inferior species, anyway.

Lawrence knew that he was fat, and that he was a cissy. Prebendary Wilson had told him that he would never be a *man*. And, although he tried to tell himself that nothing the sadistic headmaster said was true, deep down he couldn't help accepting the man's judgement of him.

Lawrence was caned several more times during his period at the cathedral prep school. He never forgot to put his football boots away again but he had no control over his inability to master the complexities of the Latin language. And Edward Wilson taught Latin from the fourth form upwards. The headmaster always brought a three-foot pea cane into class with him; he seldom failed to use it.

Sitting there in the old shelter, admiring his carpentry skills, Lawrence determined that Prebendary Edward Wilson would hang for his crimes against humanity. It wasn't just his own canings and humiliation. No, there was also the matter of Peter Harrison ... there was no time to lose. The headmaster had long since retired and might die tomorrow from old age.

Chapter Eight

Larry had looked a lot better recently, Emily decided. The weather helped, even if it was rather too warm for her. According to the weather report on television, yesterday was the hottest May day since 1976. She remembered that scorching summer only too well. Bill had been confined to bed and she'd had to keep the bedroom windows open all day. Which had meant keeping a vigilant eye on her husband – in his mental state he was quite likely to think that they were doors and clamber out. She'd had to barricade them with furniture, but even then, he couldn't be trusted. It had been a trying time but she'd go through it again just to have him back.

Now Larry was her problem.

He hadn't spent so much time in the shelter recently. She supposed that now he'd finished making his studio and dark room he was relaxing for a bit. Back to the old routine, watching late-night videos and getting up late. Although he had gone out on a photography trip last week – perhaps he was beginning to get over his agoraphobia. At least his moods had improved – he was even quite affable at times. Yesterday he'd gone into town and done all the shopping for her. All right, there were one or two things he'd forgotten – her ginseng, for a start, because he said it was a con and a waste of money and couldn't possibly do her any good at her age. And he'd bought ordinary coffee instead of decaffeinated because *he* liked it better. But at least he hadn't gone and cancelled her *Mercury* again.

Now she could hear movements out at the front and

decided to see what he was doing. She shuffled painfully across the hall to the front door.

Larry's Mini was backed up to the porch and he was loading up his camera and bags. He looked up and saw her watching him.

'I'm going to see if I can get a few pictures that might sell for magazine covers. I mightn't be back till early evening.'

It was unlike him to volunteer information. Perhaps she should capitalise on his expansive mood.

'I'll be all right. Where are you thinking of going?'

'I'll probably head for the coast, Barmouth or Aberdovey. Both are only a couple of hours away.'

'You be careful – the roads will be packed with holidaymakers off to make the most of the weekend. It's Friday, don't forget.'

'I'll be all right. If I decide to stop over I'll give you a call.'

'You do that, Larry, and don't forget because I'll only worry.' But he wouldn't stay away overnight – he never did. Wherever he went, he always came home the same day.

'Glenn isn't coming today, is he?' There was a hint of anxiety in his voice, although he tried to sound nonchalant.

'No, he won't be coming till next Friday. You go off and enjoy yourself and don't worry about anything.'

Lawrence was tense, excited, but he wasn't worried. Today was *the* day, the one he'd waited for since that humiliating session of ear-twisting, hair-pulling and head banging, culminating in the ignominious caning. Today was going to be the sweetest in his whole life.

Last week had been a reconnaissance trip. He had been back to the library and checked in the latest edition of *Crockford's* that Prebendary Edward Wilson was still listed. He was. Cliff Cottage – it had to be a coastal residence. Lawrence had written down the address and telephone number, then checked him out with a phone call. Sorry to have bothered you. Wrong number. Jesus, the old fart sounded just the same as when he was headmaster, the voice as acidic as ever, irritated at being disturbed.

So far, so good.

He had driven over, staked the place out. It was useful having the camera: bird photography was as good a reason for being up on the cliffs as any if anybody queried his presence. In fact, he'd seen nobody — the area was too remote and it was still too early in the season for holidaymakers. Still, it might be different at weekends. Which was why he'd chosen Friday again.

Wilson's tiny whitewashed stone-built cottage nestled in a hollow a few hundred yards back from the cliff face, and was reached by an unsurfaced road from the tiny hamlet down in the valley. Lawrence had left his car in the adjoining village. There were several parked by the harbour, so it didn't look out of place.

He'd headed along the shingle beach until he was out of sight of the village, then found a cliff path that led upwards and inland. He followed his sense of direction and in about half an hour came upon the hollow from the north side. He stretched out in the heather. Christ, that pull had taken it out of him!

At first he thought that the cottage was empty. There was no car in sight — maybe Wilson and his wife had gone off shopping or visiting. He focused his binoculars on a rear window. Nothing seemed to be moving inside.

Shit, it was just his luck to come on an away day! Maybe the old bugger was in hospital. Or worse still, maybe he'd died since the latest *Crockford's* was typeset. Lawrence began to steel himself for the possibility that all the planning and anticipation had been a waste of time.

Until the front door opened and Wilson came outside.

Lawrence focused his lenses on the stooped figure below him. His overworked heart stepped up a gear. It was him, all right! Edward Wilson still wore the long cassock like a black shroud, and the pipe was clenched between the remnants of his teeth the way it always used to be. His shock of grey hair, a few shades whiter, blew in the stiff offshore breeze. Yes, it was unmistakably him. But he no longer seemed like an imposing figure. He leant on a stick and seemed unsteady on his feet as he made his way down the narrow garden path. And he was heading this way.

Lawrence edged back into the gorse bushes, oblivious of

the sharp thorns that penetrated his patched jeans, his pulse racing with excitement. He considered putting Phase Two into operation now. No, he checked himself sternly, this had to be a recce; he needed to know more about the man and his daily routine.

Wilson stopped within ten yards of where his former pupil lay hidden, puffed out his cheeks, wheezed and almost lost his grip on his pipe. There was something odd about him, Lawrence thought, something more than the frailty of old age. It was the eyes, he decided. Behind those heavy lenses the eyes were completely vacant. Then the thin lips moved, muttering, conducting a conversation with himself. Spittle ran down the pipe stem, hung in a string.

Wilson stood there for ten or fifteen minutes, his mutterings interspersed with bronchial coughs, leaning on his stick as if the walk had tired him. Then he stumbled onwards.

Lawrence trained the glasses on him again. The old man was following a well-worn sheep track that meandered through the rough terrain in a circular direction. Evidently he was heading back towards his cottage, approaching it from a north-westerly direction. It was an afternoon constitutional, no doubt about that, a breath of fresh air on a fine day.

Lawrence wondered where Mrs Wilson was. She was a good ten years younger than her husband, he remembered. Probably she had gone off somewhere in the car. She was his only worry.

Lawrence was back at the same vantage place overlooking Cliff Cottage. As on his previous visit, the heat of the day was pleasantly tempered by a sea breeze.

Gulls clamoured on the shoreline below the cliffs, but the cottage was still and silent. Mrs Wilson had obviously gone out in the car again. Lawrence pictured in his mind the old Standard Vanguard that used to stand outside the school back in the fifties. He could just imagine them still owning it, preserving it like Frank Coleman had kept his Vauxhall. Clinging to the past, bemoaning the passing of time.

Lawrence willed his old headmaster to emerge from the

cottage, to come this way again, but the hours slipped past, and there was no sign of life from the cottage. The blue sky was hazy now with high cloud but it wouldn't rain. Perhaps a sea mist would creep in later; that would be an advantage.

If he had not been so tense, Lawrence might have dozed. It was pleasantly warm, and the sound of the sheep bleating contentedly behind him was soothing, yet his thoughts continued to circle restlessly, spiralling into depression. It was all going to come to nothing, he knew it would. Like everything else he undertook. He'd toiled away, building his gallows, but it would end there.

And what if Glenn decided to visit after all? He would not be able to get into the shelter but he might start taking things away again. Stealing, that was what it was. Things didn't have to be worth anything to be stolen. Glenn was a thief.

He would give it another couple of hours. Then, if there was no sign of Wilson, he would walk down to Cliff Cottage and knock on the door. *Fancy seeing you here, sir. You remember me, don't you? Let me remind you. You used to twist my ear and pull my hair, bang my head hard on the desk. And for kicks you thrashed my bare arse. I'm a fool and a cissy, and soon I'm going home to Mummy again.*

Suddenly, he heard footsteps, somebody coughing. He sat up and saw a lean, black-clad figure stumbling towards him, barely ten yards from him.

The prebendary must have taken his daily constitutional in a reverse direction. Probably walking the same track, the same way, day after day, became boring. He wasn't going to pause for breath here, that was certain. He seemed to be in a hurry.

'Good afternoon, sir.' Lawrence was on his knees, struggling to stand up. 'Sir' came habitually, not out of respect. He winced at its use, hoping that Wilson hadn't noticed.

'Uh?' Wilson halted, peered around him, his pallid features screwed up into an expression of irritability at being disturbed in his musings. 'Who's there?'

'It's *me*, sir.' Damn, it had slipped out again.

'Who's "*me*?"' The scrawny neck was thrust forward and the eyes glared definatly.

'Lawrence Prendergast.' A pause to see if anything registered behind those strong lenses; it didn't. 'You used to teach me Latin.'

'Oh, oh ...' An uncertain memory struggled, the look was one of puzzlement now. 'Oh, did I? You must be an old pupil of mine, then.'

'Yes.'

'Fancy that. I don't see many of them these days. I suppose it's a long way to travel out here. I can't get to reunions now, either, so I'm a bit out of touch. An old boy did visit me last summer, though. Grown up with a wife and family, you'd possibly remember him. Bryan Inge. Was he before or after your time?'

'He was head boy when I was at school.' *And a shit arse he was, too.*

'Well, well, well. The old man chuckled. 'Did you come here looking for me?'

'Yes.'

'Well, I always go out for a walk on fine afternoons. I'm a bit later than usual today because I dozed off, overslept. You must have been knocking on the door whilst I was out.'

'That's right.'

'Well, well, even if I can't quite place you now I'm sure it'll all come back. I've had hundreds of boys through my hands over the twenty years when I was headmaster. I'm sure I'll remember you eventually. My eyesight's not what it was and you've grown up. If I saw you as a boy again. I'd remember you. But you're a man now.'

That isn't what you once told me. 'I've been looking forward to seeing you again for years, but I never got round to it until today.'

'Would you care for a cup of tea? Or a glass of my home-made wine? I don't make wine any longer, haven't done for five years, so what's left is sure to be matured.' He laughed at his own joke.

'I'd love a cup of tea. If it isn't putting your wife to too much trouble.'

'Oh, she's dead, didn't you know? But of course you

wouldn't know, would you? A year ago last March, she'd been ailing for some time. I've got used to being on my own now. My son – you'd remember Keith – he's always trying to persuade me to go and live with him and his wife. Unfortunately they're still childless. But l like it here, I don't mind being alone. Keith will pop over sometime next week, I expect. He usually phones a couple of times during the week but the dashed phone isn't working at the moment. I wonder if you'd do me a favour – when you get home, ring up and report it for me, will you?'

'I'll do that.'

'Good fellow. Now, let's go down to the cottage and have a drink. Which was it you said you preferred, tea or wine? I think there's still a bottle of my potato wine left, that really is my best.'

'Tea will suit me fine.' Lawrence stood to one side and let the other lead the way. Suddenly, everything was starting to work out.

'It was the governors who conspired to get me out.' Edward Wilson handed his guest a cup of tea, then slopped his own in the saucer as he sat down in the worn armchair. The springs sagged, protested. 'Otherwise, I should still be there. They wanted a younger man, you know, couldn't believe that somebody my age could still do the job. That was when the school started going downhill, so Inge told me. No discipline; teaching standards fell. And now they're even taking in *girls*. If it had come to that, I'd've gone anyway. Still, I have my memories.'

Lawrence sipped his tepid, weak tea, and decided to give Wilson a cue. 'They don't cane the pupils any longer, so I've heard.'

'So Inge told me. They expel them if they do something really bad but they don't give them the cane. I would, I tell you, and if the authorities didn't like it, they could dashed well lump it! One breed of softies breeding another! A good caning never did anybody any harm. Did I ever cane you ... what did you say your name was?'

'Prendergast.'

'Ah, that's right, you'll have to forgive my memory. Did

I ever you you two of the best? Or four? Or six?' The old man was alert now, eager to relive yesteryear with another who remembered. He leaned forward heedlessly, slopping his tea on his lap.

'Several times.' Lawrence felt himself begin to shake with anger. He hoped that Wilson hadn't noticed. 'I remember the time when I forgot to put my football boots away ...'

'Ah, yes, you needed to be taught a lesson in tidiness.' Wilson put his cup and saucer down on a side table and rubbed his bony hands together. 'That'd be four, with your trousers down. Really hard. I expect you smarted for days afterwards.'

'That's right. And you twisted my ear, pulled my hair and banged my head on the desk.'

'You remember every bit of it!' An almost childish chortle. 'How marvellous! See, it made an impression on you − you never forgot. I'll warrant you don't leave your things lying about the house these days. Your wife has me to thank for that!'

'She'd love to meet you, sir, she really would.'

'And I'd love to meet her.'

'Why don't we take a ride and I'll introduce you? If you're not doing anything in particular, perhaps I could take you over later on?' Lawrence held his breath.

Wilson fell silent, nodded to himself. He was pondering on it. 'It's a possibility. I don't go out much these days, not since my wife died. She used to drive me. My eyesight isn't good enough for driving, and the doctor advised me to hand in my licence. So I let Keith have the car. I did tell you poor Edna was dead, didn't I?'

'Yes, it must have been a happy release for her.' *From you.* 'A trip out would do you good. Better if we went later on − it can get a bit hot in the car in the daytime.'

'Perhaps we will. Edward Wilson knocked out his pipe in an ashtray and reached for a polythene pouch off the table by his elbow. 'D'you smoke, Prenderhouse?'

'No, sir.'

'Well, if you ever do, go for a pipe. And a decent tobacco.' He held up the pouch, displaying the stag's head emblem. 'Exmoor Hunt is the best you can buy − smoked it ever since I was at university. The broad cut, not the fine. Pipe smoking's gone out of fashion. These cissies today aren't man enough for a pipe. You take a tip from me, smoke a pipe.'

'I'll have to try it some time.'

'They'd like to ban it, you know. Like they've banned the cane. Ban anything that's reminiscent of bygone days, they would. That's why the world's in such a mess. No discipline.'

'They don't even hang murderers these days, sir.'

'Absolutely! You've hit the nail on the head. If I had my way, I'd bring back the rope tomorrow.' Wilson paused, a match posed above the bowl of his pipe. 'The nine o'clock walk. Or was it eight?'

'Can't remember, but it'd be great to see hanging back again. I'm glad you'd like it, too, sir.'

'I would.' He dropped the match into the ashtray, struck another. 'Is it far to your place, Peterhouse?'

'Only a short ride, sir.'

'Then we'll go. Later, as you say. I've got a bit of salad for tea — would you care to join me?'

'That's very kind of you, sir. I'm honoured that you'd like to meet my wife.'

'Love to, but I don't want to put her to any trouble getting tea, so if we go after we've eaten then she won't have to bother. Where have you parked your car?'

'I've left it down in the village. I didn't really know where you lived, so I came on foot. I didn't think it'd be quite this far. Still, that's no problem. After tea I'll walk back and fetch it.'

'You're sure it's no trouble?'

'None at all.'

It was dusk by the time Lawrence left the cottage and set off in the direction of the village. He fought against the urge to hurry.

An hour later, when he backed the Mini up to the front door of Cliff Cottage, Prebendary Wilson was waiting eagerly on the step, peering into the darkness. He wore the dark overcoat and black homburg which Lawrence remembered from his schooldays.

It was as if he had dressed nostalgically for the occasion.

Chapter Nine

The journey took a full two hours.
 Lawrence had had some difficulty getting Edward Wilson into the passenger seat of the Mini, since the space was cramped and the old man's arthritic limbs seemed incapable of bending. At one stage Lawrence almost despaired. Plan Two for transportation was to render his victim unconscious, but that was a last resort. The bastard might have died on him and thus escaped the justice which awaited him. Also it would have increased the risk factor: lately the police were stopping vehicles for random checks.
 'I really think I won't bother after all.' Wilson attempted to extricate a leg, but his foot was stuck fast against the seat lever. 'I really can't do with all this performance.'
 'You're fine now, sir.' Lawrence pushed him firmly into place and slammed the door shut.
 'This is the most uncomfortable car I've ever been in.'
 'It won't be for long.' *And now you're in, you're certainly not getting out.*
 'I go to bed at half past ten.'
 'We'll be home long before then.'
 Lawrence eased the car down the rough track until he came to the road below. The engine seemed sluggish, jerky. *Christ, please don't break down on me!*
 'I don't like travelling at night.' Wilson kicked his feet petulantly. 'Never did drive after dark myself. This journey seems to be taking a lot longer than you said, Porterhouse. I think I'd prefer you to turn round and take me back home.'

'We're almost there,' Lawrence lied.

After that his passenger fell silent. Later, when Lawrence glanced sideways furtively, he saw that Wilson's head had slumped forward, his glasses hanging precariously. Thank God, the old bastard had fallen asleep. So far everything had gone like clockwork. Plan One had worked beautifully.

The Mini threatened to cut out on a long, steep hill; Lawrence held his breath but somehow it chugged its way to the top. It cut out on most junctions unless he revved the engine. Once when it died it took a minute or so to get it going again. But Prebendary Wilson never stirred. After a while he began to snore loudly. Something fell and bounced on the floor: his pipe.

He leaned sideways against Lawrence. Lawrence resisted the urge to shove him roughly back into his seat. The longer the bastard slept, the better.

Something was badly wrong with the Mini: even with the accelerator pedal pressed down to the floor it wouldn't go above thirty mph. Lawrence began to seat. On his left he saw a police patrol car in a lay-by. *Stop there, you bastards*! They did.

Finally, with immense relief, he saw the gateway of the family home. He swung in off the road and let the engine die. Christ, it had been bloody close!

'We're there!' He prodded his passenger, who reacted with a protesting grunt. 'Come on, sir, time to get out.'

'Uh? Where are we?'

'My home, sir. Now, let me help you out and we'll go and meet the family.' *And I just hope Mother isn't standing on the doorstep wondering where I've got to.*

But there was no sign of her, and he silently thanked God for her poor hearing. She must have missed the sound of the car drawing up. He helped Wilson out of the car.

'I wonder you don't install some outside lighting, Penthouse.'

'It's not working at the moment, the electrician's coming tomorrow.' Lies were coming much more easily now. 'Don't you worry, sir, I know every inch of this path, I don't even need a torch. Just lean on me.'

'Drat it, I forgot my stick. I shouldn't have come. I

can't stay long, anyway. I have to be in bed by half past ten.'

'You'll be fast asleep by then, I can assure you. Now, hold on to me and mind the steps.'

Wilson stumbled and Lawrence's grip on his arm tightened. 'Drat it, where the devil are we going?'

'We have to go in through the basement, sir.'

Lawrence found his key and fitted it in the lock. There was a sharp click and the heavy door swung inwards. He closed it behind him and locked it before switching on his makeshift lighting.

'Good Lord!' Edward Wilson stared in amazement. 'Where on earth have we come to?'

'My den.'

'This is schoolboy stuff.' The old man's eyes roved the oblong underground room. 'And that thing there, it looks like ...'

'A gallows, sir,' Lawrence laughed. 'That's exactly what it is.'

'I thought you were taking me to see ...'

'This!' Lawrence stepped to one side. Deprived of his support, Wilson tottered unsteadily. 'This is what I've brought you to see. Sit down on that chair, please.'

'Look, if this is some kind of a joke ...'

'It isn't, it's deadly serious.' Lawrence wasn't laughing any longer. 'For your information, Edward Wilson, you are a condemned man. You stand charged with assault on an unspecified number of schoolboys. Not to mention murder.

'*Murder*! You're mad, boy. Stark raving mad. Let me out of here this very minute. That is an order.'

'Unfortunately', Lawrence held up the key, dropped it into the pocket of his jeans, 'you are no longer in a position of authority. You can't give orders. In fact, you can't do anything at all. Now, *sit down*!'

Shakily, Wilson sat down on the old chair. 'I'd be glad if you'd explain what all this is about, Pilsworth.'

'Prendergast, actually,' Lawrence leaned back against the wall. 'Now, first of all, do you confess to the charges?'

'They are quite preposterous.'

'Fair enough, you deny them. Do you deny that, over a period of several years, you caned young boys, six mornings a week except during school holidays?'

'I caned hundreds of boys, yes. I was merely doing my job.'

'Good, at least you confess to that. It saves a lot of trouble.'

'What's going on?' Wilson made as if to get up but Lawrence pushed him firmly back into the chair. 'I demand ...'

'Shut up and listen. You are also charged with the murder of one Peter Harrison on 9th October, 1959.'

'Peter Harrison!' Wilson's mouth dropped open, and his glasses slid down his nose again. 'Of course I remember him, poor boy. He played rugby that afternoon, then complained of a headache afterwards. In the evening he was rushed to hospital with a headache so bad that he was screaming with pain. By ten o'clock he was dead. A brain haemorrhage. The coroner put it down to a knock on the head, possibly a kick. I remember, I shall never forget it.'

'*Because you killed him, Edward Wilson*!

'What on earth are you saying? How dare you!'

'On the morning of 9th October', Lawrence continued relentlessly, 'Peter Harrison was sent to report to you. He had lost his school tie, and his so-called crime was that he went to the harvest festival service wearing an open-necked shirt. Not only did you cane him, you grabbed his hair and banged his head on the desk. *Didn't you*?'

'I ... I really can't remember.' Wilson's anger had turned to fear.

'Because you got rid of your early-morning bad temper by banging most boys' heads on the desk before you caned them.'

'Yes.' It came out as a whisper. 'It never did them any harm, shook them up a bit.'

'It killed Peter Harrison.'

Edward Wilson was deathly white. 'No. No, it couldn't have.'

'It did. The charge is murder, Edward Wilson, *not* manslaughter. Because you meant to kill the boy — the rugby game was a convenient let-out for you.'

'I wouldn't have harmed the boy, I swear it.'

'Let me explain your motives. On the afternoon of 7th October, a Saturday, you went pheasant shooting with Peter Harrison's father. Peter came along with you. During the course of your afternoon's sport, you fired both barrels of your twelve-bore at a low-flying pheasant. Unfortunately, there were some farm workers behind the hedge, and one of them was peppered with shot. Not badly, the range was long, and most of the pellets lodged in his clothing. There was an altercation; Harrison, senior, was nearest to the men, and they blamed him. Not wishing to offend his guest and the headmaster of his son's school, he apologised and tipped the unfortunate man very generously, and the matter was concluded. Except that Peter had seen the whole thing and knew who was to blame. A shooting accident is one thing, but to be known to have stood back like the arrant coward you are and let somebody else take the blame, would not have enhanced your reputation as either a headmaster or a man of the cloth. Am I right?'

'I shot the man,' Wilson was cringing, shaking visibly, 'but I assure you, it had nothing to do with Peter's death. I swear it.'

'You murdered him and you've covered it up for over thirty years. Now you are found guilty of murder!'

'You're mad! I demand that you let me out of here. What . . . what on earth are you doing?'

Lawrence had tugged something out of the back pocket of his jeans. It looked like a handkerchief, except that it was black. Lawrence shook the square of material and draped it over his head. From a distance he reminded his prisoner of an orthodox Jew. His eyes were fixed and staring, and his huge frame trembled — with excitement.

'Edward Wilson, you have been found guilty of murder. You are sentenced to death by hanging. The sentence will be carried out tomorrow morning.'

'That's crazy, impossible. You can't.'

'Can't I?' Lawrence removed his black kerchief and

stuffed it back into his pocket, then gestured towards the gallows. Suddenly they seemed huge and real, an instrument of grim death.

Lawrence stepped forward and gripped the frail man's arm. He hauled him to his feet and propelled him towards the open door of the former lavatory.

The condemned cell.

'What would you like for your breakfast, sir?'

There was scarcely room for both of them in the confined space. The bare walls were whitewashed, and the only item of furniture was a sagging camp bed. Alongside it was a plastic washing-up bowl in case the prisoner should need it. Lawrence didn't like cleaning up messes.

'Breakfast?'

'What do you usually have for breakfast, sir?'

'Two slices of toast and a cup of tea. but ...'

'Then that is what I shall bring you tomorrow. In the meantime, sleep well.'

'Look here Prenderhouse ...' Wilson made a despairing grab at Lawrence but he was already outside. The heavy door crashed against Wilson's arm and sent him staggering back. Lawrence heard him fall as he slammed the door and locked it.

'I shall have the police on you!' The threat came out as a pathetic cry. Wilson's frightened wailings died away as Lawrence locked the outer door after him.

The shelter was virtually soundproof — shouts and screams could not be heard outside. Only his own hammering had been audible in the house during that brief period when he was forced to work with the door open. Even Frank Coleman, making coffins in his workshop on the other side of the mutilated hedge, would not hear Prebendary Edward Wilson's cries for help. But those cries would have been silenced by the time Frank started his day's work.

Lawrence was ecstatic. The feeling reminded him of those Christmas Eves when he was a small boy. He knew that he would not sleep tonight.

He stood listening in the darkened hallway but there was no sound from upstairs, no stealthy footsteps on the landing. It was unlike his mother not to creep out of her room to check if he was all right. He did not like exceptions to rules.

But then elation swept aside all other considerations. He went into the kitchen and delved into the ice-encrusted freezer in search of a pizza. He was ravenous – tonight he would enjoy a celebration feast.

Chapter Ten

'I never heard you come in last night, Larry.' Emily, crept almost apologetically into the kitchen, clutching her unbelted housecoat around her. 'I took my pills early, I must have gone right off to sleep.'

He didn't look up from buttering two slices of toast on the working surface. 'I was late. I'd've rung you if I was stopping over, like I said.' He poured tea into a cup and reached for a plate out of the cupboard.

'Did you have a good day?'

'Not bad. I took plenty of pics; now I'll go and develop them, see how I've done.'

'I thought you sent your transparencies away to be processed?'

'I took some black and whites as well.' He picked up the plate of toast in one hand, the cup in the other.

'Wouldn't you sooner eat before you got out there?'

'Why?' He eyed her suspiciously.

'No reason, I just thought it might be more comfortable to sit at the table rather than to breakfast in that awful place.' She noticed a dirty plate and cup by the sink; this was probably Larry's second breakfast. So much for his diet! 'Are you going to be long?'

'I don't know, it depends how it goes. Why?'

'I was hoping you'd do some shopping for me.'

'Later. I want to do a bit more work on the pond first.'

'Oh, Larry, no! You know what happened the last time you did some digging – you ended up with that terrible nosebleed. And you still haven't been to the doctor. Arthur can finish the pool off next week.'

'There's only a bit of shaping I want to do, fill the bottom in a little. You said yourself that it was too deep.'

'Oh, all right.' She knew that he wouldn't take any notice of her, anyway. 'But don't you go overdoing it, d'you hear?'

'I won't, just stop nagging.'

She held the door for him. 'D'you want me to come and open the shelter door for you, Larry?'

'*No!*' It was almost a scream.

'All right, calm down. You're overtired, Larry, that's your trouble. You've had a very late night, you ought to catch up on some sleep.'

But Lawrence was already gone, shambling his way down to the old shelter, slopping tea as he went.

'Mornin'.' Frank Coleman's face appeared in the gap in the privet, with the usual cigarette smouldering in the centre of his lips. 'Nice morning again but we're going to be in some trouble if we don't get some rain soon. 1976 all over again. You're not going to spend all day in that stuffy old shelter, are you?'

Lawrence restrained himself from yelling 'fuck off, you nosey old bastard', and muttered, 'I've got a lot of work to do.' He disappeared down the flight of steps. Everybody was getting on his nerves this morning.

Silence and darkness greeted him as he unlocked the door and fumbled it open. He switched on the photographic lights and saw that the small door on the right was still closed. He hadn't expected to find it any other way: there was no way that Wilson could have escaped.

'Breakfast, sir.' He spoke to break the awful stillness, then found himself listening as he inserted the key in the lock. He had expected to be greeted by a plea to be set free, an anguished wail from an aged, cowardly bully.

Just silence. Oh, shit, the bastard hasn't gone and died on me, has he?

Edward Wilson was slumped on the camp bed, his back against the wall and his head drooping on his chest. So limp and lifeless, so pale; not so much as the twitch of a muscle, just a string of saliva hanging from his mouth.

'Wake up, sir!' Lawrence shook him roughly. *Please*, wake up.

Wilson stirred, groaned. Oh, thank God! An eyelid flickered open, the lips moved. He mumbled incoherently; it would take a few moments before everything came back to him.

'Where ... am ... I?' He stared about him, a puzzled expression on his face. 'What's ... what's going on?'

'You'd better have your breakfast first.' Lawrence glanced at his watch – it was just a quarter to nine. 'Then we can have a chat.'

Wilson accepted the plate of toast and slurped down the lukewarm tea. 'Why am I here?'

'We discussed all that last night.' Lawrence stood with his back to the door. 'Don't you remember?'

Wilson struggled to remember, then gulped suddenly on a swallow of toast. 'I must have dreamt it!' His face was alert now, alarmed. 'A nightmare. I was accused of killing Peter Harrison. I was sentenced to hang.' He tried to laugh; it sounded forced. '*You* were going to hang me. How ridiculous.'

'It's true.' Lawrence smiled. 'You didn't dream it, it all happened. You were tried and found guilty of murder. I *am* going to hang you!'

'Look ... I mean, if this is some kind of joke ...'

'It isn't, it's deadly serious.'

'You can't. You daren't. That would be *murder*!'

'Not in my book. Now, hurry up and finish your breakfast, it's ten to nine already.'

Wilson pushed his plate of cold toast to one side. 'Open the door and let me out. If you don't, I'll have the police on you.'

'Let's not waste any more time.' Lawrence reached up to a small shelf in the corner and lifted down a dogeared bible. 'Aren't you going to finish your toast? I'm sorry there isn't time for me to get you some more tea.'

'I'm not hungry.'

'Would you care to take holy communion?'

'I should not. You are not ordained; it would be blasphemy.'

'Perhaps you'd like to pray then.'

'I always say prayers after breakfast.'

'Carry on, don't let me stop you. Would you like to smoke your pipe?' Lawrence produced the pipe which he had retrieved from the car. 'Just half a bowl, there's time.'

The hectoring facade of the headmaster was beginning to crumble. Wilson reached for the pipe with shaking hands and began to stuff the bowl with coarse stranded tobacco. He fumblingly lit a match, then puffed out a cloud of aromatic smoke. 'This is some sort of sick game. You're trying to frighten me because I caned you at school. That's what it's all about, isn't it?'

'I want to frighten you, but I'm not bluffing. I'm going to hang you, sir.'

'You're mad. What did you say your name was?'

'Prendergast. Lawrence Prendergast.'

'Dashed if I can remember you.'

'My brother Glenn was at your school, too. 1947–53. I was there 1953–56. We were both dayboys.'

'Ah, that's why I don't remember you. Part-timers. A pupil needed to board to receive the full benefit of private schooling.'

'I should have flogged you first.' Lawrence had begun to tremble. The pent-up rage was stirring, threatening to erupt. 'But I don't have anything to do it with.'

Edward Wilson's lower lip trembled beneath his pipe stem. 'It was only for your own good, Prendergast. There was nothing personal in it. Discipline. I wanted to make a man of you.'

'You enjoyed every second of it, don't deny it. You loved to inflict pain; it gave you a sense of power. Now all that's come to an end.'

Suddenly Wilson seemed to realise that Lawrence meant what he said. He looked tired, old, resigned. 'I've been waiting to die ever since my dear wife was taken from me. Every night I've prayed to God to let me join her. I once thought about taking my own life. That was a sinful thought, the devil was tempting me. I resisted it, asked the

Lord to forgive me for even having contemplated it. I'm not afraid of dying, just the manner.'

Oh, shit, he actually wants to die! It was almost an anticlimax. Lawrence looked at his watch again: five to nine. 'Take off your collar, please. and I'll have to ask you to put your pipe out.'

Wilson laid his pipe on the floor. Lawrence was surprised how deftly he undid the stiff collar.

'Stand up, please, and put your hands behind your back.'

Wilson did as he was ordered, a pathetic figure now. He could scarcely straighten his back; the night on the damp collapsible bed had aggravated his arthritis. He made no move to resist as a length of red plastic binder string was wound round his wrists, pulled tight and knotted.

'It's time to go.' Lawrence pushed him gently in the direction of the door. At a prison execution there would have been a chaplain; Wilson could fulfil that role himself.

Wilson did not look up at the scaffold as he was guided on to the trapdoor. Lawrence had made a chalk mark where the condemned must stand. He dropped to his knees, pulled out another length of binder twine and slipped it around his victim's ankles.

'It's a bit tight.' Wilson whispered. 'It might cut off my circulation.'

Lawrence straightened up and held on to Wilson as a wave of dizziness came and went. His blood pressure must have soared with the excitement of this moment. He took a few deep breaths to calm himself. 'I'm afraid you'll have to wear this, too. I've cut a nose hole so that you can breathe.'

This time the old man resisted, tried to move his head. Lawrence grabbed a handful of grey hair, making sure he pulled hard, for old times' sake. Wilson gave an anguished shriek. He tugged again, left to right and left again, felt some of the hairs come out by their roots. Jesus, he was tempted to bang that head on the gallows upright, maybe drop the old man's trousers, too. It smelled like Wilson had already shat himself.

Wilson's cries were muffled now. Lawrence held him with

one hand as he struggled feebly, and, with the other, reached down the rope.

The smooth woven hemp was sensuous to his touch. He let it run through his fingers. It was like a long snake, uncoiling in readiness to strike a death blow with its poisoned fangs. The brass eyelet glinted menacingly. Then the noose was around Wilson's scrawny neck, pulled just tight enough to chafe the wrinkled skin.

'Stand still, fuck you!'

A gurgle answered him. Wilson's shoulders were hunched; he might be on the verge of collapse.

Lawrence checked his watch yet again. Sixty seconds and it would be nine o'clock. He was trembling – from nervousness, not fear. Hanging was a definite art, an age-old tradition that was handed down, you'd have to be damned lucky to do it to perfection the first time. His mind was filled with doubts.

Suppose the trap didn't drop. Suppose it jammed because of his amateurish joinery. You were allowed three goes. After that ... No, Wilson could not leave here alive. Suppose the drop didn't kill him – neither strangled nor dislocated his neck. It had to. Suppose ...

Ten seconds to go.

'May God have mercy on your soul.'

There was no answer. The cloth mask didn't puff out any more. Wilson seemed to have sagged, supported only by the rope around his neck. He might have died already from fright.

Lawrence jerked the lever.

The body shot from view as the hinged door bumped against the brickwork of the old dumbwell, thudding and vibrating. The rope was taut, spinning. Creaking. Then, suddenly, it was slack. There was a soft thud from the depths of the pit.

Lawrence was sweating, and he experienced a sudden urge to pass water, to empty his bowels. By Jesus Christ, he'd done it – he'd hanged the old bastard like he'd always planned to! The rope must have snapped above the noose. You were supposed to calculate weight against the breaking strain of the hemp. Lawrence had just guessed it, basing his calculations on a quarter of a century of memories. Wilson must have put on weight since his retirement. But he had to be dead.

All the same, Lawrence was scared to look. He shied back from the edge of the pit, found himself listening, afraid in case he heard something writhing down there, groaning. But all he heard was the pounding of his own heart and a roaring in his ears.

He wished he could have walked right out of the shelter, locked the door behind him and never gone back. *Don't be bloody stupid, you have to dispose of the body.* With that thought, he steeled himself and crept towards that yawning square in the floor. The rope that disappeared down into its depths still twisted and spun like a broken swing on a playground. No groans, no dying pleas for mercy came from the depths. So he bent forward, peered downwards, and instantly threw up.

The stout hemp had not snapped. Nor had it slipped free. The raw, bloody neck was still clamped in the noose, and the head hung downwards, trailing bloody sinews. The body lay huddled in a corner of the disused cesspit, the protruding neck stump bleeding freely.

Oh, Jesus alive, I've pulled his fucking head off!

Lawrence vomited a second time and then found he was retching on an empty stomach. Below him the severed head swung to and fro, a macabre metronome that was slowly losing its impetus. Gradually, the bloody neck was slipping free of the noose; the masked head hung lower and lower. Finally, it fell, hit the brick floor beneath with a sickening crack and rolled towards the body as if it sought to join up again with the torn neck.

Lawrence rested awhile and then he knew what he had to do.

'Larry, are you sure you're all right? It's awfully hot out there.'

Emily was standing in the patio doorway. She couldn't see down to the pool excavations from there but she must have heard him digging.

'I'll be packing up in a few minutes, Mother.' He leaned on

his shovel, sweat stinging his eyes and blurring his vision. At least the decapitated corpse was out of sight, buried beneath a bag of lime and two feet of sand at the base of the pond diggings.

'I'll put the kettle on.' He heard the door close. Even in the hottest weather Emily always kept the doors closed; locked, too, when she was on her own. Like the windows. Because he had taught her to do so. She was learning to leave the curtains closed, too, and had stopped opening them whenever he was away from home.

God, he was knackered! He had waited his chance until Frank next door went into the house for his ritual mid-morning coffee. You could set your watch by the retired undertaker – every morning he downed tools at ten-thirty, shut the shed door, and shuffled back up the garden. He returned at eleven-fifteen sharp.

Half an hour in which to drag the body from the shelter, drop it into the bottom of the deep hole and get it covered in case anybody came. That had meant an hour and a half alone in the shelter with that mutilated, hanged corpse for company. Lawrence might have gone crazy, rushed out screaming and told the world that he'd hanged Prebendary Wilson at long last and would somebody please go and clear up the mess.

Instead, he revelled in his triumph, forced himself to hate the old man more than he had done all along. He just wished that the bastard had lingered, suffered, prolonged the final agonies. But that didn't stop Lawrence from taking his revenge on the bloody remains.

He crept out of the shelter. He knew that there were some old pea canes somewhere in the shed; it took him ten minutes to find them. He took two three-footers, a precaution in case one snapped off, and drew them between his finger and thumb to remove years of dust. Then he climbed down the step ladder into the pit.

Somehow he seemed stronger than ever today, both physically and mentally. He grabbed Wilson's ankle, and managed to drag him back up to floor level. Then he went back for the head. He was sweating profusely, and his jeans and shirt clung damply to his overweight body, but he ignored the discomfort. His body odours were the sweet smell of success.

Leaving the hands and feet still tied, he draped the corpse, neck first, over the base of the gallows. He could hear the blood dripping back into the pit below. He pulled the bag off the head. The eyes bulged in their sockets in an expression of sheer terror. With difficulty he set the head up on the table in the corner, facing it towards the scaffold. So that it could watch.

He gathered up the blood-streaked cassock and draped it over the folded body. Then the braces. Lawrence snapped them, tugged down the grey flannel trousers and longjohns. Christ, what a bloody stink! Wilson had let everything go, most of it evidently before death, because it was drying on him. That, in itself, was pleasing. A lot of boys at school, including himself, had shat themselves out in the corridor before going in to take their punishment.

It had to be six strokes. Nothing else would do.

Lawrence cut into the dead flesh with every downward stroke. Weals became lacerations; then crisscrossed gouges. Because he could not stop at six. Nor twelve. And when the bamboo finally snapped under the strain, he grabbed for the second. And continued until that broke, too.

He left the flogged corpse hanging there, and turned towards the head. Jesus, it had seen, all right, knew what had happened, even felt the pain — because you could see it in those dead eyes. *Remember how you used to pull my hair, you bastard*! Lawrence was surprised how easily the grey tufts came out of the scalp. In no time at all the skull was completely bald.

The cranium was already cracked, but he split it deeper and wider as he banged it against the wall, holding it by the protruding ears. Afterwards, it didn't look like Prebendary Wilson at all.

Now head and body were lying in the sand at the base of the pond excavation, burning in hot white lime, searing and fizzing. He smoothed the base over with the back of the spade, then climbed out with difficulty. He lay flat, stretched downwards and erased his footprints with the broom which he had left in readiness for that very purpose.

It had been a good day. Really good. Excellent, in fact. After a change of clothes he sat in the cool of the kitchen sipping his tea.

His mother continued to fuss around him. You look tired, Larry. You shouldn't have worked in the pond today after all that driving and photography yesterday. It's not good for you.'

'I'm going to have a sleep this afternoon.' He gave a tired smile.

A brief respite and then it would be time to start planning again. There was still a lot of that pond crater that needed filling in so that it would meet with his mother's approval. Emily Prendergast had a dread of deep water.

He went upstairs and lay on his grimy, unmade bed. Strangely, annoyingly, the desire for sleep had deserted him. He lay thinking; not about his schooldays – they were over and done with. Dead. He thought he could forget them now, something which had been impossible before today. Now he had moved on, into adolescence.

Into banking. And again he was trembling with the rage and frustration of injustice.

Chapter Eleven

A week had gone by and still there were no reports of the missing Prebendary Wilson.

His son Keith had raised the alarm. The phone was out of order so he had driven over to check on his father. The cottage was locked up, and when he let himself in, he found that only his father's hat and coat were gone – no overnight clothes, nothing to suggest that the old man might have gone to stay with friends.

Keith went straight to the local police station. A uniformed constable accompanied him back to the cottage to search the premises.

'Now sir, you're sure your father didn't have any plans to go away?'

'No, I *told* you. He's just disappeared.'

Keith bore a distinct likeness to his absent father: the same pinched features and prematurely greying hair, the same distinctive stoop of the shoulders and long white fingers. Keith, too, was a headmaster, but his ambitions went far beyond his little-known private school. He, too, would have used the cane with relish had corporal punishment still been permitted.

'I'll make a report and get a search party organised.' The officer went back to his car and spoke into his radio. There was no immediate panic, not when a guy was verging on ninety. The chances were they'd find the body quite close, maybe at the foot of the cliffs or in the woods beyond. Senile dementia often led to suicide, particularly after a partner's death. Or it could be an accident: old folks wandered off, got lost or fell and broke a leg and weren't able to attract attention. Hypothermia could finish them off. Unless you were a close relative, you didn't get upset. It wasn't like something happening to a child. You had to be realistic.

That afternoon a party of police, assisted by villagers, combed the surrounding area. But there was no sign of Edward Wilson.

Detective Sergeant Adam Kent rarely read the newspapers. He wasn't interested in either sport or politics. Just crime. And crime reports all came from press conferences given by the police. You usually knew the facts; invariably reporters got them wrong, or else they elaborated on them in order to sell more papers. So there wasn't much point in reading what they had written. Except out of idle curiosity whilst you were waiting for Sunday lunch to be served.

Like today when he flipped idly through the pages of the local Sunday newspaper. The publishers presented it as 'family reading', but even so they liked to splash a good sensational story across the front page.

RETIRED LOCAL HEADMASTER MISSING

'My God, you're actually reading the paper!' Brenda Kent came through from the kitchen carrying a dish of mixed vegetables. 'A year of marriage and this is the first time I've seen you open up the paper.'

'Boredom.' He didn't look up from the feature. His abrupt reply might have sounded rude to someone who didn't know him well — but not to Brenda. It was one of the reasons she loved him: he never wasted words; he only spoke when he had something to say. 'A man acts out of character when he's bored. As an ex-WPC you should know that.'

'Which means you found some "shop"'. She regarded him fondly.

Short and well built, with close-cropped fair hair and lived-in features — Adam Kent gave the impression of a healthy outdoor type. A husband who came home in the evenings and then went out jogging or playing squash. The impression was misleading. If Kent went out then he was on a job, otherwise he stayed in; he conserved his energy like he did words, used it when he had to. He had plenty in reserve.

'So what's so interesting?' she asked curiously.

'A retired headmaster just walked out of his home a week ago, hasn't been seen since. No body. No clues.'

'People go missing every day of the week.'

'Sure, but when you're touching ninety, you're usually found, either dead, or wandering around with amnesia.'

'He lived on the coast. She leaned across him and read the opening paragraph. He's off your beat, Adam.'

'Now he's retired, he is. But he spent most of his life a couple of miles from here. He was a prebendary at the cathedral as well as being a headmaster.'

'All right, Sherlock', she ruffled his wiry hair, 'he might have made enemies over here.'

'It's a possibility.'

'You were always telling me to stick to *facts*,' she reminded him. 'Why the sudden interest?'

'Just a feeling in my bones.' He gave one of his rare smiles.

'Because you don't read the papers enough you leap on the first thing you see. There'll probably be a small column on page twenty-five next week to the effect that Prebendary Wilson was found drowned in a woodland pool. Or else the tide washed his body up. Right, let's eat and don't you dare mention it again. You're off duty so don't go looking for trouble.'

It wasn't any of his business, she was right. It was the Dyfed force's problem. He sat down at the table and pensively began to eat his roast beef.

'Penny for your thoughts.' Brenda smiled at him across the table.

'Still thinking about Prebendary Wilson, the old guy who's gone missing. He couldn't've walked far — they should have found him by now. Too old and doddery to do a disappearing act, and if he'd killed himself he wouldn't've gone to a lot of trouble to make sure they didn't find his corpse — there wouldn't be any point. So we can only conclude that somebody's done something to him.'

'According to statistics, there are two murders a day in Great Britain. Why are you so worried about one old man you'd never heard of until you picked up the paper?'

'Because it doesn't fit.' He stared at the wall beyond her. 'Murder, suicide, whatever, there would be a body. There isn't so that means that there was somebody else involved. Somebody has got him somewhere, alive or dead. He's not rich or famous enough to kidnap, and there's no evidence of robbery in the cottage, so what have they taken him for? If it was murder, why not kill him there? A corpse is easier to remove than a living person. Whoever it was meant him harm, obviously, so they must've taken him somewhere. Where? Why?'

He caught his wife's quizzical expression and smiled ruefully. 'All right, it's probably just a coincidence. Maybe I'm just letting my imagination run riot. It's wierd, though, little things that aren't in any way related suddenly all knit together.'

'Because you're a policeman.' She stretched a hand across the table, found his. 'Which was why I resigned from the Force, Adam. Two dedicated coppers don't make a marriage. One has to stay at home and do the understanding.'

'And very understanding you are, sweetheart. You're quite right: it's not on my patch and I couldn't give a toss whether the Dyfed force find Prebendary Edward Wilson or not.'

All the same, the case left Kent with a nagging, uneasy feeling. He was glad it was out of his own area.

Chapter Twelve

The queue of customers spilled out through the door of the bank and on to the step. Tradesmen eager to bank their takings before the weekend had left it until the last possible moment, ten minutes before the bank closed. It was the usual Saturday morning crowd: the rotund butcher in his blood-smeared off-white smock clutching a wad of notes in his hand; Matheson, the suburban postmaster, who needed enough change to see him through until Saturday evening; the dapper John Rollason, chairman of Rollason dyecastings, who always cashed his cheque on Saturday mornings. The line of customers fidgeted impatiently, cleared their throats, coughed meaningfully, irritated because there was only one cashier serving. And Lawrence Prendergast had a reputation for slowness.

Miss Lovecraft could have collected her weekly housekeeping on any day of the week, but she *always* tottered into the bank at precisely eleven-twenty each Saturday morning, leaning on her silver-handled walking stick. Her arthritic fingers were scarcely capable of holding a pen; she scorned ballpoints, preferring the dip pen and inkwell on the counter. She could have prepared her cheque in advance but she always waited until it was her turn to be served. She did not believe in taking unnecessary risks; somebody might have snatched the cheque out of her hand and run off with it.

'What's the date?' A half-whispered question that carried with it a note of reprimand. The cashier should have remembered to tell her before she asked. He knew she couldn't read the calendar on the wall behind him, even with her glasses, and she had left them at home today.

'July the fourth, Miss Lovecraft.' Customers must always be addressed by name; it made them feel important, as Deane, the sub-manager, was always reminding his duo of staff. Rollason was addressed as 'sir'. And customers must never be kept waiting.

Somebody coughed and the crowd shuffled, seemed to close in on Lawrence like vultures that had spotted carrion. Only the wide counter kept them at bay. He trembled with nervousness. Where the hell had Sally got to? She was supposed to open the reserve till at busy times, and she knew damned well the last quarter of an hour on Saturday mornings was frantic. Deane was in his room with a client and the door was closed, thank God. Otherwise he would have been blaming Lawrence for the log jam of customers.

'What did you say the date was?'

'July the fourth.' She was deaf as well as nearly blind.

'That's American Independence Day. Did you know that?'

'Yes, Miss Lovecraft, I did know.'

She was scratching away with the pen, muttering to herself. The inkwell was probably empty. Deane would blame *him* for that, not Sally. He never blamed Sally for anything – he mightn't have got what he was getting if he did.

Lawrence swivelled round and rapped on the top of the counter partition behind him. 'Would you come on the counter, please, Sally?'

There was no answer. He could hear the tapping of her typewriter from somewhere behind. She was a stubborn cow, particularly on Saturdays.

'How much bloody longer have we got to wait?' It was Rollason's voice, addressed to nobody in particular, intended for Lawrence to hear. Lawrence's fingers shook as he ripped the cheque out of Miss Lovecraft's book; of course she never tore it out herself. She always had her money in pound and ten shilling notes, new ones, crisp from the printers. She would not accept used notes. On the one occasion when the bank had run out she had written and complained to head office. Deane had blamed Lawrence for that — he should have kept some back for her.

'There you are, Miss Lovecraft.' *Now piss off!*

Sally was still typing away. A chair scraped in the manager's room; the interview was at an end. Any moment now Deane would emerge from his private office and see the queue. Lawrence's mouth went dry in anticipation.

The typing stopped and the counter door banged open. Sally appeared and stamped her way down to the No. 2 till. Her attractive features were flushed with annoyance, but somehow she managed a smile in the direction of the clustered customers, just a parting of her full red lips. Her short fair hair was permed, not a strand out of place. A full bosom pushing at her tight-fitting jumper; her short split skirt revealed shapely legs.

'Can I help you, Mr Rollason?'

Lawrence scowled. Rollason would be the perfect gentleman now, eyeing her up all the while. *Don't build your hopes up, mate. Deane's getting all of that, after I've gone home and they're supposedly working late.*

'What's this?' The sub-manager's head and shoulders appeared over the counter partition. The sight was not an attractive one: thinning grey hair plastered over a head that was too large for his body; a military-style moustache in keeping with the rank of 'captain' which he had retained in civvy street; uneven teeth stained with nicotine. A show of surprise and anger for the benefit of his audience from whom he concealed his *sub*-manager status. The fact that he was answerable to the manager of the parent branch was a closely guarded secret. '*Mister* Prendergast, why is everybody being kept waiting?'

'I'm doing my best, Mr Deane.' Lawrence thought he detected a snigger somewhere. His dampened finger slipped as he flipped his way through the butcher's wad of meat-impregnated pound notes. Shit, he had to start all over again. A loud sigh drew attention to his mistake.

'Then you'll have to learn to do better. Good morning, Mr Rollason.'

'Morning, Mr Deane. Bit slow this morning, aren't we?'

'We'll be all right now that Sally's come on to the counter.

I was busy, I hadn't noticed the build-up. apologies on behalf of the cashier.'

Lawrence felt a movement beside him. Slim fingers with scarlet-painted nails opened the lower till drawer and scrabbled through the 'reserve' one hundred-pound bundles of pound notes. He was tempted to slam the drawer shut with his knee and trap the trespassing limb.

'I've taken two hundred,' she announced, turning away.

'Hey, you're supposed to initial my reserve book for . . .'

'She can do that later,' Deane snapped. 'Our priority is to attend to customers as quickly as possible.'

The bastard broke the rules when it suited him – he wouldn't have allowed his male cashier to get away with that, but his nineteen-year-old floosie could do no wrong.

Lawrence bit back an angry retort and tried to focus his thoughts on Janice. Seeing her this afternoon might compensate for the hellish morning he'd had. They were going to a photographic exhibition in the city, and it might just give him the chance he needed to get the relationship going. He hadn't had much success with girls up till now, but at least he and Janice had a shared interest in photography. And she was a stunner . . .

'At last!' Frederick Deane swaggered down the empty banking hall, jangling a bunch of keys, and locked the outer door with a flourish. He turned back and looked at the clock, then shook his head. 'Ten to twelve. We'll be having some bloody complaints, Prendergast, probably via head office, if we can't clear the customers sooner than this on a Saturday. I can't for the life of me understand why you're so slow. Damn it, you've been in banking for five years now – you ought to be able to eat the job.'

Lawrence lost count again.

'Balanced first time?' There was a smugness in the way Sally shut her heavy cash book.

'*Good* girl!' The emphasis was intended for Lawrence's ears. Come on, Prendergast, be as quick as you can.' The 'mister' was dropped once the bank doors were closed.

Lawrence had difficulty in concentrating. Twice he had to scratch out figures and rewrite them.

'Balanced yet, Prendergast?'

'Not, yet.'

'Do hurry up, there's a good chap. By the way, I want you to represent the bank at the Samaritans' annual summer fayre down at the hall this afternoon. Miss Lovecraft's on the committee, and somebody from here has to be seen to be there.'

Lawrence's head jerked up. This couldn't be happening. He couldn't not take Janice out this afternoon, couldn't risk losing her. He tried to keep his voice steady. 'I can't! I've already got on appointment.'

'Then you'd better cancel whatever you've got planned, hadn't you, Prendergast?' Deane leaned on the counter, lit a cigarette and blew smoke in Lawrence's direction. 'The bank comes first, as your old man told me innumerable times when I was chief clerk in his branch. Damn it, I've cancelled dozens of private engagements to oblige *him*.'

'I *can't*.'

'You'll have to, you don't have any choice. Now, let's have no more nonsense. I'll expect to hear that you were there this afternoon.' He bared his yellowed, uneven teeth in a leering smile. 'Talking of your old man, I bumped into him in town the other week. He asked how you were getting on. I could've lied and said okay, but I don't like telling lies. I told him how disappointed I was in you, that either you weren't trying or else the job was beyond your capabilities. I'm surprised he hasn't spoken to you about it.'

William Prendergast *had* spoken to his son after his meeting with Frederick Deane. The retired bank manager hadn't let up about it for a whole week, but Lawrence wasn't going to give Deane the pleasure of hearing about it.

'Now do hurry up and balance, Prendergast. I want to get the cash locked away and get off. I'm playing golf this afternoon. And I don't want you to be late for the fayre.'

Lawrence didn't balance. He was a hundred pounds short. He checked and rechecked his cash and figures but he couldn't locate the error. In the office behind the counter Sally was giggling at something her boss had whispered in her ear.

'How much longer are you going to be, Prendergast?'

Lawrence felt physically sick. 'I'm short, Mr Deane. A hundred pounds.'

'I don't believe it!'

Lawrence swallowed and stood back as Deane rushed round to the counter and began checking the till and the cash book, ticking figures in red ballpoint like an angry teacher marking homework. Cigarette ash showered over the page and elastic bands flipped as bundles of notes were unbanded for recounting.

'You're a bigger fool than I thought you were, Prendergast! In fact, I don't think I've ever met as big a fool as you. Apart, perhaps, from your old man. How on earth he ever got to be a manager, I'll never know. I carried him most of the time I worked with him. If half of his blunders had come to light, he'd've been sacked. But I can't cover up *this* blunder. You're in trouble. Big trouble!'

Lawrence felt as though his legs were about to buckle beneath him.

'Well, unless it turns up by Monday morning, I'll have to report it to Mister Thomas. He'll come out here from the parent branch, humiliate us all with a thorough check, and then he'll report it to head office. That, I'm afraid, will be the end of your banking career, Prendergast. What will your old man have to say to you then, eh?'

Lawrence didn't respond. He was frantically checking the paying-in slips.

'Well, we'll just have to leave it for now. I'm due to play golf at one-thirty.' Deane began scooping the contents of the till into the heavy wooden box which was locked in the safe at the close of business every day. 'I don't expect you'll have a very good weekend, Prendergast — I know I wouldn't if I'd just lost the bank a hundred quid. Still, don't let that stop you from attending the Samaritans' summer fayre. You can worry about it there just as well as you could at home or wherever you'd planned to go. And you can please yourself whether you tell your father now or on Monday.'

Lawrence had planned to tell Janice all about it but she wouldn't listen.

'I want to go to the exhibition! I don't want to go to a crummy jumble sale and eat home-made cakes and drink tea out of plastic cups. You promised ...'

'Jan, I *have* to go. Deane said ...'

'Damn Deane! Is he God? Haven't you got a mind of your own, Larry? You can tell him on Monday that *I* insisted that you took me to the exhibition. You either do that or I go on my own, and if I do then you needn't bother phoning me again!'

Frederick Deane won. Janice stormed off to the exhibition; Lawrence went to the fayre, and it was three weeks before they saw each other again. A lot happened to Lawrence during those three weeks.

The missing one hundred pounds was never found. The stern but fair Emlyn Thomas came out from the parent branch on Monday morning in answer to Deane's telephone call and rechecked cash and figures.

'Well, it isn't here.' He shook his head in despair. 'I'm afraid I'll have to go and phone head office. They'll send the inspectors, I've no doubt.'

Lawrence noted that Sally was wearing a new two-piece; she had also bought herself new shoes. And the diamond ring which she wore on her engagement finger was not a cheap replica. He presumed at the time that Frederick Deane had to buy her favours. Later, he wasn't altogether convinced about that. He had no proof, just nagging suspicions.

The bank inspectors grilled him like CID interrogators. They examined his private bank account, extracted all his paid cheques from the voucher drawers in the basement, queried every payee. What did he spend his money on? How much housekeeping did he give his mother? Did he have a girlfriend? The fact that his father was a retired bank manager was no guarantee of the son's integrity. He didn't by any chance back horses, did he – a violation of his contract of employment? Or do the football pools?

Lawrence was suspended on full pay throughout the enquiry. Which meant that he was confined to the family home except when the inspectors sent for him to question him again. One thing was certain: he would not be returning to the small three-man branch, whatever the outcome of the enquiry.

'To think that a son of mine lost a hundred pounds!' William Prendergast's only small consolation was that he never for one moment thought that a Prendergast would be guilty of dishonesty. Just foolishness and incompetence.

The enquiry was closed, left on file. If Lawrence had stolen the money then he had covered his tracks. They would be watching him closely from now on.

Lawrence was transferred to the largest branch in the city. Amongst a staff of 130 he lost his identity but he didn't mind that. To add to his punishment, he was barred from any job that involved contact with cash, which meant working as a ledger clerk. The work was monotonous and there was no chance of promotion. He was set to work as a drone until he was old enough to retire.

Deane's leering, yellow-toothed smile grew larger. 'You're a fool, Prendergast!' Lawrence tugged frantically at the door handle, desperate to escape. It was jammed; it wouldn't turn ...

He woke, sweating, in a tangle of sheets. The nightmare was so vivid, it took some time before he realised where he was safe in his own bed. But the memories had been rekindled; he could not forget. Then, out of the swirling chaos of his thoughts, another memory resurfaced.

Shortly after his father's death, when Lawrence resigned from the bank, he had heard a rumour about Frederick Deane. The bullying sub-manager, who had even lied to his own wife that he was a fully appointed bank manager, had been reported to his superiors for subjecting his typist to sexual harassment. Apparently, Sally herself had reported him. Deane had been retired early as a result.

Perhaps the bastard had not paid enough for her favours, Lawrence sneered to himself. Deane's wife had left him and died shortly afterwards.

Deane continued to live in the big house on the other side

of the city. Lawrence decided to check the entry in the telephone directory.

Deane, Fredk, Capt.
That was all he needed to know.

Chapter Thirteen

Captain Frederick Deane, even at the ripe old age of eighty-four, enjoyed a life of affluent leisure. His inheritance from his late wife had made his bank pension seem meagre. He had always emphasised the benefits of marrying into money – love came a poor second. You could find that elsewhere, have your cake *and* eat it.

Ursula had pressurised him into maintaining his social status, and he had found all the entertaining she insisted on exhausting. Since her death, life had been much more relaxed. Nowadays he did all his entertaining at the golf club, mostly at the expense of his acquaintances. A retired bank manager with the added bonus of a wartime commission, even though the only action he had seen was a German bombing raid on Merseyside, was doubly respected.

Nevertheless, Frederick still got the urge for a woman from time to time. Not a contemporary – women of his own age could only provide platonic companionship. No he longed for a much younger member of the opposite sex.

Sally had been his downfall, the silly bitch. But in his fantasies he still lusted for her. She hadn't had anything to complain about; she had just become complacent and arrogant. Damn it all, he had bought her jewellery, clothes, given her spending money. And all he had asked in return was that she slipped her frilly little knickers off for him.

He had enjoyed best their sessions on the thick pile carpet of his office; the back seat of his car had been both cramped and stressful. Always thinking that he heard somebody outside, rearing up to glance nervously out of the windows, wiping a patch clear of condensation so that he could see. Steamy in the wrong sense of the word, he chuckled to himself at the memory.

He could not understand what had got into her at the finish, the stupid wench. She always used to giggle and fend him off when he put a hand up her skirt during office hours. Good clean fun, no harm in it at all. Then one day, without warning, she'd slapped his face. Really hard. It had stung, made his eyes water.

'You dirty old man!' She had rounded on him. 'Don't you ever dare touch me again!'

She had still accepted a lift home after work, though she had refused to speak to him in the car. It had gone on like that for a whole week.

The following Monday she had been more affable so, after Hewitt, Prendergast's replacement, had gone to lunch, Frederick had tried his luck again. Sally's thigh's had snapped shut, trapping his fingers between them.

'I warned you!' She got off her stool and stormed towards the telephone. Even then he had thought it was a bluff. Later than afternoon he knew it wasn't when a grim-faced District Staff Superintendent from head office arrived.

Frederick had been retired the following week on full pension. He had told Ursula that the bank were making way for up-and-coming whizz-kid managers. She wasn't pleased at the prospect of having him around the house all day, every day, and informed him that he'd better find himself a part-time job somewhere; one that carried status, of course.

A month to the day of his retirement, she had suddenly confronted him about his affair. He had never seen her so infuriated; she was beside herself with rage. At least, he consoled himself, 'affair' sounded more respectable than sexual harassment. He tried to bluff his way out of it, but failed.

'Ursula had packed her bags, then fired one last parting shot at her husband: 'And another thing – you've been lying to me for years. You weren't a manager, you were only a *sub*-manager, a glorified chief clerk!'

Somebody had shopped him; to this day he had never

found out who. It wouldn't be Sally – she wouldn't do that to him. He wondered about Prendergast; no, he'd never have the guts. Possibly it had been Thomas, the manager of the parent branch, aggrieved that his sub-manager had brought his bank into disrepute.

Months later Ursula had suffered a stroke and died. It was after the funeral that Frederick read in the *Mercury* of Sally's marriage to a city estate agent. She was a gold-digger, nothing less. All the same, he wouldn't mind shagging her again. He wouldn't get the chance, of course. But he still had his memories. Reality was out of the question.

Until the telephone roused him from a doze in the deckchair on the terrace one very warm July afternoon. Barefooted, clad only in a pair of bathing trunks, he padded indoors to answer it.

'Captain Deane speaking.'

There was just the crackling of the line but he knew somebody was listening on the other end. Possibly it was a wrong number and the surprised caller was about to ring off. Or it would be kids making nuisance calls from the kiosk down the road. Then a deep male voice spoke.

'I'm a friend of Sally's, Captain Deane.'

His heart shifted up a gear. 'Sally? Sally *who*? His voice shook slightly. What the hell was going on?

'She asked me to call you, Captain.'

'Why?' He began to tremble. It was inconceivable after all these years. Sally would be in her forties now, probably had grown-up children.

'Because she can't call you herself. For obvious reasons.'

'What's she want?' Damn it, she could always have used the phone when her husband wasn't around or else sneaked out to a call box.

'She wonders if you still remember what colour the carpet in your office was, Captain.'

It *was* a genuine call, then. Deane thought he detected a snigger on the other end of the line. 'I don't know what you're talking about.'

'I don't either, Captain, but she asked me to say that – I presumed it was some kind of code between you. Anyway, she asked me to tell you that she'd like to see you again. If *you'd* like to see *her*, that is.'

There was an uneasy pause. Deane hadn't seen Sally for at least fifteen years, not since that fateful week when she'd phoned and reported him to the bank's staff department. What did she want with him now? Blackmail? Hadn't she harmed him enough already? Was she out to drag his name through the mud again, maybe threaten to tell them up at the golf club all about him?

'Well, do you want to see her again or not, Captain?'

'Why should I?'

'I think she wants to apologise to you about something, I've no idea what, she didn't say. All she said was that maybe you could let bygones be bygones and that things could be like they once were. I'm only repeating what she told me.'

'Who are you?'

'Just a friend of Sally's. Perhaps I shouldn't say this, but I do know that Sal and her husband haven't been hitting it off for some time now. Apart from that, I'm phoning because she asked me to.'

Because Sally was regretting what she'd done, didn't dare make the initial approach herself. That figured. Deane's free hand strayed down inside his loose-fitting trunks, a habit of his when he got to thinking about the past. 'All right, I'll see her. Where? When?'

'It's got to be a bit secretive. I'm sure you'll understand, Captain.'

'Naturally' At least the fellow, whoever he was, spoke respectfully. He sounded genuine.

'She said that if you were agreeable I was to arrange a time and place for you to meet her, then take you to where she'll be waiting for you. Okay?'

'Okay.'

'Right. Now, do you know the common on the north side of town?'

'The one beyond the golf course where the army have a firing range? I shot on it once.' There was a note of pride in his voice: he had fond memories of those wartime years.

'You've got it. Well, there's a rough track that leads up

on to the common just past the fingerpost. Be there at ten-thirty tonight. Leave your car at the golf club car park, it's only about ten minutes' walk away. I'll be waiting up the track for you, in a Mini.'

'I'll be there.'

'Good.'

'And tell Sally . . .'

But the unknown caller had already rung off.

It was ten-fifteen when Deane pulled on to the golf club car park. He usually parked in the directors' bay adjacent to the main entrance, but not tonight. On this ocassion he wished to arrive and depart incognito. He backed his BMW into a vacant lot by the gates and sat for a few moments in the half light cast by the illuminated building.

A feeling of clandestine excitement, not experienced since his banking days bubbled up: the nervousness experienced by a burglar as he surveys the house he has targeted for his night's work. Frederick lit a cigarette. He still smoked Senior Service — he hadn't pandered to that effeminate fashion of smoking filter-tips. He drew on it deeply, letting the smoke filter out through his nostrils. Tonight he felt thirty years younger. Whatever Sally had done to him in the past, it didn't matter. He would be well compensated. It would cost him, of course, but he had come prepared for that; he had been just in time to catch the bank before they closed, and a wad of notes was crammed into his wallet. It would be money well spent.

Approaching headlights dazzled him as a car turned in off the main road. Golf club members often came on here from the Horse & Jockey so that they could continue drinking into the early hours. Frederick went through the motions of looking for something in the glove box, ducking his head. He didn't want to risk recognition. An invitation to join in a round of drinks could be exceedingly embarrassing.

Once he had the car park to himself again, he got out and locked the car with a shaking hand. He kept up a brisk pace until he was clear of the club, then took the B-road that forked off to the right. He slowed down: there was plenty of time; he wanted to savour every moment. The night was fine with a warm breeze which carried the heady scent of heather and pollen. He wondered where Sally would be — probably drinking alone in some remote country pub awaiting his arrival. They would drive off in her car, park up somewhere ... Afterwards she would drop him off back at the golf club. He checked his train of thought — he was wishing the night away.

The Mini was parked exactly where the anonymous caller had said it would be. Deane paused a few yards from it and peered at the silhouette inside. There was somebody in the driver's seat, a huge fellow. He felt a sudden pang of nervousness, then shook himself mentally. *Come on, pull yourself together, man*!

He ground out his cigarette beneath his foot, squared his shoulders and approached the waiting car with a confident, almost military step. He tapped lightly on the window and the man inside started, then wound the glass down a few inches.

'Good evening. I'm Captain Deane. We arranged to ...'

'Get in the other side, please.'

Deane squashed himself into the passenger seat, hoping that they didn't have too far to travel. He had always been a nervous passenger. The interior smelled — a mixture of BO, chemicals and engine oil. He glanced behind him and saw that the back seat was piled with an assortment of junk. An untidy bugger, this one. Deane was obsessional about tidiness, always had been — it stemmed from his military training.

'How far are we going?'

'Not far.' The man reached behind him for something on the seat. A pile of papers avalanched down on to the floor.

Frederick peered at the other man. There was something familiar about him, even in silhouette.

'Do I know you?' he asked.

'You might.' The starter motor protested, then fired at the second attempt. The bodywork rattled and a stench of exhaust fumes filled the car.

'I'm sure I do.' Damn it, he knew that unkempt hair-style, the shape of the nose. The profile. Except for the moustache — that was new. His retentive memory clicked through its files. Somebody whom he had been in close contact with. Not recently, not at the golf club. Of course, *the bank*! 'Hey, you're *Prendergast*!'

'That's right.' The man turned his head for the first time and Deane knew that he was not mistaken. He vaguely registered that Prendergast was clutching something in his right hand, but he was too excited to wonder what it might be.

'So Sally's got you to make contact with me. Well, well!'

Prendergast had been the odd one out in those days — the office buffoon — but that was years ago. Sally had needed a contact so she'd used Lawrence. Like he had said on the phone, bygones could be bygones.

'How are you getting on these days, Prendergast? Still in the bank?'

'Working for myself actually.'

'Looking forward to the reunion?'

'It'll be nice to see her again.'

'And to shag her again.'

Cheeky bastard! Deane forced a laugh. 'Well, there's no point in pretending, is there, Prendergast? We're all in it together, it seems. Like old times, eh?'

'Yes, everything's coming together after all those years.' Lawrence made no move to put the car into reverse. 'Would you mind winding the window down a fraction? It's awfully stuffy in here.'

'Oh, sure.' Deane turned and fumbled along the rusted door in search of the winder.

That was when Lawrence hit him. A short, sharp blow just behind the ear, a dull thud as solid rubber met with bone. Deane grunted once, then slumped back in his seat, motionless.

Lawrence dropped the truncheon on to the floor behind his seat. Ironically, it was bank issue, supplied to staff who were engaged in cash transportation at the big city branch. It had belonged to Hebden, IC bullion vans, in the days before the job had been contracted out to an armoured van service. Lawrence had found it in the cloakroom and known instantly that it would come in handy one day.

Twenty years later it had.

He backed the Mini out on to the road and drove off slowly. His "sleeping" passenger was wedged securely in the seat beside him. Once again the engine was lacking power; he really must get it fixed before the next time. He would be all right tonight, though; the journey was less than five miles, a circuitous route that avoided the ring road and the city highways.

Within twenty minutes Captain Frederick Deane would be securely locked up on Death Row. The result of the morrow's trial was a foregone conclusion.

Chapter Fourteen

It was after ten o'clock the following morning when Lawrence went out to the shelter, clutching a wrapped pork pie in one hand and slopping a mug of tea in the other. Fortunately, Mother wasn't up yet. He was in no hurry: he had all day to do that which he had to do.

Frank Coleman was planing wood in his shed on the other side of the hedge. Lawrence quickened his step; he had no desire to engage in pointless small talk.

He let himself into the shelter. Deane heard him coming and began to thump of the cell door, shouted in that bullying tone which was only too familiar to Lawrence. 'Oi, what the deuce is going on? Is that you, Prendergast? Let me out! I'm going to have the police on you. You'll go to prison for this!'

Lawrence hesitated. Wilson had been frail and senile, and had offered no physical resistance. Deane, even in his eighties, was reasonably agile and fit.

Lawrence set the mug down on the table outside the door and checked that the truncheon was still in the back pocket of his jeans. He would use it again if he had to, but he hoped that it would not be necessary; an unconscious prisoner defeated the purpose of the day ahead. The frantic pummelling of fists on the heavy wooden door continued.

'Deane, sit down on the bed and be quiet!'
'I will not. I want a tom-tit.'
'Then shit in the bucket. I'll wait out here.'
'Damn you, let me out!'

'Shit in the bucket or shit in your trousers — I don't mind which.'

Silence. Then Lawrence heard loud expellations of bowel wind followed by plopping sounds. He had won the first round.

He opened the door, edged inside with the tea, nudged it shut and locked it. He dropped the key into his pocket, pulled out the truncheon and held it in full view of Deane. 'You'd better calm down otherwise I might hit you again. We've got a lot to talk about today.'

The tiny room stank of cigarette smoke, but that was a small price to pay to end a twenty-year grudge.

'Would you mind telling me what this is all about?' Deane was down to his last cigarette. It was obvious that he had not slept since he had regained consciousness.

'You've been arrested. Today you are going to be tried. On various counts.'

'You're mad, I always knew you were. Like your old man — he went queer in the head at the finish.'

'He was always crazy but that's no concern of yours. Now, drink your tea. You can please yourself whether you eat your pie now or later.'

Deane slurped his tea noisily. He was shaking. His bravado had been a facade; now it was beginning to crumble. He followed Lawrence out into the main room and stared up at the gallows.

'What on earth ...'

'Forget that. For now. Sit down. Your life depends upon your answers to the various charges.' *But you'll die, anyway.*

'I refuse to ...'

'You had an affair with Sally Sercombe during your time as a bank *sub*-manager. As a result, you were sacked. It was camouflaged as early retirement. Do you admit that?'

'Yes.' Deane's puny resistance was wilting.

'A theft took place. Money was stolen from the bank to the sum of one hundred pounds.'

'It went missing.'

'It was *stolen*! And *I* carried the can!' Lawrence shouted, momentarily losing control.

'I didn't take it.' It came out as a whine, and the lips beneath the greying military moustache were trembling. 'I swear to God that it wasn't me.'

'*Who*, then?'

'I thought at the time it might be Sally Sercombe; I couldn't prove it. She came in in new clothes and a ring on the Monday morning. I hadn't given her enough to cover them.'

Lawrence nodded and grudgingly muttered 'not guilty to the charge of theft'. There was a long silence before he moved on to the next charge. 'You are charged with false accounting. Fraud.'

'What on earth ...'

'That you opened three personal loan accounts in fictitious names, transferred the money to current accounts, and drew cash from them, to finance your affair with a young girl. You got away with it, apparently. After you were retired, I suspect that the bank failed to locate those non-existent customers who were no longer repaying their loans and wrote them off as bad debts. But *I* knew: the signatures on the cheques bore a similarity to your own handwriting.' He paused and met Deane's sheepish gaze. 'Guilty or not guilty?'

'Guilty.' The shoulders hunched; the oversize head drooped forward.

'You are sentenced to twelve months' imprisonment. In that cell.'

'*No!*' Deane half rose but Lawrence pushed him roughly back into the chair.

'Wait. There is one more charge left.'

'What's that?'

'You are charged with rape.'

'This is preposterous!' Deane spluttered. 'Nothing of the kind, she was perfectly willing ...'

'Not the *first* time.' Lawrence's eyes narrowed. from hereon it was intelligent guesswork. A teenage virgin – despite Sally's flirty, knowing manner, he was pretty sure Deane had been the first – was hardly likely to go all the way without some initial protests. Not that it would make any difference ultimately to his prisoner's fate, but he had to have a confession. He had to follow the correct procedure, have a reason for hanging. He continued implacably: 'She was a virgin before you had her.'

'Yes, but ...'

'I'll tell you what happened that first time. You started playing about with her, edging closer all the time, working her up so that you could get astride her. She was pretty far gone, almost there, when you touched her with your chopper. That was when she got scared, tried to push you off. So you shoved it right up her and shagged her. Then she was crying, scared she might be pregnant. So you bought her off. Jesus, what a lecherous bastard you are! That's what happened, *isn't it*?'

'Yes,' Deane muttered through his moustache, writhing in his seat. 'But that's not rape, that's seduction.'

'*Rape*!' Lawrence was triumphant. 'Sexual intercourse against a woman's will is rape. She didn't want to; you made her. Right?'

Lawrence's voice had risen to a shout. Deane cowered in his chair. There no longer seemed to be any point in trying to refute the insane accusations. 'Yes.'

Lawrence drew himself up to his full height and delved into his jean pockets. 'Frederick Deane, you are found guilty of rape by your own confession.'

Deane didn't know how much more of this he could stand. He wondered if he could overpower this madman, escape from here. But his strength was sapped and his head throbbed from where he had been stunned in the car.

Lawrence had found what he'd been searching for in his pocket. Deane stared at him, an expression of amazement on his white features. 'What's that?'

Prendergast had draped something over his head, something resembling a black handkerchief. Or some kind of ludicrous nightcap. Anywhere else but here it would have been comical. Cold fear clutched at Deane's heart. No, this was impossible, it was some kind of nightmare. Any moment he would wake up in his own bed, sweating out a fever.

But it was reality. And he wasn't in his bed; he was imprisoned in some dreadful place where death towered above him in the shape of a scaffold.

'Frederick Deane', Lawrence's voice seemed to echo in

the confined space, 'you have been found guilty of rape for which the penalty is death. You will be taken from your cell tomorrow morning and hanged by the neck until you are dead!'

'But ... but the death penalty was abolished twenty-five years ago!'

'The death penalty for rape still exists today in some states in America.' There was a smugness about Lawrence as he stuffed the black cap back into his pocket. 'Here, in this place, we are Americanised. The death penalty is mandatory for rape. You will hang tomorrow morning.'

Deane did not resist as he was pulled to his feet and pushed towards the claustrophobic cell. He felt faint; he just wanted to lie down.

'There's your pork pie if you get hungry.' Lawrence dropped the wrapped pie on to the bed. 'I'll bring you another drink later. What would you like?'

Deane simply stared. The man was completely mad. Bonkers.

'Water, if you don't request anything different. Oh, and what do you usually eat for breakfast?'

'I don't eat breakfast. Just a cigarette and a cup of tea.' Jesus, what was he telling him all this for?

'I'll try and get you some more fags.' Lawrence inserted the key in the lock, then turned back. 'Oh, and whilst you're repenting, spare me a thought — think about what you did to me.'

'To *you*?'

'Yes. If you hadn't shat all over me then I might not be hanging you now. But that isn't the reason you're in the death cell. You're condemned to hang for rape. That's nothing to do with me; I'm just carrying out the sentence.'

He slammed the door and locked it behind him. This time Deane didn't bang and shout protests. The guy was beaten and he knew it; he wouldn't fight any more.

Frank Coleman was standing on the step of his coffin shop, staring right through the gap he'd gouged in the hedge. Head forward, peering, squinting.

'Mornin', Lawrence.'

Thank God the shelter was soundproof. 'Morning, Frank. I've just been developing some film I shot yesterday.' An instinctive cover-up; he couldn't help himself. But it didn't really matter.

'It's a shame to spend a lovely day like today cooped up in there. You oughta be doing some gardening.'

'I don't *like* gardening.' His petulance was instinctive, unfeigned. He couldn't have thought of a better way of deflecting Coleman's curiosity.

'Ask your mother about this hedge, will you?' It's time it was trimmed, anyway, but whilst that chap of yours is at it, he might as well take a bit more off the top.'

'Mother doesn't want the hedge cut down. Arthur will clip it, I expect, when he gets round to it.'

Frank abandoned the hedge campaign for a confidence, one man to another. 'The missus is in one of her moods.' He lowered his voice, glancing back towards the house. 'Wants to go shopping today. *In the car.* I've just bloody washed and waxed it. God blimey, there's a bus past the bottom of the drive every hour. Apart from that, I'm busy, got to get a coffin ready for Friday. for Bertie Ramsgate.'

'Never heard of him.'

'Used to keep the corner shop on Victoria Road. It's been gone twenty years — it's one of them video hire places now. Ninety-two, he was. I buried his father in 1964.'

'That's interesting. I'm sorry, but I have to be going.'

'Can't you spare a couple of minutes?'

'What for?'

'Pop round and I'll show you how a *proper* coffin's made, not one of those mass-produced things. Real oak, brass hinges and handles.'

'Honestly, I can't spare the time. I've got to go shopping for Mother.'

But Frank was well into his stride now. 'Funny thing, isn't it, you spend your life waiting to die. Every day you're dying; it's one day less from the time you're born. Only consolation is, you don't know when it'll be. Could be tomorrow, next week, next year, twenty years' time. Just think — suppose we knew just when we were going to pop our clogs. It'd be like waiting to be executed, wouldn't it?'

A shiver ran all the way up Lawrence's spine. He trembled slightly with excitement. 'Yes, you've got a point, never thought of that before.'

'Imagine a condemned man sitting in his cell, knowing the date when he's going to snuff it. It'd drive you barmy. The Good Lord knew what he was doing when he kept the future from us. But if you want to know what I think, they should bring the death penalty back – then there wouldn't be half the murders there are. A guy'd think twice; he'd know what'd happen to him if he was caught. It ain't the *hanging* that's the deterrent, it's the *waiting* to be hanged.'

'I'm sure you're right.' Lawrence moved away. He *hadn't* thought of it that way before. He'd been in too much of a hurry so far. And now there wasn't any hurry. Why hang Deane the next day when he could prolong the agony, watch the man's slow descent into despair? Yes, he'd make the bastard wait.

He was almost at the house when a movement beyond the rose bushes caught his eye. He started, peered. Maybe it was Arthur – no, surely not; it wasn't Thursday.

It wasn't Arthur. The figure behind the thorny foliage was too slim, too well dressed. Arthur was big and clumsy, and always wore a dirty blue bib overall; this fellow had a clean checked shirt on. He stooped to pick something up: one of the empty margarine tubs which Lawrence filled with water for the birds. The man had a handful of them, stacked one inside the other.

'Hey!' he shouted in protest – the cheeky bugger had no right to ...

'Oh, hi, Larry!'

The man reared up into full view. It was Glenn with a slightly guilty expression on his face. 'I was just picking up a few empties that had blown about the garden.'

'I'll take them.' Lawrence held out a hand. 'I was going to refill them, anyway.' So much for Mother's promise that her elder son wouldn't take any more 'rubbish' away. But this time Glenn wasn't going to stand his ground. He'd been caught red-handed trying his sneaky clear-up.

'Actually, I'm looking for something.' Glenn sounded a trifle sheepish.

'And what might that be?' Lawrence asked suspiciously.

'The hoe attachment off the old Jalo, you know – the old hand plough, the manual cultivator Dad had years ago when we used to have a vegetable patch. When we moved I took it to use in the garden at home, then forgot about it for years. The other day I wanted to use it to hoe between some onions, but the hoe attachment was missing. I expect it's still around here somewhere. When I was a lad Dad used to keep it in the old shelter. Ten-to-one the hoe's still in there, lying in a corner.'

'No, it isn't!' Lawrence tensed defiantly.

'It's only small, about so big.' Glenn spread his fingers about six inches. 'You wouldn't notice it if you weren't looking for it.'

'I promise you it's not in the shelter; I cleared *everything* out!' Lawrence was beginning to sweat and it wasn't because of the heat.

'Well, I'd like to take a quick look, just in case. Tell you what, you can come with me to ...'

'*No!*' Lawrence shouted. His mind raced – how the hell could he put off the bastard?

'Look, I'm not going to pinch anything. We can ...'

'I said *no!*'

Glenn hesitated. His brother was squaring up to him the way he used to do when they were kids. Invariably in those days their arguments had ended in a fight, but now one of them had to back down. Glenn thought of his mother – she was very frail these days, and the slightest disagreement would upset her. He didn't really need the hoe attachment; he could make do with the small ploughshare. It did the job nearly as well.

'Oh, all right, if your den's that precious to you. He smiled. 'Anybody would think you'd got a skeleton in the cupboard there, the way you keep it locked up like the vaults in the Bank of England.'

'I happen to have a lot of valuable photographic equipment in there.' Lawrence spoke quickly as if to justify his security measures. 'There are break-ins every night round here. I can assure you that whatever you're looking for isn't in there.'

As he walked into the house Lawrence reconsidered his decision to hold the prisoner for some time before execution. It was too dangerous. Deane would hang tomorrow morning.

Chapter Fifteen

It was stifling in the small cell. Frederick Deane's body was bathed in sweat and his shirt and trousers clung uncomfortably. He contemplated taking everything off except his briefs and socks. No, it would humiliate him even further; he was already wallowing in a pit of degradation.

He had had to use the bucket again. He wasn't even granted the ignominy of slopping out; the place stank. Which was why he decided to smoke his last cigarette. Prendergast had said he'd get him some more; he'd forgotten to remind him to buy Senior Service. Odds on the fool would turn up with a packet of spatted ones. Still, he could always rip the filter tip off. More likely, the idiot would forget altogether; he used to forget just about everything when he was in the bank.

The boy had flipped, there was no doubt about that. Which was frightening when you compared him with his father. An hereditary madness that had mutated from father to son, producing a dangerous lunatic. Deane inhaled; the smoke steadied his nerves a little.

Bill Prendergast had had a terrible temper. The entire staff in his office were scared of him, including Deane himself. You always knew first thing in the morning what kind of mood the manager was in. If you received a curt 'morning' then the day wasn't likely to be too bad as usual, but a grunt, or no response, heralded a day of tyranny. Prendergast would immediately start looking for faults. It usually began when he opened the mail and a minor complaint from a customer would be blown up out of all proportion. He didn't allow his staff a mid-morning break, so you had to drink your coffee while you worked. He didn't permit cups on the counter, either, so the cashiers had to grab a slurp round the back during a lull – except on busy morning there wasn't a lull, and their drinks went cold. They weren't allowed to chat, so conversation was limited to banking matters, and that was in whispers.

Most managers worked in their private office – but not Bill. He claimed the chief clerk's rostrum which gave him an elevated position from which to survey the entire branch. But he got results; you had to hand it to him. Under his iron discipline profits increased every half year. Which was why complaints from staff were ignored, swept under the carpet. He was a legend in his own lifetime.

Deane remembered how Prendergast had begun bringing Lawrence into the office during the boy's school holidays, indoctrinating him young. At the age of twelve, he was expected to put a batch of remittance through and balance it, and woe betide him if he ballsed it up. Frederick could see then that Lawrence wasn't cut out for the job but the boy's father was determined to shave the square peg until it slotted into the round hole. He ranted and raved, humiliating Lawrence in front of the staff, and had him in tears on innumerable occasions. Then he had delegated Deane to train him, ready to blame them both if his son didn't come up to his expectations.

Somewhere along the line, Frederick had thought at the time, it had to blow up in Bill's face. It hadn't; it had blown up in his own instead. Which was why he was here in this stinking, sweltering hole right now, under sentence of death.

Frederick couldn't see that he himself was to blame in any way. Bill had made Frederick's life a misery, so it was only natural that he should try to take revenge on Lawrence. Not consciously – he had just found himself doing it. Because Lawrence was a fool; he was scruffy, overweight, lacked commonsense. Every office had a stooge, a whipping boy; it was just Lawrence's misfortune that he was posted to a small branch with a small staff. There was no choice of scapegoats: Lawrence had been the obvious candidate.

Frederick's headache increased to migraine proportions.

The small battery-operated light in the cell was dimming – another hour and he would be sitting in darkness. He wasn't hungry, just thirsty and in need of a cigarette. He cursed William Prendergast for making a monster out of his son.

It was obvious to Lawrence that Glenn was going to hang around all day. And it wasn't even Friday – Glenn's usual day for visiting. The normal routine was for him to meet his mother in town for lunch after her Friday writing class, but today they would make do with a jacket potato and salad, and then sit and talk for the rest of the day.

It was too dangerous to sneak down to the shelter. Glenn was like a ghoul – he moved silently, popped up where you least expected him. He might want to follow Lawrence inside just to check that that old hoe attachment wasn't lying around in there.

Deane would just have to go without a drink. In all probability the battery in that Oxfam night-light had run out by now and he would be sitting in the dark. So what – he wasn't getting four-star treatment. And it was too damned hot to walk down the road to the little shop and fetch some fags. Cigarettes cost money; it was just a waste when the bugger was going to die in the morning.

Nevertheless, Lawrence had work to do in there, preparing for the morrow. There was a new rope to be fitted to the gallows, a lighter one this time. He'd sussed out where he'd gone wrong before, why Wilson had been decapitated. He'd got the drop wrong, too short. So the victim had kicked and struggled, pulled his own bloody head off. It needed to be so that the feet just brushed the floor of the pit. This time he would measure his victim, get it right. Otherwise it was so messy – too much cleaning up to do.

Glenn stopped on for tea. Scrounging bastard, he was deliberately prolonging his visit. Lawrence retired to his bedroom, where he could listen to what was happening down below. He heard the clinking of crockery: Glenn was washing up. Then he heard voices in the hallway. He crept out on to the landing. Glenn was preparing to leave, but she was delaying him as long as possible, like she always did. Clinging to him.

'I don't expect I'll see you till next Friday, will I, love?'
Lawrence tensed, hanging on Glenn's reply.
'I might pop over before if I get a chance, Mother.'
Oh, shit!
'That'd be nice. I don't suppose you could find a couple of hours to finish that pool, could you?'
Lawrence's sweaty hands clenched.
'I'll see.'
'Larry's been so good digging it out but I'm worried about him. He's not at all well, and digging doesn't do him any good. All it wants is filling in a bit so that it's not so deep, and lining with polythene. Now that it's started, we may as well finish it. But I could always ask Arthur ...'
'Don't worry, we'll fix something.'
'There's no *immediate* hurry.'
That was a relief. Larry heard them moving out on to the front steps. *Oh, Jesus, hurry up and go!*
It was another ten minutes before he heard Glenn's car start up. Only then did he go down to the kitchen and switch the kettle on. Deane would be well on the way to dehydration by now. That was fine except that he wanted him in good shape for tomorrow.

'Where are my fags?' In the glow from the replacement batteries the prisoner looked haggard, exhausted. The smell from the slop bucket was overpowering.
'They'd sold out.'
'Bloody hell!'
'Drink your tea. Here's some sandwiches.' Bloater paste; there had been a couple left over from tea. 'Now, stand up for a moment.'
'I want to measure your height.'
'I'm five-eleven.'
'Stand up, I have to be sure.'
Deane was feeling faint and had difficulty in standing upright. Lawrence pushed him roughly back against the wall, then ran the retractable steel measure up his body. He made it 5.10½, that was as near as dammit.
Deane sank back down on to the bed. Prendergast was

going a bit far with this sick game. He wouldn't hang him, though. He wouldn't dare.

Would he?

'I've brought you a bible. Don't waste the batteries for too long, though.'

'I'm an atheist.'

That made it nice and easy – they wouldn't have to go through all that rigmarole about a chaplain in the morning. and as Deane didn't eat breakfast that was another chore that he would be spared.

'I'll see you in the morning.' Lawrence stood in the doorway. Frederick Deane was a pathetic sight, scarcely recognisable as the bullying, womanising banker. He wasn't going to feel sorry for him, though. No way.

He locked the door behind him and went back into the house. Tonight he would savour the anticipation of the morrow. That was what it was all about.

Deane dozed fitfully. He had shed his clothing, with the exception of his pants and socks, but the stifling heat was still almost unbearable. God, all he asked right now was a pint of lager and a cigarette.

The replacement batteries in the small night-light had run out. He should have conserved them, only used the light when he needed it. Now there was only impenetrable darkness.

The Prendergast boy was a fool. He was incapable of doing anything competently. Forgetfulness was his worst fault; like that time he had forgotten to turn the reversible daily head office letter inside out and it had arrived back at the branch the next morning, the previous day's clearing cheques inside it. 'You're a fool, Prendergast!' he yelled into the darkness of the cell. 'How on earth can we explain this away'

Then it came to him in a flash. *NOW* he understood what Prendergast was up to! This filthy hole, wherever it was, was a *bank*! Lawrence Prendergast was running his own bank because he wasn't capable of working in anybody else's. This must be the strongroom, the safe where the cash was kept. If he'd had a light he would have searched for it.

Of course, the idiot wouldn't be able to manage even his own bank so he'd kidnapped his old boss. Slavery. What a shit of an idea. Then Deane thought of something else. Lawrence had probably gone to kidnap Sally sercombe – he'd bring her here, too. Now that wasn't a bad idea ...

He began to warm to the scheme. Of course, they wouldn't have any customers; they didn't need any. They were going to have their very own secret bank. Like it was before except that Thomas wouldn't be paying them surprise visits to check the cash, and there wouldn't be any inspectors or staff department with which to lodge complaints of sexual harassment. It was all going to be great fun.

But first the place had to be tidied up, cleaned up. Organised. Then they could start. Prendergast was incapable himself, so he'd got his team together. But why the deuce hadn't he gone about it the right way instead of this pointless rigmarole? He'd only had to *ask*.

Deane felt a lot easier now that he had sussed it out. The 'trial' was all part of a demoralising procedure. It was unnecessary. He didn't need to be kept prisoner here: he'd turn up for work every day. Anything so long as he was *manager*. And the first thing that fool could do was to go and fetch him some cigarettes. Senior Service.

He felt a lot easier now. But where the bloody hell had Prendergast got to? It was always the same when you sent him out on errands. He'd be gone an interminable length of time and often when he got back he would've completely forgotten what he'd been sent for.

He was coming now. Deane got up off the bed as he heard the outer door open and close. Lights went on in the adjacent room; enough came through the cracks round the door to enable him to see. Only when he heard a key in the lock did he realise that he wasn't dressed. It didn't matter.

'Have you got my cigarettes?'

'No, just a cup of tea.' Lawrence deposited a mug on the floor.

'Is Sally here yet?'

Lawrence stared. The expression in Deane's eyes had changed. The fear had gone, been replaced by something else. Eager anticipation.

'Not yet.' Humour him, like he'd humoured Wilson at one point.

'I hope she won't be long. We open at ten, you know, and there's a lot of tidying up and cleaning to do first. We've got to make *our* bank the best, Prendergast. You'll have to smarten yourself up, you know. I am *manager*, you do realise that, don't you?'

'That's fine.' Lawrence tugged a piece of material out of his pocket, a home-made balaclava with a slit for the nose. Then he produced some knotted binder twine. 'Now, I'm going to have to tie your hands.'

'What for?' Suspicion again.

'For when Sally gets here.'

'Oh, I see', Deane grinned, 'a little of the old bondage, eh? Never knew she was into that.'

'It's been a long time, Mr Deane. And you are the manager now, not sub-manager.'

Lawrence tied Deane's hands and steered him towards the door. Then he slipped the mask over his head.

'Hey, what's going on?'

'All part of the game, Mr Deane. We're all going to play – you, me and Sally when she gets here. This is our very own torture dungeon.'

'Hadn't we better leave it until after the day's work is done?'

'Don't worry, we'll play it again then.'

Lawrence guided Deane on to the trap door, making sure his feet lined up against the chalk marks, then bound the ankles. He looked up from his kneeling position. God, Deane had got a belly on him! He'd got an erection, too.

'I read somewhere that hanging games were all part of bondage.' The voice was muffled behind the mask. 'That a lot of so-called suicides are the result of pseudo hangings gone wrong. Accidents. So just be careful what you're doing, Prendergast.'

'I will.' Lawrence consulted his watch. It was a minute to eight. 'I'm going to hang you in about sixty seconds. Is there anything you wish to say?'

'How long will Sally be, Prendergast?'

'She won't be coming.'

'But you said . . .'

'I was lying, Deane. Sally won't be coming now or ever.

The last person on earth she wants to see is you. She'll remember you to her dying day, how you took advantage of her, raped her. You've scarred her mind for life. You killed the girl she might have been, made her the gold-digging bitch she is. That's why you've got to die!'

'It *is* all a game ... isn't it?'

'No.' Lawrence's voice trembled; his hand rested on the lever. 'It's all for real, Deane. You're going to be hanged by the neck until you're dead!'

'*No!*' A scream that was blanketed by the death mask, a desperate lunge by the trussed body. But it was to no avail; the trap door clanged downwards and the body shot from view.

Lawrence stood back. Afraid to look in case the head had been torn from the shoulders like last time. Staring fixedly at the rope, the way it tautened, spun, creaked.

And snapped.

There was an awful silence and then a dull thud; not the sickening crack of splintering bone like the time before, just a heavy thump.

Then silence again.

Lawrence's sweat turned icy. It wouldn't matter that the rope had broken so long as it had done its work first; dislocation of the neck was the object of the exercise. At least it would save him the trouble of taking down the dangling corpse.

He stepped forward, steeling himself to look down into the pit. Whatever he saw would not be pleasant. It wasn't meant to be; he didn't want it to be. Vengeance was his, it must be terrible to behold.

Frederick Deane was sitting up. His back resting against the wall, his knees drawn up, he struggled feebly. The frayed rope trailed from him like some emaciated boa constrictor which had wrapped itself around his neck and was slowly throttling him. He was choking, gurgling behind the hood, sucking and blowing the material.

He was dying painfully and slowly from strangulation; dislocation of the neck had not been achieved.

Lawrence screamed down into the pit, 'Hurry up and die, you bastard!'

He wondered how long it would take Frederick Deane to die. Five minutes? Ten? An hour? Oh, Jesus, he hadn't bargained for this!

He stood there helplessly watching his victim writhe within the wrist and ankle bonds. He slid, now he was resting by his shoulders. The length of rope moved as if the reptile attacher was trying to strengthen its hold, but without an anchor its efforts were futile.

Die, you bastard!

But Frederick Deane didn't die; his struggles seemed, if anything stronger. He hitched himself up towards a sitting position. Behind his back his hands flexed in an attempt to break free of their binding. If he succeeded in his efforts, he would be able to loosen the noose.

Lawrence knew that he had to kill his victim, finish him off. Like a novice shooter who discovered that he had merely wounded his quarry, he needed to despatch him. The *coup-de-grâce*.

If only he had a gun, any firearm, anything with which he could kill from a distance. But he didn't possess one. There was an assortment of knives in the kitchen drawer: a bread knife, a carving knife, a variety of vegetable knives. No, he did not have the guts, the very idea had him starting to retch. Some blunt instrument then?

As if in answer to his prayer, his fingers strayed to the pocket of his jeans and touched the ridged, tapered solid rubber with the leather thong dangling from it. His truncheon.

Clumsily, Lawrence climbed down into the pit, stumbled, almost fell headlong on top of Deane. He steadied himself and tugged out the truncheon.

A desperate, pleading groan. It was as if the bound man sensed his nearness, begged for mercy. Through the slit in the mask Deane's nose was bleeding.

'I'm going to kill you!' Lawrence hissed.

He hesitated, again the hunter about to dispatch an injured beast of the chase but holding back because practice and theory were frighteningly different. A blunt weapon, a hard blow ... you needed to know where to strike and how.

The hood billowed, the protruding nostrils blew twin blood

bubbles, burst them. The head, of course, it was the obvious target. The back of the neck – wasn't that how his father had used to kill wounded rabbits during those childhood forays through field and covert?

But Frederick Deane's head was pressed back against the wall, wedged there by the full weight of his slumped body. Lawrence grabbed for it in panic and tried to jerk it round. Something came loose in his clutching fingers, tore free. The execution mask.

Jesus God! The sight of those features had him throwing up, spewing undigested toast and tea over the old man's wrinkled abdomen. Distended bloodshot orbs regarded him, mirrored the cauldron of pain and terror that seethed within, swollen and threatening to burst. The nose bled freely, thick crimson rivulets that poured down on to the extended, purple tongue. The neck was chafed, a bulging collar of raw flesh. The lips moved, but could not get the words past the bloated obstruction, merely dribbling pink saliva.

Lawrence snatched his fingers away, shrank back. He couldn't believe that grotesque thing on the floor was the banker. Perhaps Deane had been some hideous monster in disguise and now the human camouflage had fallen away.

He struck blindly in panic. A soft *thwack*, then warm thick liquid showered back on to him, and the hand that wielded the weapon was spotted with scarlet. Deane's right eye was gone, hanging by a sinew. Blood gushed out of the gaping socket. The body jerked up off the floor, then fell back.

And that was when Lawrence Prendergast went berserk, raining blow after blow on the unprotected head, desperate to destroy that bloated rictus, pulp it to a mulch that was not reminiscent of anything he had ever known.

But the tongue still extended from the scarlet morass wobbling between the uneven teeth that clamped it, defying death to the last. Split lips, a shattered cheekbone, a sharp sliver of bone sticking upwards as if hoping to impale the attacker. Moans like a distant wind in the hills, remonstrating rather than pleading now. *You always were an incompetent fool, Prendergast.*

Lawrence leaned against the wall, feeling as if he might faint. If he did, he hoped that he wouldn't slump across that bloody mulch on the floor. He didn't even know for sure if Deane was dead; he dared not look. The moment of triumph about which he had fantasised for so long had terminated in a dreadful anticlimax.

Some time later he climbed up out of the pit, sneaked back into the house and bathed. His blood-soaked clothing would go out in a dustbin liner on Monday.

He did not remove the corpse until after dark this time. It was a messy task and he threw up twice. He scarcely had the strength to tip in the lime and shovel sand on top, but somehow he managed it, then raked the surface level. By the light of a half moon he estimated that another couple of feet of filling in would bring the base of the pool up to his mother's approved level.

Just room enough. Two down and one to go. Then the polythene liner and the water would hide his secret for ever.

All the same, he was disappointed in himself. Two hangings, and he had bungled them both in different ways. In Wilson's case the drop had been too long — the retired headmaster's own weight had decapitated him as a result; for Deane it was too short — his feet had touched the pit floor, saving him from instant dislocation of the neck.

Not enough attention to detail, he reprimanded himself; sketchy measurements and estimated weights. Next time it would be different because he knew the body in question intimately, the height and the bone structure. Neither would have altered much over the last twenty years, not enough to make any appreciable difference, anyway.

Just thinking about it excited Lawrence in a different way from the others. It aroused him.

And he knew that this time he would get it right.

Chapter Sixteen

Goodness, Larry was actually cleaning out the stair cupboard! Anxiety quickly succeeded Emily's delight. Should Lawrence be working so hard after his nosebleed last night? Admittedly, it had not been as bad as the first one – it had stopped after twenty minutes and he had not had to drive down to Casualty. All the same, his high blood pressure was worrying. If he still refused to go to the doctor then he should take it easy for a few days. He had been spending far too much time working out there in his new darkroom lately. Hour after hour in that stale, stuffy atmosphere couldn't possibly do him any good. And what a waste of this beautiful summer, too.

She stood on the lower landing, holding on to the bannister for support. She debated with herself whether or not to go downstairs. Larry could be bad-tempered if you caught him doing something which you'd asked him to do, and which he'd either put off or else flatly refused to do: a kind of climb-down that went against his nature. You just had to let him get on with it and pretend not to notice unless he actually drew your attention to it.

Oh, dear, what should she do? She didn't relish the prospect of spending half the day upstairs in her bedroom; it would probably take Larry at least that long to make a good job of the stair hole. Unless, of course, he was just looking for something and was planning to put all the rubbish back again when he'd found it. that wasn't beyond the bounds of possibility; he'd done it before.

She leaned furtively over the stair-rail and peered down

into the hallway below. Empty boxes of all shapes and sizes were strewn as far as the front door: grocery cartons, chocolate boxes, cereal packets, padded jiffy bags and large envelopes. She noticed that he had piled all the non-recyclable rubbish up against the dining-room door. Oh dear, yet another room was going to be out of action.

Lawrence was blundering about amidst the debris. He trod on something that cracked and splintered, muttered 'fuck it' and kicked away whatever he had broken. The remains tinkled like glass.

She saw his emerge from the hallway clutching something in his hands. It looked like that fort which her father had made for Glenn during the war years when toys were virtually unobtainable. Afterwards, it had been handed down to Larry.

He was making room to set in down on the carved dolphin hall table, pushing everything to one side in his clumsy haste; the silver salver and the pile of dog-eared telephone directories were in danger of crashing to the floor. They rested precariously on the edge alongside the telephone with its permanently twisted cord. Larry almost always took the phone out into the porch when he made one of his rare calls, in a pathetic attempt at secrecy. Poor Larry, he felt deprived because he didn't have any secrets. Perhaps it would do him good to have the odd one or two. Just harmless ones.

No, it wasn't the fort, it wasn't big enough. Emily stared, trying to focus her failing eyesight. It was some kind of wooden structure mounted on a tall base. A signal box from that Hornby lay-out which William had bought second-hand from the Shuttleworths in 1944? No, that wasn't right, it was too big for that.

Suddenly, with a sickening lurch of recognition, Emily knew without any doubt what the mysterious object was. That *thing* was unhealthy for a small boy to play with; worse when an adult gloated over it. She was sure that she had surreptitiously deposited it in the dustbin when Larry was about nine. He must have just as slyly retrieved it. And hidden it until now.

Emily thought back to that day in 1952 when she had

first seen the disgusting contraption, at the church fete. She remembered the carnival atmosphere, the sideshows and tombolas, everybody enjoying themselves in the summer sunshine. A day of innocent pleasure – until she had seen that nauseating sideshow. Bill should never have taken Larry into that tent – their son had only been six at the time.

It was a sick spin-off from the Nuremburg trials, at a time when everybody was gloating over the nazi commandants getting their just desserts. And old Joe Heathcote had seen a way to make a few quid for the church organ out of the executions. A carpenter by trade, he had built a miniature gallows and mounted it on a base with a trap door that dropped down into a pit below. He had also painted up a lead soldier to look like Hitler and made a tiny bag to go over its head. It was a perfect working model.

The condemned Führer stood on the trap door with a rope around his neck, and the audience paid their two pennies and filed in one at a time. Joe pulled the lever – down went Adolf – and then opened up a little door in the base so that you could see the hanged model swinging. It was so lifelike, that was the worst part about it. Many of the visitors went outside and rejoined the queue; Bill had done just that, mainly because Larry had been so fascinated that he wanted to see it again. And again. And again: twelve performances in all. Bill had called a halt after a couple of bob's worth.

Larry had talked about nothing else for weeks afterwards. Emily had expected the boy to have nightmares but he slept soundly, woke up the next morning and chattered on about it again. Then Bill had met Joe Heathcote in town and the result of their meeting was that Joe had given Bill the model gallows, because he didn't have any further use for it after all the complaints he'd received at the fete. Emily had suspected that her husband had bought it to keep their son quiet. It had certainly done that: he spent hours up in his bedroom hanging and re-hanging Hitler. After three years, finally she had seized an opportunity to dump it. Or she thought she had.

Now she stared in fascinated horror as Larry carefully hung the miniature noose round Hitler's neck. *Click!* The lever functioned as smoothly as it had always done and then Lawrence was unclipping the tiny door in the base, chuckling to himself as he looked inside.

Emily felt nauseated. A sudden, searing pain flared in her arm. She gasped aloud at the intensity of it, then clung to the bannisters as it receded.

Larry was coming upstairs, carrying his toy scaffold with great care, almost lovingly.

'Mother!' He almost bumped into her, stared in surprise. 'How long have you been there?' Accusing, angry because she had spied upon him.

'I was just on my way downstairs.' Emily cleared her throat nervously, the way she always did when she was embarrassed. She felt decidedly guilty. 'Having a clear-out, are you?'

'No, I was just looking for something. Don't fret yourself, Mother, I'm going to put it all back shortly.'

Which was exactly what she had feared. She sighed. 'What is it you were looking for, Larry?'

'Something.'

She had anticipated his answer; she had heard it on innumerable occasions before. Sometimes he alternated it with 'nothing'. Now he was shielding his latest find with his arm, pushing his way past her, eager to be out of her sight.

'Larry?'

'*What*?' He turned an exasperated face towards her.

'You've found that dreadful toy that you had when you were six, haven't you?'

'So what?' He held it up defiantly, taunting her with it because he remembered how much she used to hate it. She had been terrified of it then; she still was. 'It's probably worth a lot of money nowadays.'

She averted her eyes from it. 'It's morbid. Barbaric. I was very cross with your father at the time for giving it to you.'

'Hanging is a deterrent.' The justification came easily, words which he had learned by heart in boyhood from his father so that he could regurgitate them when the occasion demanded. Like now. 'If hanging was brought back the murder rate would drop by fifty per cent, I'd guarantee it.'

'We're a civilised society, Larry. An eye for an eye isn't the answer. It makes us as bad as the murderers.'

'It *is* the answer!' Her bland platitudes enraged him. 'Look how you and I have to barricade ourselves in against burglars, all the security precautions *I* have to take ... Or take the rioting in town last August: three killed and the best they can do is to give two of the guilty ones ten years apiece. They'll be out in seven, and if their appeal is successful they'll walk out scot free with a hefty compensation cheque to boot. Do you call that a deterrent? It's a fucking incentive to murder!'

Emily closed her eyes. A headache was just starting. Larry's outbursts always upset her, particularly when he used foul language. She was determined not to encourage any further discussion about his obsession. Nothing she said would make any difference to his views. But she had to know what he was up to with that dreadful contraption. 'What are you going to do with ... with that *thing*, Larry?'

'I'm going to clean it up, keep it in my room. It must've been lying under the stairs for years.'

It was pointless trying to dissuade him, but she felt some nameless fear stir inside her. Model trains, war gaming, she could have accepted those – a lot of men pursued their childhood hobbies in later life – but this was morbid, unhealthy.

'Anything wrong with that?' Belligerent, challenging her to oppose him. She capitulated, as she always did.

'No, that's fine, you're old enough to do as you please.' She decided to switch to a less contentious topic. 'I see you've done some more work on the pond.'

'How do you know that?' He tensed suddenly, and his eyes bored into her. Oh dear, she couldn't get anything right.

'I had a little walk down the garden yesterday evening.' she swallowed guiltily, aware that she had trespassed on her son's domain. 'It was really pleasant and I managed it quite well. Another couple of feet of filling in and it'll be about ready for the liner. You've done really well, Larry, and I'm proud of you. I could get Glenn or Arthur to finish it off, you know.'

'*No!*' His features darkened. She had, in all innocence,

said the wrong thing again. '*I'm* going to finish it. I want to. *I* started it, it was *my* idea. All right?'

'All right, calm down, Larry! I was only thinking of your health.'

'Then don't!' he snapped. 'I'm perfectly all right. I'd've finished it by now except that I've been too busy. Just stop mithering me, Mother.'

Emily continued shakily on her way downstairs while Larry stamped off to his bedroom. She negotiated a path through the jumble of boxes in the hall and went through to the kitchen. Tea and toast – that would sort her out.

She couldn't understand why she felt so unwell. When she got up she had been fine. Now that sharp pain was back in her arm, and seemed to be travelling upwards. It was worrying. Not for herself, she didn't care about herself. It was Larry she worried about.

How on earth would he cope if anything happened to her?

Chapter Seventeen

Kent had gone out with detective Sergeant Mike Clifford to check the abandoned BMW on the golf club car park. The Scene of Crime forensic expert would take it apart if necessary; at the moment it wasn't necessary. A guy had every right to go off without telling his friends where he'd gone. It was a routine enquiry at this stage, just in case.

After they had checked the car, Don Baker, the golf club secretary, served them coffee in the deserted lounge bar. 'It's certainly very strange. Captain Deane comes in here most nights, weekends as well. Widower, no family, nothing else to do, if you understand me. He needs company, though you wouldn't have thought it if you knew him – outgoing sort of chap, life and soul of the party. Any functions we wanted to put on, he'll organise 'em. But', he lowered his voice in an exaggerated air of confidence, 'he is one for the ladies, you know.' He winked.

'A womaniser?' Kent did not believe in skirting issues. He was already compiling a mental dossier on the missing man. He needed a profile.

'Oh, no, no!' Feigned shock, an expression of embarrassment. 'Nothing like that. As far as I know, anyway. Dash it all, he *is* in his eighties. but he knows how to chat up the other chaps' wives without causing offence, flatter those that are in need of flattery. Perhaps he did strike up a relationship and has gone off with a woman. Though I haven't heard of any of our members who are missing a wife.' He laughed, a self-conscious giggle.

'A widower, you said?' Kent prompted.

'Yes.' Baker dried a glass meticulously as though right now it was the most important job of the day. 'His wife left him a few years back, so I understand. She died shortly afterwards.'

'Why did she leave him?'

'Well ...' Baker hesitated momentarily in a vain attempt to appear discreet. 'Rumour has it, and I'm only repeating club gossip, and there's plenty of that, most of it unfounded ...' He held the glass up to the light, polished off a slight smear. 'They *say* that he was messing about with a young girl in the bank. I know for a fact he did get early retirement, but people regularly put two and two together and make five. Don't they?'

'Sometimes,' Kent agreed, his expression impassive. 'Who was the girl?'

'Oh, I've no idea, I'm not interested in scandal.'

'I see.' Kent would find her if he had to.

'The odd thing is, apart from not having seen him for a week, that he parked his car down the end of the car park. Normally uses a space in the officials' sector just outside the main entrance. He isn't an official although he has been nominated for the committee, but he is a kind of fixture here. Everybody respects the Captain – he'll help you if he can. He was in banking, and some of the local businessmen who come in here sometimes ask his advice on financial matters. He could have made himself a nice little earner out of consultancy if he wanted to, but he isn't that kind of man. Well off, you know, his missus was loaded.'

'So he left his car in an inconspicuous place, locked it up, and hasn't been seen since. He took the keys with him so he obviously intended to return.' Kent briskly summed up the key facts. 'We'll have to search the golf course and the common at the back.'

'Oh, he wasn't suicidal, I can assure you of that.' Baker spoke hastily.

'Very few people are.' Kent glanced at his companion. Clifford was a good cop, worked by the book; he was obviously thinking on the same lines. 'We have to follow a procedure. We'll have to check his house, too. Just to be sure.'

'There's always the possibility that he's gone abroad, perhaps with a lady friend.' The secretary was loyal to his members, they paid his salary. 'The airport's only twenty minutes' drive from here. They could have gone in her car. Or it could even be a male companion. I'm sure the Captain would have told me if he'd been leaving his car here but possibly the arrangements were made in a hurry. He might be back in a day or two to pick it up.'

'Possibly.' Kent doubted it. 'But why not leave his car at his own house? His companion, male or female, could have picked him up there. Or met him at the airport.'

'I've absolutely no idea. Now, if you gentlemen have finished, I've got rather a lot of paperwork to catch up on. Help yourself to more coffee, if you want it. Our barman doesn't come on duty until midday.' Evidently Baker wanted to make it clear that the menial role of temporary barman had only been undertaken to help out.

'I think you've told us all we need to know at this stage.' Kent stood up. 'Just one other thing ...'

'Yes?'

'Did you by any chance know Prebendary Edward Wilson?'

'The name rings a bell. Vaguely.'

'He used to be headmaster of the preparatory school up by the cathedral many years ago.'

'Ah, that's why I know the name. One of our members sent his son there. Oh, it would be a long time ago; the fellow's as old as the Captain. The father, I mean, not the son. Rollason's a pal of Captain Deane's – they used to play billiards together. I remember him telling me once about this headmaster fellow. A sadist, if what he said was true – used to cane boys every morning, delighted in it. But, again, that's only gossip. I don't take much notice of what people say.'

'Thank you.' Kent smiled. 'We won't trouble you any further just at the moment, Mr Baker. We may be back, though. Our chaps might want to go over Deane's car, but we mustn't jump to any conclusions yet.'

Detective Chief Inspector Borman was a stickler for playing

things by the book. Concentrate on priority cases, he told his men, put the rest on file, categorise them. Deane was not a priority case, whatever hunches Kent might have about him. They didn't have the manpower to mess about with gut feelings.

Deane was not listed as missing; nobody had reported him as missing. The fact that he had no immediate next of kin was immaterial. The abandoned car in the golf club car park would have to be explained in due course; they couldn't do more than just call at his house, to check whether he was home or not. He might have gone on a world cruise without telling anybody − he had the right and the money to do just that. Or he could be dead in the lavatory or bathroom, anywhere out of sight of the ground-floor windows. If, after a reasonable length of time, there was still no sign of him then they would force an entry. He didn't have milk or papers delivered, just the mail; the post office had not received a holding order. He might have overlooked that − even the most organised of people were permitted the occasional lapse. At the moment there were no grounds for undue concern. The regular police patrols would keep on checking. The BMW was safe where it was; it could remain there. The police were doing everything that could reasonably be expected of them.

Kent had a fortnight's leave due to him. Overdue. If he didn't take the backlog soon he would lose it. Brenda had mentioned a break − maybe a week on Jersey (and forget Bergerac). He stalled her on that one. He could use a week at home just winding down.

'Which means you're going to take on the Deane case unofficially. It might not *be* a case, and you could end up getting your knuckles rapped. An old chap has decided to go off without telling anybody, maybe with some young tart. Blow his smoke screen and you could be in a lot of trouble − he sounds an arrogant so-and-so. I'm always wary of men who use military titles in civvy street.'

'It's the car that worries me − that's the one fact that doesn't fit. He had no reason to leave it where he did. If he was sneaking off for a dirty week and didn't want anybody to know, why park the car where questions are bound to be asked?'

'An oversight, he's an old man.'

'No, far too shrewd for that. He went to meet somebody at an appointed place near the golf club, or else he was picked up from there in another car. He didn't know it then, but he wasn't coming back. He won't be now. He's as dead as a dodo, I'll guarantee it. All we lack is the body. Just as we do in Wilson's case.'

'So you're going to spend your week's leave trying to find the body?' She wasn't surprised: had been expecting something like this. She turned back to the sink and began stacking the dishes in the rack, because she didn't want him to see how her eyes had misted up. She could have cried with frustration but she knew she wouldn't. Because Adam would go right out there and do what he thought he had to do and blow Detective Chief Inspector Borman. She wouldn't even try to talk him out of it.

'There's a body somewhere,' he was adamant, 'but there's no guarantee I'll find it.'

'Why's it so important to you, Adam, when there are confirmed murders on the unsolved files? You don't even know for sure that a crime has been committed.'

'Not *a* crime. Two crimes,' he corrected her. 'They still haven't found the prebendary. And he's officially listed as missing.'

'Good God, you're not linking the two?' She turned round and stared at him. 'That's just a wild supposition.'

'A hunch.' He came across and kissed her. 'When I get one as strong as this, I have to follow it up. The disappearances are identical – two guys in their eighties just walked out of their homes and haven't been seen since. The only reason they're not being connected at this stage is because no crime has been proven and they happened in different parts of the country. What connects them for me is that Wilson came from around here. He could be closer than we think. His body, I mean.'

This time she didn't challenge him. There was an indisputable logic to his 'hunch'. Adam had a first-class record. the fact that he was still a DS was because his superiors wanted it that way. Proving your bosses wrong didn't earn you promotion.

'This has all the hallmarks of serial killings,' he continued softly. He wasn't being dramatic; if anything, he was playing it down. He just needed somebody with whom to share his thoughts. 'All we're lacking is bodies. But the FBI didn't find the bodies until they found Dahmer, did they?'

'Oh, God!' Put that way, it was terrifying. 'Adam, please be careful.'

'Maybe I'm wrong.' He was trying to reassure her now, perhaps regretting that he had spoken his suppositions out loud. 'And even if I'm not, my chances of finding either bodies or killer are about fifty thousand to one. But I have to try − you understand that, don't you, Bren?'

'I know you do.' She kissed him, trying not to let him see how shaky she felt. She didn't ask him where he was going to start because he wouldn't tell her. When an ex-WPC married a DS there were a lot of things her husband didn't tell her. She knew that from the outset. Especially when the husband was Adam Kent.

'I'll be toing and froing.' Which meant, expect me when you see me and don't worry if you don't. 'You never know, we might even make it to Jersey next week, depending upon how I get on.'

They wouldn't be going away; she had scrapped that idea already. There were several jobs she wanted to do around the house, anyway.

'If I find Wilson, I'll find Deane.' He reached for a dishcloth. It was unlike him to help her with drying the dishes: evidently a kind of penance for not going away on holiday. 'And if I manage that, I'll find their killer. That's the only certainty in all this.'

Afterwards he changed into a sweatshirt and cords and went into the hall to use the phone. Brenda closed the adjoining door. She would not eavesdrop on him. She didn't want to know who he was ringing because she couldn't help, anyway. Hers was the hardest role of all.

Staying at home and waiting. And, though she would not have admitted it to her husband, praying.

Chapter Eighteen

Janice Peters was beautiful.

She was tall and well built, with long dark hair that fell almost to her waist. Her large dark eyes smiled as readily as her full lips; her shapely nose wrinkled mischievously when she was amused. Her every movement was graceful in spite of her height. At boarding school she had held the record for the cross country and been captain of the netball team. Her academic record was equally successful: at university she had achieved a BA with honours. At twenty-four she had an exciting future before her.

She was even more beautiful naked.

Like she was now as she posed in Lawrence's bedroom studio. During her university vacations she had earned pocket money by modelling for the art school; this was no different. She had perfected her pose, sitting so that lusting male eyes were unable to feast upon her inner thighs.

She could sit motionless for hours, letting her thoughts drift, divorcing herself from her audience.

It was the flash of the camera that disturbed her most, dazzled her. She was sure that she would have her eyes closed in most of the pictures. She found herself wincing, anticipating the sudden blinding light.

'Just turn slightly towards me, Jan, please.'

She did as she was requested, moving her body without uncrossing her legs. He moved closer, dropped into a kneeling position.

'My father would have a fit if he ever found out.' She giggled nervously, guiltily.

'Well, he won't, will he?' Lawrence blinded her yet again.

Her father, a retired brigadier, openly disapproved of Lawrence Prendergast. He had forbidden his daughter to carry on seeing "that scruffbag of a wastrel". Bank managers were well below brigadiers in the social scale and that boy wouldn't even make it to managerial level. 'Your mother and I want to see you marry *well*, my dear.' Janice's mother would not witness that ambition – she had died the previous year. Franklyn Peters became even more protective towards his daughter after his loss.

Lawrence was okay, though she had given up trying to convince her father of that, particularly after that business of his unfair transferal from the local bank. Lawrence was an introvert and a recluse, but his father had made him that way. They both needed a break from parental domination. Maybe if she helped Lawrence, he would help her.

Lawrence's father approved of her socially but he objected to her worn jeans and moccasins. For starters. She didn't conform to his ideal of the prospective banker's wife. So she usually met Lawrence in town. They were at Lawrence's home today because his parents and his brother had gone to Corfu for a fortnight.

Janice was a virgin. She wasn't deliberately 'saving herself', it was just that she wasn't very interested in sex. When she felt the urge she was usually alone and she had learned to satisfy herself. She took a fatalistic view: when sex happened, it would happen. Lawrence had never molested her, but she found his shyness endearing.

Which was why she had had no qualms about taking off her clothes in his studio. She kept her thighs together by force of habit. He probably wouldn't want to look there, anyway.

She sat and watched him take the film out of the camera. She wondered why he didn't go in for photography as a career; she might even suggest it to him one day.

'I could develop these pics right away.' He put the film on the developer. 'In fact, I could have them all printed before you go home. If you'd like that.'

'Why shouldn't I like it?' She moved close to him; she hadn't dressed but it wouldn't matter.

'We'd have to stop in here in the dark for some time.'

'I don't mind.'

He switched off the lights, plunging them into stygian blackness except for the dull red developing light. It was relaxing after the dazzling glare from the photographic lights, much cooler, too. And something else, it was *romantic*. She'd better not tell Lawrence that, he'd think she was flaunting herself.

Janice might have got dressed except that she couldn't remember where she had put her clothes and she might knock something over if she tried to find them. It didn't matter.

'There, we've just got to wait now.' Lawrence wiped his hands on a towel and moved away from the sink. His fingers found hers. She gave an answering squeeze.

She was trembling and her heart was beating madly. Her father would go berserk if he ever found out; Lawrence's too. But they wouldn't.

She wanted him to kiss her. He was always shy about kissing and when he got round to it, it was usually no more than a wet compression of their lips. Edward, at university, really knew how to kiss, and she never had to initiate things with him.

This time Janice made the first move. They bumped noses because Lawrence wasn't expecting it. And giggled.

He was clumsy, ill at ease. He trod on her foot, but did not seem to notice. It hurt but she didn't want to spoil everything by telling him and embarrassing him. She was reminded of her childhood days when she lived with her parents in married quarters in Whittington Barracks. Adjacent to the barracks there was a field in which a donkey was kept. Sometimes she used to go down there to give it a carrot. One day, the donkey, in its haste, had stepped on her foot. The bruise had stayed for a fortnight. She didn't mind if Lawrence did bruise her.

She didn't mind what he did to her.

'Oh, Lawrence!' She moaned softly, found his lips again.

'What?'

'I love you!' She blurted it out because she knew if she didn't say it now she never would.

She felt him tense suddenly. She was scared in case she had offended him. After all, men were supposed to say that to women first.

'I'm glad, because I love you, too, Jan.'

Then he was holding her awkwardly, trembling. She felt something hard pressing against her thigh; she knew only too well what it was. It was both exciting and frightening. Edward used to get an erection when they kissed but she had flatly refused to let him do anything. She'd let Lawrence, though. *If* he wanted to.

She guided his hand up to her breasts. He squeezed and pinched; somehow she managed not to cry out. Down below he was pushing himself at her, rubbing against her.

And this time she wanted it desperately.

'You can if you want to, you know.'

He was silent. Her stomach seemed to contract; her mouth went dry. Serve her right if he told her to get her clothes on and get the hell out of here, called her a hussy. She couldn't blame him if he did. But he didn't.

'I'd like to.'

'Go on, then,' she said gently and removed his fingers from where they were clamping a nipple and guided them downwards, put them where it was all soft and wet and tingling. 'We could lie on the floor, I don't mind.'

He had some difficulty getting his clothes off. Something toppled, clattered. 'Don't worry about that.' His stomach was huge, seemed to spread out over her own. Something else was huge as well.

'I've never done it before.' She wanted him to know that in case he thought otherwise.

'Neither have I,' he confessed. She knew that he was telling the truth.

Things happened very fast after that. It was all over so quickly, an anticlimax. It didn't hurt her like the women's magazines always said that it did. She would willingly have suffered pain if it could have gone on longer. But he was backing off, leaving her with the overpowering urge to rub herself to a climax except that she was too embarrassed.

Nevertheless, she was glad that they had done it. Next time it wouldn't be so fraught, they would relax and enjoy it.

They had the house to themselves for the best part of two weeks. They made love, and Janice became quite domesticated, tidying up Lawrence's bedroom and cleaning it. When the Prendergasts returned from their holiday they had to revert to meeting in town after Lawrence finished work at the bank. Janice refused to come home with him. William Prendergast had made no secret of his disapproval of her. And, anyway, he told his son, you shouldn't even *think* about a serious relationship until you've got your first appointment. You couldn't afford to support a wife. Concentrate on passing your Institute of Bankers examinations, then you can look round for a wife to suit your position.

Emily was surprised at the tidiness and cleanliness of Lawrence's bedroom. 'You haven't had that girl in here by any chance whilst we've been away, have you?' Her husband would fly into a rage at the mere idea of Janice being here in his absence.

'I haven't seen her for weeks.' The lie came instinctively.

'That's all right, then.' Secretly, Emily would have encouraged the relationship but she dared not oppose Bill. Larry swore that he hadn't had Janice in the house whilst they were away and that was good enough for her. She had checked up on her son, exonerated herself.

'I wish we could get engaged,' Janice told Lawrence one day in the milk bar after work. 'It'd mean falling out with my father, though.'

Lawrence's pulse raced. The idea both shocked and excited him. Life could be idyllic married to Janice. There were problems, though; he didn't have any money and his father would most certainly oppose the idea. The latter was a frightening prospect.

'I'd like that,' he said.

'You don't sound very enthusiastic.'

'I *am*!' He tried to sound convincing. 'I'd have to talk to the parents about it first though.'

'Sod your Father! You're a grown man, Lawrence. An adult. You'll have to break with your parents sometime, you know. and as you hate the bank so much, why don't you look for another job? In photography, for instance. You'd be much happier. We could both be happy. *If* that's what you want!'

He was carried along by her enthusiasm. 'I'll tell my folks.'

But he didn't. He agonised over the decision, put it off. He tried to think of a compromise; maybe if he took a flat in the city ... Even that would mean a confrontation. And Janice's father would do his utmost to part them. One way or another, Lawrence didn't stand a chance.

Then Janice stopped meeting him. He tried to phone her but Brigadier Peters answered the phone and Lawrence replaced the receiver with a shaking hand. He wrote to her; there was no answering letter.

One evening a month later the telephone in the hall rang. He heard his mother answer it, say 'just a minute please'. Her footsteps were coming upstairs, hurrying; he could always tell when she was flustered.

'Larry, it's for you,' she whispered, glancing down into the hall to check that her husband was still in the lounge watching television. 'It's ... it's *that girl*!'

'Oh!' Surprise. Delight. A nervousness that had Lawrence's mouth going dry.

'Be quick, Larry. And ... keep your voice down – you know what your father's like when he's in a bad mood.' William Prendergast wasn't actually in a bad mood at that moment – but that could change within seconds.

Lawrence stumped downstairs and picked up the telephone with clumsy haste. 'Hi, Jan.' His mother was standing on the landing: he knew she was listening. Probably for the sound of her husband getting up out of his armchair and coming through to ask who was on the line.

'Lawrence, there's ... there's something I have to tell you.' She sounded tense, edgy. Hostile, almost.

His stomach knotted and he gripped the receiver as though

he meant to crush it. 'Go on.' He glanced back towards the stairs, knew that his mother was still listening, straining her ears.

'Lawrence ... I'm pregnant.'

His vision blurred. He leaned against the dolphin table for support and tried to speak but he couldn't get the words out.

'Are you still there, Lawrence?'

'Yes.' It sounded weak, a shell-shocked whisper.

'Did you hear what I said?'

'Yes.'

'Well?'

Oh Jesus, what could he say? There was an awful lot he wanted to say but couldn't. I'd marry you except that your father and my folks wouldn't allow it. I couldn't afford it, anyway. I wish I could marry you, I really want to. I'm in love with you. We'd better meet and discuss it. Except that he couldn't say any of those things because his mother would hear.

'I ... I ...'

'As I thought, you don't want to know!' Her tone was scathing. 'Don't worry, don't even give it another thought. I don't want to upset your folks — that would be a major catastrophe, wouldn't it? But you needn't worry, because I'm going to have it taken away. I'm going to have an abortion.'

'No, please, let's talk first ...'

'I don't want to hear from you again, Lawrence.' She was crying now. 'Please don't phone me, don't write. Just forget that there was ever anything between us. At least talking to you has proved what I already knew, that I would never ever be able to drag you away from your darling mummy and daddy!'

The line went dead.

'Jan, please ...' Despair, a surge of panic.

'Larry, what's the matter?' Emily was standing at the top of the stairs, aghast at her son's white face. 'What did that girl want?'

'What on earth's going on?' The lounge door burst open

and William Prendergast stood there, angry at being distracted from his television programme. 'Who was that on the phone?'

'It was a wrong number.' Lawrence made for the stairs, pushed past his mother. 'Nothing for anybody to worry about.'

That was the last time he ever heard from Janice Peters. He wrote a pleading letter: *Don't kill my baby.*

She didn't reply. But he knew only too well in the years that followed that she had had an abortion. She had murdered his baby.

Now the hurt was greater than ever. It had festered like a slow-growing cancer. Sadness had become grief; sorrow had merged into hatred.

Lawrence was ready for her now but he knew that Janice was going to be the most difficult one of all. But that would not stop him, because there was nothing else left for him.

Chapter Nineteen

'I haven't seen or heard anything of Frederick Deane for almost twenty years', Sally Satchwell smiled briefly, coldly, 'and if he's gone missing then all I can say is that he's been missing from my life since they retired him from the bank!'

Kent accepted a cup of tea. He noted from the washing basket in the corner of the kitchen that she had a teenage son and daughter. He had timed his visit to perfection: the children were either at school or college, and her husband was at the office.

He had traced her through the city branch of the bank, after a casual conversation with a cashier there.

'Do you happen to know if Sally Sercombe still works for the bank?' He hoped that if she did then she wasn't on the staff here − a business hours meeting might have caused her embarrassment. He had found out her name by chatting to a long-established customer of Deane's former branch. Sercombe was a starting point; she was probably married by now. She might still be a bank clerk − perhaps a part-timer earning her own spending money.

'Sercombe?' The cashier's forehead furrowed. 'Sercombe ... the name rings a bell. Oh, I know, you mean Sally Satchwell. She worked here up until about five years ago, still banks here. She lives up on Caldwell Rise, can't remember the number but it's the third house on the left. She's often in here on Fridays to cash her housekeeping money.'

Kent had found the house without any trouble; now he

had to play down his visit. The truth as it stood right now was least likely to arouse her suspicions.

'It's only a routine enquiry. In all probability there's nothing wrong and he's just gone off somewhere. I'm just making a few advance enquiries in case we do have to go looking for him.'

'He's probably gone off with a woman. He's a dirty old dog and I wouldn't think he's altered much, even at eighty whatever.' There was venom in her tone.

'A womaniser, eh?'

'A womaniser, a cheat, a liar and probably a lot of other things I never found out.'

'I've heard his wife left him because he'd been messing around with some young woman.'

'Who told you that?' Her expression froze. Kent read alarm and guilt in her eyes. He'd hit the right nail on the head — too hard.

'I heard it somewhere, can't remember exactly where.' Oh, shit, he'd put his foot in it.

'I reported him to the staff department for sexual harrassment.' She lit a cigarette with shaking hands. 'He used to touch me most times he passed my desk. I put up with it because the branch was a cushy number. But when he groped up my skirt one day I decided enough was enough. I lost my rag. That way why they 'retired' him early.' She was blushing and avoiding his eye.

Kent knew she was lying. Deane had been screwing her, that was obvious.

'Did he have many enemies?'

'Me, for one. Afterwards. I never *liked* him before but I tolerated him.'

'How many other staff were there?'

'Just one, a guy named Lawrence Prendergast. He was a real slob, I couldn't stand him either.'

'What did Deane think of him?'

'He used to bully him. Anybody else but Prendergast and I'd've felt sorry for him but the guy was ... ugh! He was overweight, lazy, incompetent, wouldn't say boo to a goose. No sense of humour. Moody, hateful sort of a chap.'

'Did he hate Deane?'

'Must have, but he was the worm who wouldn't turn. His old man was a bank manager, gave him hell, too. He was forced to work in the bank – just his luck to have Deane as his boss. If he hated Deane, he never showed it. He must've brooded, unless he was so hardened to that sort of treatment that it just washed over him. I heard he packed the bank in after his father died, and was just living at home with his mother. He's probably still living with her if she's alive today. Me, though, I don't want to dig up the past; it's best left buried as far as I'm concerned. I want to forget it.'

'Thank you, you've been most helpful.' Kent stood up. 'I hope I won't have to bother you again.'

There always had to be a starting point in every enquiry. Sally Satchwell had provided him with the first link of a long trail that might be going nowhere. He would follow it until either he found what he was looking for or else it petered out.

Adam Kent was that kind of man; he thought positively, optimistically, but he knew a dead end when he came to one. Right now it was looking as promising as he could hope for at this stage. Captain Deane was the kind of man who made enemies.

Kent needed to know if Prebendary Edward Wilson had made enemies, too. He was already forming profiles of the missing men – profiles that would not appear on any official CID files.

Chapter Twenty

Janice had often wondered over the years, particularly during the last twelve months or so, just what life would have been like if she'd married Lawrence Prendergast. However bad, it couldn't have been any worse than having Ben Frame for a husband.

She had become progressively disillusioned with Ben. He had changed, there was no doubt about that. Little remained beyond a physical resemblance to the man with whom she had walked down the aisle on that heady July day in 1976. The height of the hottest summer on record, as if she needed a landmark to remind her.

Ben was tall and muscular, and looked more like a manual labourer than a cost accountant. He played on it, too, created an image within his own mind. Everybody fantasised – there was nothing wrong in that, except when you took it to the extreme. As Ben did. Fourteen years her senior, he was a cowboy enthusiast. His perpetual complaint in recent years had been the decline of the Western film, but he had remedied that with the video – he had his own personal library of classic cowboy films, shelves of paperbacks and stacks of comic books accumulated since his youth. She could have tolerated that, but it didn't end there. He bought Western clothes and replica guns, even paid a fortune for a supposedly genuine USA marshal's badge. And then he discovered that there were places in the UK where one could go and spend a 'Western holiday' – dress the part, swagger around a specially built 'frontier' town, fire blank cartridges in the street and ride a horse, albeit a docile one. They even staged mock gunfights and battles with red indians.

No way was she going to play cowboys and indians for a fortnight. If Ben was set on going, then he could go on his own. Which he had done. But it was after his homecoming from this fantasy holiday that things had really begun to go seriously wrong between them. It was as if Ben hadn't come back, but had been replaced by a lookalike stranger. Because, for him, fantasy had replaced reality.

The only redeeming feature as far as she was concerned was that he had never actually hit her. He had come close on several occasions, trivial disagreements which escalated into full-scale rows. Beans and bacon were fine now and then, a makeshift meal once, even twice, a week. But not every day. If he wanted to live like that then he could damned well get his own food!

Looking back, she realised that it was his macho image and rugged looks that had attracted her in the first place. She hadn't associated him with the legendary Wild West then. He had simply seemed like the kind of man who would look after a woman, protect her. He was highly intelligent, too, and he had just achieved promotion in his job in the motor industry.

Five years later he was made redundant. She now suspected that he had been sacked, possibly over a stupid quarrel with one of his superiors. He never got another job after that.

She took a part-time job, because she needed the money and also because she would go crazy if she had to spend all day, every day, at home with Ben. He had become morose and quarrelsome, but she made excuses for him – it was humiliating for any man to have to stay at home whilst his wife went out and earned the money to provide them with those luxuries that the dole didn't budget for.

The local art school had advertised for somebody to teach adult classes on Wednesdays and Friday mornings and they were going to need an evening class teacher after half term. Janice got the job. Things had gone wrong after her first session.

There was one male student in the class. Harry Law was seventy-five, a widower and a perfect gentleman. He had decided to take up painting to give him an interest. Janice had known him for several years and had no hesitation in accepting a lift home afterwards. Harry was a slow and careful driver, and he insisted on taking her right to the door of her home. He raised his trilby as he drove off. He really was a dear.

As she entered the hall Janice saw that Ben was standing on the stairs. He was dressed in a blue checked shirt and Wranglers, and sported his marshal's badge. But there was no welcoming smile, just a glare from his piercing dark eyes. there was no mistaking the accusation in his expression.

'What the hell's going on?' He was too angry even to put on that pseudo transatlantic accent which he had been trying to cultivate.

'What on earth do you mean?' She had no idea what he was accusing her of.

'What's the idea, a bloody bloke bringing you home?' He advanced on her, towering above her.

'Don't be ridiculous!' She was angry in spite of her fear. 'That 'bloody bloke', as you call him, happens to be a student in my class. He's seventy-five and a gentleman. He offered me a lift home. I accepted. I also saved a pound bus fare. Now, does that satisfy you?'

'No, it doesn't. I want you to pack the job in.' His fingers closed over her arm and squeezed viciously.

'Hey, that hurts!' She was tempted to slap his face with her free hand. She might have done, except for his expression. 'No, I damned well won't give the job up. We need the money desperately.'

'Then you'd better not have a lift home with that old bastard.' He was obviously trying to save face with a compromise. 'Got it?'

Ben had always been jealous, possessive to the point of total domination, not just of her body but of her mind; she even felt guilty thinking her own thoughts. She knew that she was in danger of becoming paranoid. Like him.

He brooded for days afterwards. Her lift home with Harry Law was obviously preying on his mind, clouding it with suspicion. On Friday she asked Harry to drop her off at the shops and walked the rest of the way. she even wondered if Ben might start following her, spying on her. It all stemmed from his tough cowboy image. He treated her the way his heroes had treated their women a century ago in a raw frontier land. He should see a psychiatrist. He wouldn't, though, and she would never dare suggest it.

Ben's other obsession was as bad, if not worse. Sex.

In the early days of their marriage she had tolerated it. Because it was her duty. But always there was the fear of pregnancy. She was haunted day and night by the guilt of her abortion. If she could have had her time over again she would have had the baby, brought it up as a single parent, and found the love she desperately sought. But now she didn't dare go through childbirth – it would have revived too many painful memories.

The years passed and somehow she didn't become pregnant. Ben had hinted once that he was sterile. She half suspected that he had undergone a vasectomy because he didn't want kids. That was okay by her – she wasn't going to ask any questions.

She didn't want sex, she didn't like it, but she did everything that Ben asked. And more. Lately, it was getting too much. Money was short – they needed every penny they could get – but he frittered pounds away on porn mags. That was where all the OTT ideas came from, she was sure. His demands were getting more outrageous every day. She dreaded to think what else he might ask of her.

'Been a long time, haven't you?'

Ben was waiting for her as she emerged from the bathroom, his eyes narrowed with suspicion. She saw a footstool on the landing and thought for a moment that perhaps he had been changing a light bulb. Then she understood. About a week ago, on returning from shopping, she had found that the opaque pane of glass above the bathroom door had been replaced by a piece of transparent glass. Ben had told her that he had been fixing the new roller blind and had accidentally poked the rod through the glass. Rather than go to the expense of frosted glass, he had bought plain. That made sense. She had seen no cause to doubt his word. It didn't matter. Until now.

'I enjoy a bath.' She tried to force herself not to feel

guilty — baths were one of her few indulgences. 'Why, what's the hurry?'

'Always wondered why you locked the bathroom door.' He was sneering. 'Now I know.'

'I haven't a clue what you're on about!' She tried to push past him but he was blocking her way.

'Convenient for you that the window was all steamed up, isn't it? Lock the door, take all the time you want. I bloody heard you, though, you made a helluva noise when you were coming!'

'That's a lie!' Her cheeks flushed. She had not masturbated since before ... before Lawrence. She could not bring herself to do it afterwards. Sex with Ben was a concession — the last thing she needed was self-stimulation.

'You're a bloody liar!' He grabbed her by the hair. 'Telling me you never toss yourself off! I've known all along.'

He was furious because the condensation on the top window had prevented him from looking in on her. But in his mind he had seen what he wanted to see.

'Let go of me, Ben!'

'Let's go into the bedroom.' His voice was lascivious now. He slackened his grip slightly and steered her towards the bedroom door. She felt physically sick.

He pushed her on to the bed and tugged the bathrobe so that it fell away, revealing her nakedness. 'Now as I missed out, show me what you were doing in the bath.'

All the inhibitions of her youth seemed to close in on her. She found herself huddling in on herself, pressing her thighs tightly together, crossing her arms so that they hid her breasts. 'All I was doing in the bath was trying to relax. Nothing more. If you choose to think otherwise, Ben, and it turns you on, feel free.'

'*Show me!*'

'*No!*' He had pushed her as far as she was going to go. She had consented to his every whim up until now but there was no way she was going to debase herself any further.

He took a deep breath, then turned away. He crossed to the window and stood looking out, his back towards her.

'I think you're having an affair.' He spoke scathingly, bitterly. 'I've thought so for some time now. You never want sex on the days you've been teaching.'

'That's ridiculous!' Janice's fear was momentarily replaced by incredulity. 'How would I fit it in, anyway?'

'You'd find a way.' He turned to face her and the expression on his face suddenly chilled her to the marrow. 'Well, *are* you?'

'Of course not.' Her voice trembled. Even to her own ears, the words seemed loaded with guilt.

'All right.' He sighed loudly. 'I'll have to take your word for it. But I'll tell you this – if I *ever* find out that you've been with another man, I'll fucking well kill you. And him!'

He strode from the room. She listened to his heavy footsteps going downstairs, then the front door slamming.

She lay there, staring up at the ceiling. The most frightening thing of all was the trapped feeling. She'd been aware of it for years, accepted it, but now it terrified her. She had to account for every minute of her day – she couldn't even have ten minutes to herself in the bath. This was how it would be for the rest of their married life. The future was bleak, frightening.

It was sometime before she was able to cry. And that was when she made her decision to leave Ben. Not now, not tomorrow, nor the day after. Perhaps next week. It would take time, because there was a lot of planning to do. Like finding somewhere to go.

Her father wouldn't help her. He wouldn't accept a failed marriage – it would be a slur on his reputation. If her mother had still been alive it might have been different; between them they could have talked him round.

Her father hadn't approved of Ben any more than he had of Lawrence; it was just that she had learned her lesson the first time round. She should have stuck to her principles then, had the baby. The situation could not have been any worse than it was now. She understood Lawrence now. Parental domination was not invincible – it only lasted as long as you let it. Maybe Lawrence had wanted to marry her, had wanted a family; it was just that he had baulked at the first hurdle. Like she had.

She found herself wondering what he was doing now. She had heard that his father had passed away, which meant that he was probably coming to terms with life. She could not have tolerated him the way he was then, but he might have changed. *She* could have changed him if she had only been able to get him away from his domineering parents. In the same way that she had 'escaped' – just walked out and married Ben. That had turned out to be a disaster; now she was going to have to walk out again, start afresh.

Ben would look for her, she knew that. His possessiveness, his jealousy, knew no limits. His threat had not been an idle one. She gave up trying to make excuses for him.

She would leave him to his cowboy and sexual fantasies. She began to think more positively, planning what she would take with her, how she would travel. A couple of suitcases, a train going south. Running. Hiding. She would find some casual work somewhere, enough to feed her and put a roof over her head. Only then would she take stock of things, try to plan for the future.

She began sorting out a few things that she would take with her. She wasn't committing herself; just acting positively. If she was ready to go, decided to go, then she *would* go. The thought made her feel better.

Tonight she had stood up to her husband for the first time. It could be that was all that was needed. She didn't know – she was too confused to try to sort out his problems.

She packed a holdall bag, put it at the back of the wardrobe and hid it under a pile of jumpers. At least it was ready if she needed it. That was a comforting thought.

Ben came home just after eleven. He had probably been to the pub.

'What's for supper?' He switched on the television.

'There's some bacon in the fridge.' She made no move to get up.

The smell of frying came through from the kitchen. Shortly afterwards she heard him eating. He usually brought his supper through to the living-room. Not tonight. Nor did he make her a coffee.

She went up to bed around midnight. He did not follow her.

The next morning when she came downstairs he was still asleep on the couch.

She thought again about walking out. Maybe she would next week if things hadn't improved. Next week was always a comforting thought – it was there if she needed it.

Chapter Twenty-One

Kent approached everything in life systematically. This evening was no different. Rule number one: begin with known facts. After that, play your hunches. Deane was missing so he started at Deane's house.

Kent parked his Fiat in the driveway and walked round the outside of the building, a large red brick house with half turrets. The latticed windows seemed to follow his progress like suspicious eyes and the evening sunlight glinted angrily on the glass as he peered into the ground-floor rooms. *You've no business here; you're not on an official police enquiry.*

Nothing appeared to have been moved since his last visit. The officers on patrol had instructions to check the premises nightly, just in case of break-ins. At this stage the chief thought that was sufficient. Kent didn't.

He completed his circuit, then stood staring out across the spacious lawn in the gathering dusk. Baker had said that Deane had a private income, and this place certainly went beyond the means of a run-of-the-mill banker. If it was a kidnap then there would have been a ransom demand by now. Wilson didn't have any money so he wouldn't have been snatched for that reason. But Kent was still linking the two disappearences; somewhere there had to be a common denominator. It was just a question of finding it.

He weighed up the facts and balanced them on his own scales. Two elderly men had gone missing; a banker and a clergyman. One had money; the other didn't. Who had snatched them and why?

He needed to do a reconstruction of Frederick Deane's

last known movements, a meticulous piece of guesswork. Okay, we start from the front steps. Deane would have emerged here from the house and gone to get his car out of the garage.

Kent walked to where the Fiat was parked and slid in behind the wheel. Fiat or BMW, it made no difference at this stage. He drove slowly, set the trip and checked his watch. Three-point-two miles to the golf club, twelve minutes and twenty-two seconds. He reversed into the space by the entrance – the one where Deane had parked – sat there and waited for it to get dark.

He tried to think himself into Deane's situation. He would have been edgy in case somebody recognised him, but nobody had seen him. After that, either a car pulled in and he joined the driver or else he walked somewhere to an appointment. From which he never returned.

Kent locked up his car and went into the club house.

Baker was drinking at the bar, doing his usual PR job on the members. He glanced up in mid-conversation and saw Kent. His eyes narrowed before his lips smiled a token greeting. The police were not welcome here – the bar regularly stayed open until midnight or after. It was a tradition. They had never had any trouble before and he didn't want any now.

'Good evening, *Mister* Kent.' He turned away from his audience, lowered his voice. 'Not official, I hope.'

'No, I was hoping to speak to somebody. Mr Rollason, you mentioned his name the other day.'

'Oh, yes, that's him on his own at the far end of the bar, the tall grey-haired man. Be careful, he's a bit prickly. He's upset quite a few members over the years.'

'I'll be discretion itself.' Kent promised. 'After all, Deane was a mate of his.'

Charles Rollason was definitely ex-military, Kent decided. The clipped moustache, the short hair, the way he tapped an unfiltered cigarette on his thumbnail before putting it to his mouth. Probably a wartime colonel who had chosen not to retain his title in civvy street. He had made his name in engineering, and an MD carried more status in business circles. Kent had researched Rollason and knew that he had retired in 1975, when his son had taken over the family business.

'Mr Rollason?' Kent's approach was direct. He shook Rollason's hand firmly. 'Adam Kent, I'm just making a few discreet enquiries about Frederick Deane.'

'Police, eh?' Rollason regarded him with steely blue eyes. 'Dashed slow in getting off the mark, aren't you? Damn it, Freddie's been missing for ten days now. *I* know something's wrong.'

'It's unofficial.' Kent kept his voice low. 'I feel the same as you; I think something should be done. That's why I'm here.'

'Now that's what I call initiative. Too many chaps these days work by the book, won't lift a finger outside nine till five. What are you drinking?'

'Just a Kaliber.' Kent felt a surge of relief. 'I'm a teetotaller.'

'Drop of the good stuff never did anybody any harm.' Rollason signalled to the barman. 'Still, if that's what you want. Kaliber, please Jeff.' He turned back to his companion. 'What do *you* think's happened to old Freddie, Kent?'

'That's what I want to know, and I won't be able to find out until I've talked to somebody who knew him well.'

'It *could* be a woman but as far as I know Freddie didn't have anybody in tow. He'd've told me, he always did.' A wink. 'Hope to goodness it *is* a wench and that before long old Freddie'll show up knackered. Likes 'em young, you know. The younger the better.'

'Is that so?'

'He's got a way with him. A bullshitter, but he's convincing. He's got money, too. His missus left him half a million. I know because I know her background. She was a Jameson of Jameson Engineering Plc. Her father started the business from nothing then sold out to a corporate. It was nationalised and went downhill, but old Bertie Jameson had banked his lolly by then. Yes, she set old Freddie on his feet. Pity he had to go and blow his marriage for a bit of skirt. His missus died shortly after she left him, else I reckon she would've changed her will. All for a young wench, a flighty bit of stuff at his bank. Got him the sack, too, but it didn't do him any harm. They covered it up, called it early retirement.'

'What was the girl's name?'

'Um, let me see, Sally something or other ...'

'Sercombe?'

'Yes, that's it. Funny name, always tickled me. You'd've thought her family was Jewish, wouldn't you? Sercombe ... circumcise, get it? Ha, ha.'

Kent laughed politely, unamused. After a decent interval, he confessed, 'I thought it might be her. I've already spoken to her.'

'That's damnably clever of you.' Genuine admiration was complemented with a swig of whisky. 'One step ahead of the game, eh? That's what I like to see.'

'It wasn't just Frederick Deane that I wanted to speak to you about, Mr Rollason.'

'Oh? who, then?'

'Prebendary Edward Wilson.'

'The old headmaster?' Rollason's smile vanished. 'Good God, he'd retired when you were a lad, Kent! I don't see how ...'

'He's missing, too, in almost identical circumstances. That's why I want to talk to you about both of them.'

'Oh, I see. Well, Freddie never knew Wilson, I can assure you of that. He wasn't *that* unlucky!'

'No, I appreciate that, but your son went to the cathedral prep school, didn't he, Mr Rollason? When Wilson was headmaster.'

'Peter had a most unfortunate time there.' Rollason's expression hardened and his eyes narrowed at the memory. 'Wished I'd never sent him there, but in those days state schools weren't what they are today. A boy needed a public school background if he was going to make his mark in life and so you had to send him to a prep school first. My wife insisted that Peter be a dayboy, otherwise I'd've sent him further afield. Wilson left his mark on him, and I don't just mean weals from those beastly canes of his!'

'A sadist, eh?'

'You can say that again. The old bastard flogged pupils every morning for the most trivial, contrived offences. Really enjoyed it. He wouldn't get away with it today, though, I don't need to tell you that. I didn't know half the story until after Peter had gone on to public school. My wife begged the boy not to tell me, made sure that I never glimpsed his backside. If I had ... ' Rollason's knuckles whitened. ' ... I'd've knocked seven sorts of shit out of that devil, prebendary or no prebendary!'

'So there must have been a good many who hated Wilson?'

'Odd you should say that, Kent. Peter doesn't bear him any malice at all. The old codger was a kind of living legend in his own time. Some of the boys virtually revered him. Peter was an introvert – I blame Wilson for that – but he shook it off along with his schooldays. Today he's on the board of the parent company with a whacking salary, and in for an MBE with a bit of luck. Can't say that in the long term it did him any harm, but at the time he must've gone through bloody hell.'

'Wilson must've had enemies, though, pupils or parents who still hate him for what he did?'

'Oh, I expect so.'

'Did Frederick Deane have many enemies?'

Rollason paused. His eyes were searching out his companion, suspicious again. When he spoke it was in a confidential tone. 'Freddie was a bit of a bully at work, too, you know. Oh, not like Wilson, but he knew how to make life hell for his staff. A kind of power game, you know. He only had a small branch; he had to make it big in his own way. I guess he took a lot of his frustration out on junior clerks. If they were female he shagged 'em; if they were male ... well, he just made life as intolerable as he could for them. He had his own idiosyncrasies, liked everything done *his* way, and God help anybody who didn't pander to him. Now I think of it, there was a fat slob of a cashier in his branch who actually went to school with my Peter. A lot of good a public school education did *him* – he couldn't even run a till efficiently. God, the times I've stood in a queue in the bank while he pissed and farted about! Now you couldn't blame old Freddie if he'd kicked that boy's arse from here to next week.'

Kent's neck prickled; there was a familiar tightening of his stomach muscles. But he took a sip of his non-alcoholic lager before asking casually, 'You don't by any chance remember his name, do you?'

Another pause. Rollason screwed up his face in deep thought and drew hard on his cigarette, letting the smoke wisp out of his hairy nostrils. Kent's guts were balling. Finally, Rollason spoke: 'Damn it, I can see the fellow now, standing behind the counter, fumbling through a wad of notes with his fat fingers. One of those aggravations you never forget. Don't remember him at school but Peter spoke of him. You know the type – overweight, no good at sport and not very clever in class, either. I *should* know who he is. I did at the time – Freddie used to go on about him, knew him before the bank days ...'

Oh, Jesus shit, just give me a name.

'Yes!' A finger went up. Rollason almost shouted aloud, ecstatic because his memory had not failed him. '*Prendergast*, that's it! Can't remember his first name; perhaps I never did know it. But I'll tell you how I remember his surname.' A schoolboyish enthusiasm, the answer to the clue that completed a teasing crossword. Self-pride; that was all that mattered. 'His father was a bank manager in the branch where Freddie was chief clerk. Old Prendergast gave Freddie a rough time. Some of the things he told me were almost unbelievable. You know, the old school of disciplinaria. And Freddie got landed with the son. Now it all ties up!'

Kent felt light-headed, as if the barman had given him real lager instead of non-alcoholic. 'I guess I can find him.' He resisted the urge to down his drink and go – that was a rookie reaction. You played a hunch but you didn't take anything for granted. Not yet, anyway.

'Are you interested in young Prendergast, then, Kent?'

'I have to follow every lead.' Kent tried to sound casual. 'Even the obvious dead-end ones. A process of elimination. I don't for one moment suppose that Prendergast has any bearing on this. And, in any case, at this stage we have no evidence that any criminal act has been committed. Just that two men have walked out of their homes and not returned.'

'But you're looking for somebody who might have cause

to hate both Wilson and Freddie!' Rollason stabbed a finger at Kent. 'Right?'

'That's one angle of approach, certainly.'

'Well', Rollason pursed his lips, shook his head, 'I hate to disappoint you, Kent, but that fellow Prendergast wouldn't be capable of kidnapping a geriatric in a wheelchair.'

'You're probably right.' Kent put his empty glass down on the bar top. 'Well, I'd better be getting along. The missus will be wondering where I've got to.'

'Always did admire a bloke prepared to put in a bit of his own time. I wish you luck. For Freddie's sake. Yes, with hindsight, having known him all these years, I'd say it's a bit of stuff, some young wench who's fallen for his pitter-patter. Old Freddie knows how to turn on the charm.' He laughed. 'I'll bet you that right now he's holed up in some posh hotel, screwing the arse off her. And the very best of luck to him, only wish I could be so lucky.'

'I hope you're right.' Kent said. He left the crowded bar and went outside to his car.

It shouldn't be too difficult to find this Prendergast fellow. He made a conscious effort to curb his hunch. It was getting too strong. Again, he had to establish known facts. It was all part of the elimination process. All too often you ended back where you began. Then you started all over again. Disappointments were an occupational hazard.

He almost succeeded in convincing himself that this was going to be another disappointment. Almost, but not quite.

Chapter Twenty-Two

Lawrence had barely slept all night, just uneasy snatches, waking and peering at the luminours dial of the old bell alarm clock, wishing the nocturnal hours away. He reminded himself repeatedly that on this occasion there was no hurry. Both Wilson and Deane had been old, many years over their allotted lifespans; they could have dropped dead any day, cheated the hangman. But Janice was young, younger than himself, and unless she suffered from some terminal disease or an unexpected fatal accident befell her, then next week or next month was soon enough. Even next year.

Then he remembered his mother. No, he could not wait that long. She was continually pestering him to finish the garden pool. If he did not complete the job soon then she would ask either Arthur or Glenn to do it. Lawrence could not risk that happening.

Only yesterday he had had a heated exchange of words with her over the unsightly excavations behind the shelter.

'I'm absolutely fed up with having a crater in the garden, Lawrence.' She dropped the 'Larry' when she was really annoyed. It wasn't like Emily Prendergast to work herself up to this extent – she must have been brooding on it for days. 'You've always been the same, going to do this or that, "just leave it to me", but it *never* gets done. There are dozens of jobs around this place waiting for you to do them; that's why I have to live in such a pig hole!'

'What's the hurry? It's not going anywhere.'

'That's just the point.' Her tone was icy. 'I only wish it *was* going somewhere. I want it finished by Saturday week.

A few of my friends from the art centre are coming round for afternoon tea and I want to show them the garden if it's a nice afternoon. It's Mary's birthday and ...'

'Take them to the art centre café, then.' He fought off a surge of panic.

'I will not. This is my home and I'll have my friends in whenever I please. And the same applies to you — you can have anybody in when you like.'

You didn't say that when I was going out with Janice. 'I'll get round to it, I'll have it finished before Saturday week.'

'Can I have your word on that?'

'Of course.'

'All right, but I warn you, if it isn't almost completed by Wednesday week, then I shall ask Arthur to do it when he comes in the next day. And if for some reason he can't make it, I'll get Glenn to do it when he comes over on the Friday. Do you understand?'

'All right, *all right*!'

Later that day Lawrence had gone into the lounge and found his mother holding a photograph, staring at it as if she thought it might provide the answer to some insoluble problem. He went closer, curious to see what she found so interesting. It was his father, dressed in his bank suit, scowling at the camera.

'Mother, I'll never understand to my dying day why you married Dad.'

'Whatever are you talking about?' The pain had returned in her arm and she felt suddenly faint.

'Well, just look at *me*. I'm just like him, aren't I? You've said so yourself on numerous occasions.'

'Yes, you are like your father, you always have been. What's wrong with that?'

'Plenty. That's why I'm like I am, not just ugly but queer in the head.'

'Lawrence!'

'It's true.' There was a note of despair in his voice. 'If you hadn't married dad then either I wouldn't have existed or else I'd be different.'

'That's not a very nice thing to say, Lawrence!'

'Well, it's true. Just look what an ugly bastard I am. there's something wrong with my brain, too. Always has been. It comes from Dad.'

'Please, Larry!' Emily was frightened. Bill *had* been strange, and there was undeniably something ... odd about Larry, but she couldn't bear to think that her son could turn into the monster his father had been. *I pray God that you're not right, Larry.*

Lawrence turned away and stamped upstairs. He was going to lie down in his room. He had a lot of things to think about.

He was edgy with excitement. Because that afternoon he had located Janice Peters. She was married, her name was Frame now. Finding her hadn't been easy. He was cautious of making direct enquiries, so he had taken to frequenting the art centre café − it was the kind of place she might show up. She hadn't but by sheer chance he had eavesdropped on a conversation between two middle-aged students at the next table.

'I used to know Mrs Frame years ago.' The plumper of the two ladies sawed away at a piece of brittle toast. 'She used to attend evening classes in Miss Green's day. You remember Miss Green, don't you, Barbara?'

'Vaguely,' her companion replied, 'but I did get the feeling I'd seen Mrs Frame somewhere before.'

'Yes, it's Janice Peters that used to be, daughter of Brigadier Peters.' Lawrence started, then strained to hear every word. 'A lovely family. Sadly Marina died a few years back. Cancer, you know, suffered terribly, poor dear. The brigadier still lives in that magnificent house on the Old Burton Road. But I was really surprised when Janice let slip that she lives on the Dimbles estate. My goodness, what a comedown after her family home! Reading between the lines I would think that she's married beneath herself and the old man has kicked her out − it's the sort of thing he would do. She's probably teaching art to try to make ends meet.'

Lawrence had all the information he needed. He checked the telephone directory: there was a B. Frame listed on the Dimbles. He made a reconnaissance in the Mini and found the house. There was a man sitting outside in a deck chair, dressed in gaudy pseudo-cowboy attire. Lawrence felt a pang of jealousy. Jesus, what a nutter! Janice must have lost her marbles.

That night he knew that he could not leave it any longer. He trembled with excitement, remembering Prebendary Wilson and Frederick Deane; he was glad it had worked out the way it had. Both hangings had been different. Individual. He had memories to savour. Right now, though, he savoured anticipation.

He had loved Janice, still did, but that didn't stop him hating her. Not because she had walked out on him but because she had murdered his child. He imagined pronouncing her sentence. *Found guilty of murder. Sentenced to hang by the neck until you are dead.*

He would hang her naked. And afterwards he would photograph her corpse, from every angle. *I want to take a picture of you, Janice.* The thought gave him an erection; he hadn't had a hard-on for a very long time. *And I want to screw you, Jan, just one more time.*

Sometime after dawn he fell asleep. When he awoke it was mid-morning, but that didn't matter because he had the whole day to himself. He couldn't do anything before nightfall.

Except make a phone call.

Lawrence went out to the shelter and busied himself preparing it for the forthcoming execution. He found a clean sheet in his mother's linen cupboard and put it on the camp bed. Janice had a thing about cleanliness.

The rope was of the same thickness as the one with which he hanged Deane. Whatever happened he could not risk another decapitation – it would spoil her for the photographs. He loaded his camera and checked that the flash was working.

He had bought a box of turkish delight – fancy packaging with a red heart and tied with a pink ribbon. He left it on the bed. There was no last wish that he would refuse to grant her – except her life.

It was two o'clock when he went back indoors. The house

was cool after the sweltering heat outside. He switched on the kettle. There was no sign of mother. Maybe she was in the lounge or the dining room, enjoying an after-lunch nap. She must have gone back to bed – she had not looked well yesterday. He would take her a cup of tea. He felt guilty about the way he had spoken to her yesterday. Perhaps he would apologise. In an oblique sort of way. He was inhibited where apologies were concerned.

He took the cup of tea upstairs and was aware of the silence, just the humming of the fridge and the buzzing of bluebottles that had somehow infiltrated his defences of closed doors and screwed down windows.

He stumbled over an extension cable on the landing, slopping some liquid on to the carpet. *Sod it!*

His mother's bedroom door was closed. He tapped on it, waited. There was no reply. She was probably asleep.

He debated whether or not to disturb her. He could always reheat her tea; he wouldn't waste it.

He edged the door open a little, enough to enable him to peer inside. The room was gloomy, like every other room in the house. He could just make out his mother in the centre of the bed, a frail, huddled shape beneath the blankets and eiderdown.

'Mother?' His whisper seemed to magnify in the stuffy atmosphere, almost to a hoarse shout.

There was no answer.

He was starting to edge back out on to the landing when something stopped him. A sudden thought – she might be ill, perhaps a fever; it was his duty to check. If necessary, he would call the doctor. But she was probably all right. She had an amazing resistance to ailments in spite of her fraility. He shuffled across to the bed.

'Mother, are you all right?' *And I'm sorry about yesterday.*

Still Emily Prendergast did not reply.

Lawrence set the mug of tea down on the bedside table. He considered leaving it there, tip-toeing back downstairs. He would return later to see that his mother was all right. Except that then her tea would be cold and undrinkable.

It seemed such a shame to disturb her. He could always

make her some fresh tea. Maybe, though, he should just nudge her into a state of drowsiness, enquire after her health. Then, if she wanted, she could go back to sleep. There was nothing wrong with her, there couldn't be, it was just her age. Doctor Bilton had said that a few weeks ago when she had gone in for a check-up. Lawrence would have felt happier if that pronouncement had come from Doctor Clark.

Lawrence touched her shoulder, shook her gently. 'Mother, I've brought you some tea. You don't have to drink it now if you don't want to.'

There was no response, no flinching of aged slumbering muscles. Nothing at all.

'Mother!' Concerned, he gripped her shoulder and shook it more firmly. She seemed so rigid. It was probably her arthritis. Cold, too. Even in the height of summer she insisted on using the bed warmer. Old people felt the cold. Doctor Bilton had said that, too.

Suddenly there was a movement. Her head lolled to one side; her grey eyes stared sightlessly up at him. Her mouth was open and he saw that the tongue was tucked to one side.

He froze in his crouched position. His fingers dug deep into her bony shoulder, shook it frantically. But there was no reaction. Her staring eyes did not blink; no sound came from that open mouth.

Nothing at all.

'*Mother*!' A hoarse disbelieving cry. She was sleeping heavily, that was all. His fingers relaxed their hold and he staggered back and stood there looking down upon her. She was all right, just sleeping. He would leave her tea where it was and if it had gone cold by the time she awoke then he would make a fresh brew. She needed her rest. *And I'm sorry about yesterday, Mother.*

Lawrence refused to accept that his mother had died in her sleep. She would be up and about shortly. He would leave her in peace until she was fully rested.

And he would fulfil his promise to her and have the pool finished by Friday week.

Chapter Twenty-Three

Lawrence went through to the bathroom and vomited into the cracked pan. After that he was all right, just shaky because Mother had given him a fright. He had thought she was dead and he would never be able to face up to the thought of life without her. But she wasn't; she was just sleeping, exhausted. This heat, day after day, didn't do her any good. She would probably spend a few days in bed. He would look after her, bring her food and drinks. If she was too tired to eat or drink then he would take them away again, and bring her something fresh later. There was nothing to worry about, no need to call the doctor. If Doctor Clark hadn't retired he might have asked him to call and check her over, but he didn't want Bilton here, the supercilious bastard.

He went back downstairs.

He didn't feel hungry, he would eat later. He was on a diet, anyway. He stood by the telephone. There was a number scribbled on the pad; it gave him a fluttering sensation in his stomach. He glanced at his watch. Three pm – it was too early to phone yet, she might be out at work. If she worked. On the other hand, if he left it until evening, her husband might be there. There was a limit to the number of times one could call and put down the receiver upon hearing a male voice. The husband would think they were nuisance calls; Lawrence didn't want the police involved. All the same, he had to phone sometime. He would think about it.

Then he remembered that guy sitting in the deck chair, all togged up in his ridiculous cowboy gear. An odd bod, a nutter, but the chances were Janice's husband didn't work. He was probably unemployable. Shit, that meant he would be hanging around the house day and night.

Lawrence tried not to think about his mother. She was safe in bed; if she needed him she would shuffle out on to the landing and call over the bannister. Otherwise he would just pop his head round the door from time to time; he wouldn't disturb her. She needed her rest.

He concentrated on thinking about Janice instead. Picturing her gave him an erection, brought back memories of those days when they'd had the house to themselves. She was beautiful. Naked, she was very beautiful. He had photographed her that way; sometime during those early weeks of heartbreak and anger, he had destroyed the pictures. It didn't matter, because soon he would take some more. He was tempted to do things to himself just thinking about it, but that would have been counterproductive. There would be plenty of time for that later.

At four-thirty he made up his mind to telephone her. No, he wouldn't put the phone down if that jerk of a husband of hers answered; something much more subtle was required. *Is that B.J. Frame Limited? Sorry, mate, you've got the wrong number.* There wouldn't be any need to disguise his voice. Even a second misdirected connection would not create any suspicion. *Awfully sorry, pal, I'll go through the operator, seems we've got a permanent fault.* That would account for a couple of calls, at least. Lawrence hoped he wouldn't need to try a third time.

His finger shook as be began to dial. Once it slipped out of the hole and he had to start all over again. Finally, he heard the phone ringing at the other end. He held his breath and gripped the grimy mouthpiece with an intensity that threatened to crack the plastic.

He found himself counting the rings. It was answered on the eighth.

Ben had been in a 'mood' that day as opposed to a 'mental'. Janice differentiated between abuse and sullen silence; threats and implied threats. She didn't know which was worse, a raging row or a sulk. In the past she had tried to defuse the situation with apologies, whether she was in the right or the wrong, tried to appease him in any way she could think of. None of these strategies had worked; Ben would surface when he was ready.

Today he had spoken only one word since her arrival home at one-thirty from college. 'Cow!' It made a change from 'bitch'. She didn't answer – that would only make it worse – but she was past caring anyway. She knew what the trouble was; there was nothing to be gained by going over all *that* again. She had gone to art college against his wishes. Today, as it happened, she hadn't had a lift even as far as the shops, so her conscience was clear. In addition to his continual grievance against her part-time teaching job, she had not been home to put his meal on the table at one o'clock sharp. She almost retorted that "cowboys" dined on corned beef and beans, that there was a tin of each in the larder and a real westerner would get his own grub.

Instead, she opened the tins, put the beans in a saucepan to heat on the stove, and went upstairs. When she came down there was no sign of Ben. She checked the house, then looked out into the small garden. He was nowhere in sight – what a relief. If he followed form he would go and mooch somewhere, probably in the recreation park, sit and watch the ducks on the lake and then go to the pub. He would come home late, after eleven, and sleep on the sofa.

Well, sod him! She wasn't going to waste her time worrying about him. She fixed her own meal, ate it, and sat outside in the deck chair.

God, it was hot! The lawn looked to have died; it always recovered after a heatwave but this time she had her doubts about its survival. The drought was into its eighth week now. There were stringent water restrictions and there was talk of standpipes being installed around the city if it went on for much longer.

Idly, she considered her future. Her emergency holdall was packed ready in the wardrobe, and she had filled an additional carrier bag with essentials such as toothpaste and soap, enough to see her over the first few days. It gave her some relief just thinking about it. Deep down, she knew it wouldn't happen. Because she hadn't got the guts. The sudden unaccustomed flash of honesty with herself gave her a jolt. It was true, she always put things off, left them until a tomorrow that never came. She wished that she had close friends with whom she could talk over her problems but Ben had never encouraged a social life. He had nurtured the image of the strong, silent man who was complete in himself, needed nobody. He certainly didn't need her. And he didn't want her to need anybody, either.

If she had somebody to talk to, an unbiased listener who would weigh up the pros and cons, then deliver judgement, she would be guided by his or her advice. If they said 'stay', she would grin and continue to bear it; if they said 'go', she would walk right out this very minute. She just needed a push.

The phone was ringing. She struggled up out of the deck chair and ran into the house. She had been daydreaming; it might have been ringing for some time. She got the feeling that it would cut out the moment her fingers closed over it. It didn't.

'Hallo.' She was breathless. She never gave a name or number, just in case. It might be social security snoopers checking to see if Ben was home or moonlighting.

'Janice?'

'Yes?' She thought the voice sounded vaguely familiar but she couldn't place it.

'Are you all right to talk?'

'Yes.' She spoke emphatically. Christ, she'd never needed to talk more, no matter who was on the other end of the line. 'Who is it?'

'It's me. Lawrence.'

A shock ran through her hand, as though the telephone had electrocuted her.

'Are you still there, Jan?'

'Yes. Yes, I'm here.' She lowered herself down on to the chair.

'You're sure you don't mind me calling?'

'No, not at all.' The same old Lawrence, still unsure of himself. She wondered how long it had taken him to pluck up the courage to telephone. She didn't stop to think how he had managed to find her. 'Ben's out. He probably won't be back till late.'

'I see. How're things?'

She hesitated a moment. 'All right.'

'You don't sound too sure.'

'I'm not right now.'

'I'm sorry things aren't working out for you.'

'It's the way the cookie crumbles. How's your mother?'

'She's fine, just fine.' He spoke fast. 'Ageing and rheumaticky, sleeps a lot. She's spent today in bed. As a matter of fact she was only talking about you yesterday, wondered how you were doing. She prompted me to give you a bell. I'd been meaning to for some time, actually.'

'That's nice, I really appreciate it.'

'I was wondering', he sounded nervous again, 'if ... if perhaps we could meet up. Just to chat. I know Mother would like to see you again.'

'I'd like that. I'd really love it.'

'When would it be convenient?'

'Any time. Any time to suit you, Lawrence. I'd really like to talk to you again.'

'How about tonight?'

'Yes okay.' She knew tomorrow would never come. It was tonight or never. She thought about the holdall and the carrier bag in the wardrobe. No, that was presumptious, and anyway, she wasn't looking for another relationship right now. Just an hour or two away from here. She'd try to be back before Ben. And if she wasn't ... too bad! 'Tonight would be fine.'

'Good. Eightish?'

'Yes but ... but maybe you'd better not pick me up from home, Lawrence. Just to be on the safe side. Things are a bit ... *iffy*, if you understand?'

'Oh, sure. Where, then?'

'Do you know the Dimbles?'

'Vaguely.'

'There's some shops at the bottom of the estate. Beyond them there's a stretch of waste ground where they're going to build even more houses. I'll be waiting there. At eight.'

'Sounds fine.' She detected relief in his voice. 'I've got a Mini. It's yellow.'

'I'll see you at eight, then.'

He rang off and she sat there holding the phone, staring at it unbelievingly, almost wondering if she'd dozed off in the hot sun and dreamed the whole thing. She began to tremble. She'd never done anything like this before; it was a frightening experience. Somewhere inside her a shrill voice was screaming at her, warning her not to go.

She ignored it, went upstairs and ran the bath. Whatever the consequences, she was going.

Chapter Twenty-Four

Lawrence leaned across and held the passenger door open. 'Hi!'

Janice looked stunningly beautiful in her turquoise summer dress, her long raven hair — not a fleck of grey — glinting in the evening sunlight. She seemed huge in the cramped car, big but not overweight, exactly the same as she had been all those years ago.

'Good to see you.' She was clearly nervous, tense, looking out of the windows in case anybody was watching. But the road and the wasteland that bordered it was deserted.

He let in the clutch just a little too quickly and grated the gears as he sped away. Lawrence was edgy, too, Janice thought.

'Maybe we'd better go somewhere first so we can talk.' He still had not got the timing fixed — the engine faltered at thirty-five, refused to pick up any more.

'Oh?' suspiciously. Tonight she was suspicious of everything and everybody. Even Lawrence.

'Just a thought. Don't get the wrong idea, but perhaps it would be best if we caught up on the news before we go home. Mother will be there, so the conversation will be somewhat restricted.'

'Oh ... yes, of course, I see what you mean. That's fine by me. Where are you thinking of going — not a pub or anywhere like that? It'd be just my luck to bump into somebody I know.'

'Let's go up on to Gentleshaw Common.'

'Fine.'

He parked just off the road alongside a silver birch spinney, then switched off the engine. He turned towards her. 'Tell me how it is with you.'

She told him all about Ben, hoping she didn't sound too bitchy. 'A lot of the time he can be really good.' She couldn't stop herself from making excuses for her husband. 'Usually he brings me a cup of tea in bed on Sunday mornings. I'm really trying to make our marriage work.'

'It's taking a long time.'

'I guess so.' A sigh of resignation. 'But I keep on hoping.' Then she told him about the holdall and the carrier bag hidden at the back of the wardrobe.

He noted that dusk was blending into darkness. 'You could do with a break.'

'Maybe.' She was uneasy, feeling that maybe she had told him too much. 'Perhaps I shouldn't have come out tonight. I'd really like to be home by eleven at the latest.'

He peered at his watch. 'It's just after half past nine. We'll go and have a quick coffee with Mother, then I'll drive you straight back.'

'All right, but I don't want to be any later than eleven.' Somehow, sitting there in the brightness of a summer afternoon had boosted her limited bravado; with the coming of darkness it was starting to fade. She wouldn't really walk out on Ben; it had only been a thought. Tomorrow their latest tiff would blow over. Until the next one flared up.

Lawrence started up the engine. He took the ring road that skirted the city centre and headed back out towards the countryside. Everything had gone to plan. So far. Thank goodness this would be the last time.

Janice experienced a pang of nostalgia as they turned into the long driveway with its overhanging laurels and straggling privet. In a way it seemed only like yesterday when she had last been here. It had been summer then, hot like it was now, and they had had the big house to themselves. Her train of thought led to her pregnancy. She felt an urge to cry.

'I must show you my new den first, before we go into the house.' He came round and opened the door for her, then took her arm.

'Couldn't we look at your den another time?' He hadn't

changed at all. She remembered that awful cluttered, claustrophobic darkroom he used to have. Where it had all begun. The feeling of guilt returned. *I don't want to see it, it won't be any different from before.*

'It won't take a moment.' He was holding her wrist tightly, pinching the skin so that she almost cried out. 'I'd just like you to see it. Then we'll go and see Mother.'

'Oh, all right.' It was awfully dark. She was scared of falling, didn't object to him holding her. Obviously Lawrence now had an outdoor photographic room. Probably his mother couldn't stand the mess any longer, and had persuaded him to move his rubbish out. Janice was having doubts about her earlier thoughts on her former boyfriend. She would have to weigh up the advantages and disadvantages very carefully. She wasn't going to make any hasty decisions.

They were going down some steps. Lawrence paused and fumbled in his pockets; she heard the clink of keys. He still had his phobia about burglars, then. A door swung inwards and he pulled her through. She heard the lock click behind them. Oh, God, it was dreadful in this stygian blackness; it smelled too. She was on the verge of screaming.

He switched on the lights, blinding, dazzling photographic spotlights that had her shielding her eyes. Then she saw.

And screamed.

'Lawrence, what's that ... *thing*?' But she knew what it was – there was no mistaking the hideous gallows, the noose dangling above the trap door.

'It's a gallows.' He laughed. 'An instrument of execution.'

He was crazy. He always had been. 'Please, I want to go back.'

'No chance.' He relinquished his grip on her and gestured towards a small, adjacent room with an open door. 'You're under arrest, Janice Peters. Or should I say, *Frame*? You are charged with murder. Tomorrow you will be tried and if found guilty ...'

'Is this some kind of ... game? I haven't murdered anybody, you know I haven't.'

'You murdered your baby. *My* baby!'

'*No*!' She had been accusing herself of this very thing for years. Now with this terrible accusation, the feeling of guilt swept over her anew.

'Yes, it was murder.' He was trembling, shaking violently. 'And anything you say may be taken down and used in evidence against you.'

Janice thought she was going to faint. She swayed, clutched at the small table, knocked something rolled and then thudded to the floor. It was some kind of cosh with a leather thong, and instrument of violence. She began to sob 'Please, Lawrence, take me home.' 'No you're not going anywhere.' He grabbed her arm again and began to lead her towards that open door. 'This is your cell. I've made every effort to ensure that you are as comfortable as possible.'

She tried to hold back but he was too strong for her. He dragged her through the door and kicked it shut behind them. The stench in the little room was overpowering and she gasped involuntarily.

'Lawrence, let me go. I'll call the police!' It was an empty threat and she knew it. There was no way she was going to be able to call for help in this terrible place.

'This place is soundproof; don't waste your breath. Now what do you like for breakfast?'

She mustered a show of defiance. 'I never eat breakfast!'

'Please yourself.' He shrugged his shoulders. 'I'll have to lock you in, though. There's a bottle of water in the corner. Use the bucket if you need to.'

She had to be dreaming all of this. She closed her eyes. The banging and locking of the door jerked them open again; she wasn't home in her bed, hearing Ben come back from the pub. She was in a filthy death cell, waiting to be hanged.

'The murder of the unborn child was a deliberate and calculated act.' Lawrence's features were flushed with anger; his eyes bulged. 'In no way can it be interpreted as manslaughter. Do you plead guilty or not guilty to the charge of murder?'

'Lawrence, stop being ...'

'*Guilty or not guilty*?' he screamed, his fleshy features suffused with rage.

'Guilty.' Her response was a barely audible whisper. She

sat on the concrete floor because she knew that her legs would not bear her weight. The night had been a long and sleepless one, worse after the batteries in the night-light had run out and left her in suffocating blackness. She had wept until there were no tears left. *Oh, Ben, I'm sorry, I wasn't going to run out on you. Please come and find me here. I'll even stop going to art classes if that makes you happy. I'll do anything you want me to.*

But Ben wouldn't be coming to rescue her because he would have no idea where she was. He might have contacted the police, but that was unlikely — he was probably glad to be rid of her. Even if he *had* contacted the police, they wouldn't know where to look for her.

Lawrence was mad, dangerously mad. She glanced fearfully at the gallows behind him, stark and grim, the symbol of a brutal death that had been abolished in this country quarter of a century ago. Except here: the death penalty still existed in Lawrence Prendergast's sick domain.

She looked back at Lawrence. The trial was evidently over — what would happen next? He was shaking out a square of crumpled black material, trying to smooth the creases out of it. Then he draped it over his head. Anywhere else he would have looked comical, a partygoer donning a fancy hat out of a cracker. Only it wasn't fancy; it was macabre. He stared at her; he was trembling all over.

'Janice Frame,' his voice was husky as though he had laryngitis, 'you have been found guilty of murder by your own admission. You are sentenced to be taken from that place' — he pointed vaguely in the direction of the cell without taking his eyes off her — 'tomorrow morning, and hanged by the neck until you are dead.'

The bare room seemed to tilt one way, then the other. Once again, Janice thought she was going to faint but somehow blissful unconsciousness eluded her. He didn't really mean it, of course. All this was designed to frighten her because she had walked out on him, had his baby aborted. He had brooded on it over the years; it had sent him mad. But Lawrence, despite all his faults, would never really hurt anybody.

Would he?

'Look Lawrence', she tried to smile, 'why can't we let bygones be bygones?'

'Because it won't bring back the dead. Nobody can bring back a murder victim. So somebody has to die. You do understand, don't you?'

She didn't but she wasn't going to argue. She watched him closely. He looked strange: the features that had been flushed with rage only minutes ago now looked pale and clammy, and he seemed to be struggling to breathe. He mopped his forehead with the piece of cloth which had served as a black cap.

Then, without warning, his nostrils gushed bright scarlet, a twin deluge of blood that flooded the lower half of his face like a vampire that had looked up from its feast. He said something through bloody lips – she didn't catch the words – and then the dark cloth was clutched to his nose. His head went back and he groaned.

Hope materialised out of despair. This was a welcome intervention that might bring her freedom. She scrambled into a sitting position. 'I'd better go call a doctor for you.'

He ignored her. His eyes were closed; he might have been slipping into unconsciousness. She turned away and glanced in the direction of the heavy outer door. It was locked; the key was in Lawrence Prendergast's pocket.

'Lawrence ... give me the key. I'll go to the house and phone ...'

He mumbled through the blood-soaked rag: 'Sit down!'

Janice obeyed. *Oh, please, God, let him lose consciousness*! It was a wicked thought but she didn't care; she didn't care if he died. Because she knew now, without any doubt, that he planned to execute her.

The square of material was now saturated. He squeezed it out and sticky blood speckled the concrete floor. His grubby shirt was crimson; his face was blood-smeared. He was a thousand times more terrifying to behold awash in his own life's blood.

She wondered if he might have a stroke. No, it was unlikely – what she was witnessing was his safety valve, his overflow, in operation. Otherwise he would have had a cerebral attack. It had been a toss-up between life and death. Life had won by a narrow margin. This time.

'I'll be all right.' He had sat for what seemed an eternity with that rag held to his nose. Now he removed it and Janice saw that the blood was drying, already beginning to congeal. His grotesque appearance reminded her of an illustration in a book that had both fascinated and horrified her as a child. The legendary Dun Cow devouring its freshly killed prey, an horrific bloodied beast raising its head in defiance at the appearance of a knight in armour.

'I'm sure you will, Lawrence.' She could not disguise her disappointment. 'You'll need to rest, though.'

'I shall.'

'I thought you were going to take me to see your mother.'

'She's not well, she's stopping in bed today.'

'I'm sorry, I should love to see her again.'

'That's not possible.' He stood up uncertainly. 'I'll bring you a cup of tea shortly. What would you like for lunch?'

The thought of food almost made her retch. 'Just a cup of tea will do fine.'

'I'm afraid I'm going to have to lock you back in your cell. Please take off your clothes.'

'No, Lawrence, please.'

'Take ... off ... your ... clothes.'

She saw his expression and began to unbutton her turquoise dress. It made no difference whether she was clothed or naked: Lawrence had seen it all before; he had photographed it. With her consent. God, she must have been crazy.

She felt so much more vulnerable unclothed. His bloodshot eyes roved over her body, and she instinctively clamped her thighs together. Unable to bear his scrutiny any longer, she got up and walked dejectedly back towards her cell.

Her eyes rested momentarily on something on the floor. At first she thought it was some revolting creature, an elongated rat with a knotted tail. Then, with relief, she saw it was an inanimate object: the cosh. It must have fallen from Lawrence's pocket and rolled under the table. He did not seem to have missed it.

The door thudded shut behind her with a dull echo of

finality. She stood there, listening to his receding footsteps. The outer door opened and closed.

Then there was just silence. That was when Janice collapsed on the bed and sobbed her unrelenting hopelessness.

Because there was no doubt whatsoever that on the morrow she would hang.

Chapter Twenty-Five

'*Where have you hidden the body?*'

Ben Frame was visibly shocked. Janice's disappearance had infuriated him, which was why he had telephoned the police. He was not unduly concerned about her safety – that she might be in any danger never occurred to him. *I'll teach the fucking cow a lesson – she'll look a right idiot when she finds the cops are out looking for her*! With a bit of luck she might even find herself in trouble like that woman he'd read about in the paper who had gone off screwing with a couple of blokes. She was scared to go home afterwards so she'd got them to tie her up and dump her in a ditch to make out she'd been kidnapped. She ended up in court for wasting police time. Yes, he'd teach Janice a lesson she'd never forget, and if she *had* been with somebody else, he'd bloody well kill her – and the other guy as well.

Suddenly everything had backfired on Ben. This hard-faced cop had made him feel a berk. There was undisguised contempt in his eyes as he took in Ben's fringed buckskins and chaps. The cocky sort who didn't believe a word you said. And now he was accusing Ben of *murder*.

'What ... what d'you mean?' Ben stared in disbelief, thinking that maybe he'd heard wrong or misunderstood.

'Just what I asked you.' Detective Sergeant Adam Kent was tight-lipped, his inscrutable steely blue eyes boring into the other man, looking for signs of guilt. Accusing. 'Where've you hidden your wife's body? It'll be easier for you in the long run if you come clean.'

'I ... I ...' Ben wanted to empty his bowels into his new

Levis. 'Jesus Christ, I haven't *killed* her! D'you think I'd call you if I had?'

'Yes I do.' Kent was unmoved, totally emotionless, a cop who was doing the job he was paid to do. 'That's usually step one — try to throw the police off the scent. It doesn't work, though.'

'I swear I haven't done anything to Janice. Shit, I want her back. Alive.' For the first time he began to worry in case Janice wasn't all right.

'Do you?' Kent's gaze roved the room. This guy was obviously a cowboy freak. He even had his childhood cowboy and indian models adorning the mantelshelf, and toy six guns and a replica Winchester 73 were displayed on the walls. His missus probably couldn't take any more, so she'd just walked out. Casually, he asked. 'Can you ride a horse?'

'No, I've never been on one. Why?'

Kent didn't bother to answer. These cowboy nuts never got down to the nitty-gritty of their hobby; their interest didn't go beyond saloons and gunfights. You could slot them into a category, cardboard cut-outs that would fit one on top of the other.

The detective was getting that familiar feeling again. He dispelled it; it was too early yet. His first day back on official duty and he had a missing wife to investigate. Now, if it had been some guy in his eighties ... *Stick to facts; play your hunches later*. This was just routine. Janice Frame would probably return home or else phone to say she wasn't coming back.

'I'll take a look over the house.' Kent headed towards the stairs. 'We might want to dig in the garden later.'

Ben tried to look unconcerned. 'Feel free.'

'Was she having an affair?'

'Christ, no!'

'What makes you so sure?'

'Oh, shit.' Ben licked his dry lips. 'There was an old guy who gave her a lift home from the art college once. Just once. I put a stop to it.'

'Know his name?'

'I did but I've forgotten it.'

'Never mind, I'll find him if I need to. Did she go out much? Alone, I mean.'

'Never.'

Which is probably why she's gone now, Kent thought and pushed that nagging hunch away again. This was a straightforward case of a wife doing a runner because she'd had enough of her husband. She couldn't stick her domestic prison any longer and had kicked over the traces, like the horse he'd never ridden.

'D'you think ...' Ben was almost afraid to put his worst fear into words, 'that ... that she *has* gone off with somebody else?'

'It's a possibility.' Kent left the room.

Upstairs he found the packed holdall and plastic carrier in the wardrobe. He brought them down to show Ben.

'Well? What do you think these are for?'

'I ... I dunno. Looks like she just ... kept a few things ready.'

'In case she left you. She'd obviously thought about it. But when she went she didn't take her things. Now that *is* strange.'

Kent was puzzled. Either Janice had left in one hell of a hurry, a spur of the moment decision, or else her intention was to return. There was time yet; she had only been gone one night. Unless something or someone had prevented her from coming back ...

'We'll circulate her details and photograph. 'He walked out into the bright sunshine. 'Stay by the phone in case she calls. Our chaps will be in touch with you later.'

If somebody had got her, it was probably too late. Mostly the victims of sex killers were dead within the hour; after that you were hunting a corpse.

He thought about it on the drive back to CID headquarters. And about Wilson and Deane, too. A serial killer, according to an FBI definition, was someone who aggressively sought out potential victims and committed three or more homicides with cooling-off periods in between. Typically, serial killers would continue until stopped.

So far there were two victims. Neither had been found yet. It needed one more to make it a serial killer. Janice

Frame was an outside possibility. So far the police were not linking the first two. Kent was. He wasn't sure about the third; it was a long shot.

He had never got round to seeing that fellow Lawrence Prendergast. He would try to contrive a call sometime this week.

Right now he was too busy with offical business.

Chapter Twenty-Six

'Warm, innit?'

Lawrence started, spilling tea from the mugs which he carried in either hand. Oh, shit, that stupid old bastard, Frank Coleman, was peering through the mutilated hole in the hedge. If only he'd sodding well left the privet alone.

'Yes, very warm.' Lawrence would have hurried on except that he had scalded his fingers and so was forced to set the mugs down on the ground while he dried himself with his grubby handkerchief.

'Ever seen a baby's coffin?'

'No.' *And I bloody well don't want to, either*! He had begun to feel edgy about Coleman — the man always seemed to be hovering around by the hedge. He tried to calm himself down. It was probably only boredom — he just wanted to chat to somebody.

'Come on round, then.' The retired undertaker inclined his head towards his workshop. 'I've just finished a real beauty. It's for the Lomas's — you know, the son of Rickman Lomas at Grange Hall. One of these 'ere cot deaths. They're loaded. They wanted the best so they came direct to me, cut out the middle man.' He winked. 'It don't come any cheaper, though.'

'I'm rather busy right now.' Lawrence stooped and retrieved his mugs. 'Later, perhaps, or tomorrow.'

'Thirsty, are you?'

'Sorry?'

'Two mugs of tea.'

'Oh ... yes, it's the heat.' Nosey bastard. 'I've got a big developing job on.'

Coleman had no interest in photography – he didn't want to get involved in the techniques of film processing. 'How's your mother? I haven't seen her lately.'

'She's been a bit off colour, so she's staying in bed. She'll be all right, though. I think it's just the heat. But I really must be going.'

'Don't forget, pop round and have a look. They're collecting it tomorrow afternoon.'

The last thing Lawrence needed to be reminded of now was an infantile death. It fuelled his anger.

Janice was lying on the camp bed. It was too short for her so her legs were draped over the edge. He couldn't help noticing that they were slightly apart. Just a fraction; not enough for him actually to see between her thighs but enough to make him try. She looked tired, drained to the point of exhaustion.

'Cup of tea.' He bent to set the mugs on the floor by her feet and glanced slyly upwards. Just a few wisps of black, curly hair; the rest was in shadow. 'I'll stop and drink mine with you.'

'That's very magnanimous of you.' She smiled weakly. 'Considering you're going to execute me.'

'That's beyond my control now,' he answered brusquely.

Her flesh goosepimpled in spite of the heat. He was probably right. She leaned over to reach for her tea, opening her thighs another inch or so in the process. 'Lawrence, I've been thinking ...'

'That's good.'

'About the baby, my baby.'

'Mine,' he corrected her.

'All right, yours.' Undeterred, she sipped her tea. 'All right, it was wrong of me to have it taken away ...'

'Not "taken away"; murder, a capital offence,' he corrected her again.

'She ignored his interruption. 'Nothing either of us could do would bring it back, but – her' thighs eased apart another inch and the light from the main room feel directly in between – 'we could always have another.'

Lawrence stared at the shiny pink flesh half hidden amidst pubic hair. *I'm going to photograph you, Jan. Afterwards.* The thought started to give him an erection.

'There wouldn't be any point.' His gaze was riveted; he was trying to work out some means by which the lips could be held open for the camera. Dead flesh might not be co-operative. He'd think of something.

'Why not?'

'I couldn't possibly hold you prisoner for nine months, it isn't feasible. And it's against the law to hang pregnant women. Furthermore, it wouldn't alter the fact that a murder has been committed. I'm sorry, but I'm sure you understand.'

Her body seemed to wilt, and her legs came back together. It had been a good try.

There was one last hope remaining. 'I thought you might like to sleep with me, anyway.'

'I'm going to. Afterwards!'

She almost spewed back her tea.

'We have to discuss the execution.' His voice was devoid of emotion. 'I want to make it as easy as I can for you. Mother's got some sleeping tablets that the doctor gave her, strong ones. They take about fifteen minutes to work. If you took one ten minutes before the execution then it would ...'

She shook her head. 'No, I don't want to go that way.'

'Shall I bring you a bible?'

'I'm an agnostic.'

And she didn't eat breakfast, either. There was nothing left to do except to hang her.

Lawrence took a cup of tea up to his mother, put it down on the bedside table and removed the one that was cold with a dark-brown scum on it. She was making a habit of dozing off and forgetting to drink her tea, lately.

'I've brought you some fresh tea, Mother,' he whispered. A couple of bluebottles buzzed up from beneath the sheets and settled on the headboard, ready to drop back down again as soon as he was gone. He made sure that the bed warmer was still switched on. She really felt the cold these days. 'I'll see you later.' He paused in the doorway. 'I'll cut you some banana sandwiches for tea. And a slice of madeira cake. You can dunk it if you like.'

He went downstairs and filled the big chipped enamel jug from the cold tap in the sink. Then, slopping it as he walked, he carried it outside.

Most of the empty margarine tubs around the garden were sure to be empty. Either the birds would have drunk the water or else it would have evaporated in the heat. He had been too busy to refill them these last few days.

All the tubs were gone! He searched the rose beds, the edge of the shrubbery. No sign of them. They must have blown away; they were light enough when they were empty. But there had been hardly a breath of wind for weeks.

Suddenly, he realised what had happened and began to shake with anger. Glenn had removed them all, slyly collected them up, taken them away to dump them. And after he had told him to leave them alone! His brother wouldn't even bother to try to find a plastic recycling bank; he'd just drop them in the nearest litter bin. The bastard!

'Good afternoon.'

For the second time that day Lawrence started, whirled around. He thought for one moment that it was Glenn standing there in a navy blue shirt and dark brown cords. Except that this man was too short. And there was no beard; the hair was fair instead of dark. Whoever it was, the fellow had a bloody cheek wandering around the garden as if he owned it. He was probably a rep or an insurance agent. He might be selling anything from double glazing to life policies. Well, neither Lawrence nor his mother wanted either of those.

'Lawrence Prendergast?'

'Yes.' His defiance began to melt. There was something definitely "official" about the man, a confidence that bordered on arrogance.

'Detective Sergeant Adam Kent.'

Lawrence felt his pulse start to race. There was a sudden void in the pit of his stomach.

'I was wondering if you might be able to help me.'

Lawrence couldn't think of anything to say. He just stood there looking helplessly at his visitor.

'Maybe we could go inside out of the heat, Mr Prendergast?'

'Oh, sure.' Anything to get the fellow away from the shelter and the pond diggings. Lawrence thought he had detected a smell of decomposing earlier, though it might have been the fertiliser which Arthur scattered round the rose bushes. 'Follow me.'

Kent half wished that they had stayed outside. The living-room was a clutter of junk, and it smelled stale and stagnant as if it had not been aired for years. Lawrence moved piled newspapers off one of the chairs, spilling some as he did so.

'Would you like a cup of tea, Sergeant? I've just made some for my mother. She's in bed, not at all well. I'm afraid the heat doesn't suit her.' *Which is why you won't be able to talk to her.*

'No, thanks, I had one just before I left the station.' Kent didn't fancy drinking anything here – the cups were probably never washed. 'I'm sorry about your mother but it's you I called to see.'

'Oh?'

'I believe you worked in the bank some years ago?'

'A long time ago.'

'You were in Frederick Deane's branch.' A statement, not a question this time.

'Er ... yes.' Lawrence hoped that his unease didn't show.

'He's missing, and we're trying to find him.'

'Oh ... I see. Well, I haven't seen him since he retired ... that must be getting on for twenty years ago. In fact, I'd almost forgotten him until you mentioned him. I'm surprised he's still alive – he must be getting on.'

'In his eighties. You see, I'm exploring all sorts of possibilities. He might just have gone for a holiday without telling anybody, or gone to stay with distant friends. Was he a ... a popular man? Did folks like him?'

'I wouldn't know. He mixed with customers but I was always left to look after the branch.'

'With Miss Sercombe?'

'Yes, Sally. Haven't heard of her for years, either.'

'How did you get on with Deane?'

'Just a working relationship. He was the boss; I did as I was told.'

'You didn't *like* him, though.'

'Sally told you that?'

Kent didn't answer. He wondered why Lawrence had smears of dried blood on his neck. He looked for a shaving nick but he couldn't see one.

'He was having it off with Sally. *She* got him the sack. Early retirement, they called it. He didn't lose out on his pension. In fact, he gained financially.'

'But he didn't like you?' Kent was sticking his neck out here, but it paid.

'No, because he knew that I knew. Between them they nicked a hundred quid out of my till and got me a demotion. They wanted me out of the way but they got their comeuppance. I couldn't give a monkey's about either of them, actually. It doesn't worry me whether the old fart turns up or not, frankly.' Lawrence stopped, aware that he was giving too much away.

'I see. You also knew Prebendary Edward Wilson, didn't you? Wasn't he your headmaster at preparatory school?'

Lawrence's guts churned. He hoped his baggy jeans would hide his shaking legs. 'That's right. He's dead for sure by now.'

'We don't know. He's gone missing, too.'

'Has he? Blimey, what's going on?'

'I'd like to know. I was just hoping that perhaps you could give me a lead on anybody who might have cause to hate him. Deane, too.'

'I guess if you went through the school's register of pupils from around 1940 through to 1965, you could extract several hundred names and ninety-five percent of those wouldn't throw him a rope if he fell in the river. But you forget those sort of things after you've left school, don't you, sergeant?'

'Most of us do, Mr Prendergast.'

'Well, like I said, I wouldn't help him, but neither would I run him over if I found him walking along a deserted country lane in the dead of night. I just wouldn't give him a lift.'

'Dislike rather than hatred, eh?'

'You've got it.'

'I'm glad I called.' Kent got up and edged towards the door. 'I was really looking for specific enemies. It would seem that both men were disliked rather than hated maliciously. I have to make enquiries, you understand.'

'Of course.'

'It just happened that I discovered during the course of my routine investigations that you knew both men so I thought it was well worth speaking to you in case you could shed some light on their disappearance. Oh, and there's a funny thing — I found out this afternoon that you knew somebody else who's recently gone missing.'

'Who's that?' Lawrence hoped it sounded casual. He would not be able to hide his shaking much longer.

'Janice Peters. Her name's Frame now.'

'Oh, Janice!' It was as if somebody had kicked him in the balls. Somehow he had to stop himself from doubling up. 'One of my girlfriends when I was in my twenties. A fairly casual relationship — I guess that was why we split up. I suppose she must be married by now. I don't even get a Christmas card from her and I wouldn't know where to send her one.'

'I talked to her father. He told me that you used to see her.'

'He didn't approve. Bank managers' sons aren't good enough for brigadiers' daughters. I liked her, though. I'm sorry she missing. You don't think she's ... in any sort of trouble? Just run away, perhaps?'

'I'd like to think so.' They were outside now and Kent was trying to keep his hunches in check. This guy was like some kind of hermit: an eccentric, ex-public school, ex-bank clerk living in squalor with an ailing mother. 'Maybe I could talk to your mother when she's feeling better? She must have known Wilson when you were at school. She might remember Deane, too. And Janice Peters, of course.'

'I doubt it, her memory's bad. Very bad.' He said it just a bit too quickly.

'Often old people can remember the past quite clearly whereas they forget everyday things.'

'Not Mother. She's very muddled.'

'Oh, well, I'll leave it, then.' Kent's gut feeling was stronger than ever. He didn't believe in coincidences. Certainly not triple ones.

He stood in the driveway and looked back at the house, noting its dilapidated elegance and picturing it in his mind as it must once have been. The curtains were closed, as if they hid some ghastly secret from prying eyes. Even in the hot sunshine it sent a shiver rippling up his spine.

And Kent's inbuilt alarm system seldom cried wolf; he was too hardened a policeman. His subconscious recognised signs, warned him. He had heeded his hunches, kept them in check. Now it was time to unleash them.

He prayed that he was in time. For Janice Frame's sake.

Time was running out fast.

Chapter Twenty-Seven

Christ, the bloody lock was playing up again!

Lawrence stepped back, catching the plate on the floor with his foot. Tentacles of spaghetti spilled over the edge. Fuck it! The lock on the shelter door had not been working smoothly for the last couple of days; he had ignored it because he had other things to do. So long as it locked and unlocked he hadn't worried. Now the key wouldn't turn properly. It was as if something was jamming it – perhaps a tumbler had come loose.

Shit! He stood back and held up the key. It looked slightly bent. He had had to force it the last couple of times. The duplicate was somewhere in his room – he had put it in a safe place – and it might take hours to locate it. But in all probability the trouble lay with the lock; another key wouldn't solve the problem.

What the hell do I do now? He fought down his rising panic. He dared not phone for a locksmith. Frank Coleman was a good handyman; he could do most jobs. But Frank wouldn't be content with just fixing the lock, he'd want to see inside. And, anyway, once the door was open the soundproofing was nullified. Whoever repaired the lock was sure to hear Janice in her cell.

He went back to the house and found a hammer in the dresser drawer. He placed the key flat on the patio floor; it was slightly bowed, that was the root of the problem. He tapped it gently. Harder. It flattened. Shit, it had better work now!

It did. Not smoothly but at least it turned. Later on he would look for the spare.

At least the lock on the cell door turned smoothly. 'I've brought you something to eat.'

Janice stirred. She had been sleeping. Her eyes were red-ringed as if she had been crying, too. She swung her legs to the floor and sat with her thighs pressed tightly together, resting the lukewarm plate on her lap.

'What time is it, Lawrence?' Her voice was tired as if she had given up hope, resigned herself to her fate.

'Seven o'clock.'

'In the evening?'

'Yes.

'Why are you doing this to me, Lawrence?'

'You heard all that at the trial. You're a murderess.'

'You know', she was close to tears, 'that afternoon when you phoned, I'd been thinking a lot about you. I'd almost made up my mind to leave Ben. I'd had a few things packed in readiness for weeks. If you'd played your cards right I think we could have got back together.'

He stared, his expression changing from surprise to disbelief. 'It wouldn't have made any difference, Jan.'

'No, I suppose it wouldn't. I guess I was born a loser.'

'I executed the other two, you know.'

'What other two?'

'Wilson, my old headmaster, and Deane. You remember me telling you about Deane, how he made me out to be a thief. Him and that little tart, Sally Sercombe.'

'I suppose Sally's next, then?'

'No.' He pursed his lips. 'You're the last one.'

She tried to cover her shock with flippancy.

'Gee, thanks.'

'Between the three of you, you made me what I am. Wilson flogged me, Dad sentenced me to a life of banking and Deane made sure I never surfaced.'

'And me?' Her eyes flickered nervously.

'A baby was perhaps the one thing that could have rescued me, made me normal. After that was gone, there was nothing left. Just Mother. Now there's nothing left at all.' He was fighting back sobs.

'She's dead, isn't she, Lawrence?'

'*No!*' he screamed. She thought he was going to hit her. 'She's not dead, she's just poorly in bed. Her age and the heat. She just needs to rest. After the heatwave breaks, she'll be okay.'

'Why don't you let me look after her?'

'No, I won't let anybody tend to her except me. I've been a swine to her but I'm going to make it right. It's not my fault, they made me that way. *They* are responsible; I had to punish them for what they did to her. Father, too, he was as bad, he made her life a misery for years but she just put up with it. The day he died, I got to thinking about what they'd done. They had to pay for it.'

'Why didn't you just care for her, give her the affection she'd never had?'

'I tried. God, I tried. But it was too late. The baby would have done it, Jan, she'd have doted on it. We could have lived with her, but you walked out, murdered it.'

'But I told you Lawrence, we could have another baby.'

'It's *too* late, don't you understand that?'

'Because she's dead?'

'No, she *isn't* dead, she's only sleeping. I told you that!'

'Then it isn't too late, is it?'

'*Shut up, damn you!*' He kicked out, sending the plate spinning. It smashed to fragments against the wall, spewing cold spaghetti on the brickwork – worms slowly oozing their way down to the floor. He breathed heavily, visibly trying to bring himself under control. He averted his eyes when he finally spoke again. 'Is there anything you want?'

'I'd appreciate stretching my legs; I've had awful cramp. Just out in the big room will do.'

'All right. I'll wait here. Don't be long.'

She stood up, moving with difficulty. The gracefulness had gone from her posture. Her bare feet shuffled; her shoulders were hunched and her head bowed. She heard the bed creak behind her as Lawrence sank down on to it.

Outside, she saw what she was looking for. She stooped and retrieved it, then held it behind her back.

'Are you finished?' he called out from the adjoining room.

'Just about.' She appeared in the doorway. Her stoop was gone; she stood tall and straight, almost Amazonian. 'There's still time, you know, Lawrence.'

'For what?' He didn't look up.

'To fuck.'

His head jerked up. He looked shocked. 'I've never heard you use that word before, Jan.'

'Well, you have now. Because things have changed. I'm not the girl you used to know. Or the one Ben thought he knew. If I was instrumental in making you what you are, then you and Ben between you have make me what I am now. Of course, you wouldn't understand, I don't expect you to. I feel dreadfully sorry for you, Lawrence, I mean that.'

'Don't start feeling sorry for me. Nobody else ever has.'
Except Mother

'Well, I do. Larry ...'

'*Don't call me that*!' It came out as a half-scream.

'Because only your mother ever called you "Larry"? Well, she's dead now. You won't admit it, but I know she is. Please, Lawrence, you've only got me left now.'

'I don't need you, Jan, I never did!' Rage flushing his fleshy features, he used an arm to lever himself upright. The bed creaked alarmingly beneath him.

That was when she hit him.

A swift downwards blow, too fast for the eye to follow. The thong of the solid rubber bank-issue truncheon was wrapped firmly around her wrist and her full weight was behind the blow. She saw it, felt it hit him square on the forehead with a thud like a gymnasium punchball. The skin split, a gash that oozed crimson, his eyes glazed. Then his nostrils gushed crimson.

His head was knocked backwards by the force of the blow, a slow-motion slump that over-balanced the flimsy bed. He rolled to the floor then lay still. Not so much as a flexing of a muscle. The only movement was the blood that flowed from him and began to form a pool in a slight hollow in the concrete beneath him.

She hit him a second time, because she had to be sure, thought she heard the skull crack. Then she was kneeling down, rummaging in the pockets of his dirty jeans. She recoiled as she found the rag he had used as a black cap, stiff with congealed nose bleed. She dropped it, tugged out an unwashed handkerchief. Something came with it, clattered and tinkled on the floor. A pocket knife; *a bunch of keys*.

Janice gave a euphoric cry, gripping the keys with an intensity that gouged her palm.

Aware of the scaffold, the noose which had been prepared for her, she got to her feet and ran to the door, breathless, fleeing from this bizarre chamber of barbaric death that reeked of madness and evil.

She tried the wrong key first, cursed beneath her breath. Her fingers trembled so that she could barely fumble the large one into the hole. It rattled, stuck. She twisted, pushed. Panicked. Oh, please God, let it be the right one!

It was, it went in. She thanked God aloud.

A click as it began to turn.

Then jammed.

She thought that she could move it again, but it was stuck fast. She tried exerting pressure, but it would not even click back to the left. Something rattled inside the lock but there was no movement, no play. She tried to pull it out — it wouldn't come. Pushed in case it wasn't in far enough. It wouldn't go.

'*Fuck you*!'

One hand clasped over the other, she grunted, impervious of the pain and the sweat that stung her eyes, distorted her vision. Gripping, twisting, imposing her will upon hardened steel.

The key snapped in the lock.

She staggered back, staring in disbelief at the useless stail between her forefinger and thumb. Pushing the broken end back into the hole, she prayed that it would miraculously join up again, that this time it would turn. She threw herself at the door; kicking, punching until her grazed feet and fists began to bleed. Screaming hysterically for somebody to come and let her out.

But only the echoes of her own voice answered her. Finally, even they died away and abandoned her to the grim silence of the execution chamber.

And that was when Janice finally snapped.

Chapter Twenty-Eight

'It could be that we're up against a serial killer.' Kent had told Detective Chief Inspector Borman. Which, with hindsight, was a foolish thing to say.

John Borman was in his late forties, hatchet-featured with rimless spectacles that gave him an unsympathetic look. He *was* unsympathetic.

'We don't even have bodies, let alone a killer.' There was a note of impatience in his tone. 'All we have are two missing persons listed. A third if you count the Welsh one. I'll check the computer if you like, come up with another dozen that have just walked out of their homes and never been seen since. No corpses, either. And there are folks who knew them, worked with them, probably had an affair with them. Would you like their houses searched, too?'

'No, of course not. I'm only interested in Prendergast. You should see him, the hovel of a house he lives in. He's a weirdo and he was shit scared when I called last week.'

Borman sighed and began slipping through a sheaf of papers, a deliberate sign of his lack of interest. 'There are a lot of weirdos in this world, Kent, and ninety-five percent of them either hate the police or are afraid of them. Because we intrude on their own strange world, harmless as it often is. You have to stick to *facts*. We're getting enough stick from the media over unsolved crimes as it is without wasting time on wild theories.'

'I still have to find the Frame woman.' Kent's ears had taken on a pinkish hue, the only visible sign that the chief's jibe had gone home.

'Then go and find her.'

'I'd like to question Prendergast again.'

'All right, contrive a second visit if you really must, though I don't see what you have to gain. He doesn't even have a record.'

As Kent left CID headquarters he determined that he would make Lawrence Prendergast his first call of the morning. And he would insist upon seeing the fellow's mother, too.

Arthur always worked at the Prendergasts' on Thursdays from April when the lawns first needed mowing right up until late autumn when he swept the dead leaves up.

Always Thursdays, never any other day of the week, because Mrs Prendergast was a stickler for routine. Her late husband had indoctrinated her that way. If it was pouring with rain, then she would telephone and ask him to leave it until the following Thursday. But she paid him well and she was the only customer on his gardening round – not that he ever let her know that.

This season, though, he had not seen much of her. She was old and ailing. She probably didn't even know what the weather was doing, stuck behind those closed curtains day in, day out.

Arthur didn't care much for the son, Lawrence; he never had. Bone idle and queer in the head, but he would never express an opinion outside his own family in case word got back. It wasn't worth risking his job; times were hard enough as it was. And he knew that Lawrence would have dispensed with a gardener if he'd had his own way.

'Me, I like a *natural* garden,' Lawrence had once commented sulkily when Arthur was weeding the small rockery around the giant monkey puzzle tree in the centre of the front lawn. Which meant everything overgrown and looking a sod of a mess. Like it was inside the house – though Arthur had only seen through the partly open door when he went to collect his wages at the end of the day.

Unable to have his way, Lawrence had retaliated by trying to make the otherwise neat garden look as much of a mess as possible without incurring his mother's displeasure. The empty margarine tubs he strewed around the garden for the birds to drink out of made it resemble the city's market square at the end of festival week. He didn't use the bird table, either, throwing scraps of food on to the lawn instead, so that Arthur had to rake them off before he could mow it. Silly bleeder!

Now, the elder son, Glenn, he was okay. He had his own farm somewhere and knew a bit about horticulture. It was a good job that he did live a distance away or else Arthur might have found himself out of a job! All the same, the chap had done a good job picking up his brother's rubbish.

It was just after nine when Arthur drove his battered Mazda pick-up into the Prendergasts' driveway.

It was going to be another scorcher. He had discarded his faded old bib-overalls for a pair of light denims; he hadn't been able to find a belt so he'd tied them round the waist with a length of baler twine. Two lengths, in fact: one on its own didn't quite meet around his pear-shaped stomach.

The lawns didn't need mowing. Not that he would've minded running the mower over them but it did seem a bit of a waste of time and it wouldn't do them any good in the long run. So he'd better find something else to do ...

He didn't want to disturb Mrs Prendergast and Lawrence wouldn't be up yet, for sure. Arthur pushed his cap to the back of his head and scratched his unruly greying hair. It was too early in the season to begin hedge cutting; like the lawns, the hedges had had their growth retarded by the drought. Even the privet hadn't grown much. And, anyway, once he started clipping, that interfering old so-and-so from next door would come to the hedge and ask him if there was any chance of him taking a foot or so off the top. Not bloomin' likely – Arthur worked for Mrs Prendergast, not that po-faced busybody.

So no hedge cutting, then. And the weeding was up to-date – he'd had to spin it out last week. Then he recalled something that the old lady had mentioned a week or two ago when she'd paid him. 'Larry has gone and dug out a pond, down behind the old shelter, Arthur. You mind you don't go and fall in it — you mightn't get out again! He's gone far too deep; if we fill it with water somebody might go and drown in it. It needs filling in a bit, reshaping — he's no landscape gardener. He says he's going to do it himself but I'm a bit worried about him, he's got high blood pressure, you know. Anyway, if he hasn't got round to it in a week or two — you know what he's like — then perhaps you could have a go at it. But I'd rather you didn't do it when he's around.'

Arthur glanced up at the house. The curtains were closed — that was no surprise — and there was no sign of any movement. They would both still be abed for a while yet, he told himself.

He went towards the shed in search of a shovel.

Glenn had decided that he wouldn't wait until Friday for his fortnightly trip over to see his mother. Because by Wednesday evening he had the feeling that something was wrong.

His mother hadn't phoned for a whole week. He had intended to visit last week but had decided that he ought to finish the meagre second hay harvest whilst the weather still held.

Mother was sometimes a nuisance with her phone calls. She always left it until late evening when Glenn was either still working or else too tired to sit by the phone chatting on and on about trivialities. He really wasn't interested in art-centre gossip.

All the same, when he hadn't heard from her for almost a week, he decided to telephone. If he phoned around ten-thirty Mother usually took the call herself on the upstairs phone. He let it ring for several minutes but it wasn't answered.

That was odd. Lawrence would have picked it up, for sure. Mother might still be downstairs watching some documentary on the television, in which case she might not have heard the phone. Lawrence was probably stuck out in that new den of his. Explanations that weren't entirely convincing.

Glenn tried twice more up until midnight. That was when

he began to worry. He thought about ringing Frank Coleman, asking him to go round and check, but Frank would undoubtedly be in bed, and a disturbance would invoke a return favour.

There was only one thing for it. The harvest was finished and Gary could see to the livestock, so he would drive over to his mother's the next morning. He'd get off to an early start, try and be there around nine.

No doubt everything would be fine, but at least it would give him peace of mind.

It was five minutes past nine when Glenn turned into the drive of his mother's house and parked behind Arthur's pickup. He couldn't see the gardener — he was probably weeding around the back somewhere. Well, everything looked pretty normal, thank God.

He decided to go indoors and check on his mother. He did not feel so uneasy now.

Kent did not have any definite plan of approach. All he would say when Prendergast answered his ring on the doorbell was that there were some further questions that he wished to ask him about the missing persons. The guy had been shit scared on Kent's last visit, and he knew how to work on him. If, at the end of the day, he'd made a mistake, then there was nothing lost. Lawrence Prendergast wasn't the type to go to the Police Complaints Commission. He was on safe ground.

It looked like everybody was visiting the Prendergasts' today, Kent thought as he manoeuvred his car alongside the Subaru. The truck belonged to a workman, no doubt, and the owner was probably doing a job somewhere about the place. The yellow Mini outside the garage was Prendergast's; he'd checked with the DVLC yesterday. Unfortunately, everything was in order — a minor motoring irregularity would have been a good starting point.

The patio door was open. He rang the bell and waited. In the distance he could hear somebody moving about upstairs. That was probably Prendergast having to get up early because a tradesman had arrived and spoiled his lie-in.

Kent's ears followed the footfalls. Hurrying. He detected

panic from the way they scampered. They were coming downstairs now. Running.

Something was definitely amiss. He tensed himself.

A figure crossed the doorway, checked and turned back. Obviously he'd seen him. An anguished face, pallid behind the growth of black beard, wide-eyed. Scared.

'Is something the matter?' Kent took the liberty of stepping over the threshold uninvited.

'My mother ...' The man had difficulty in getting his words out, held on to the doorpost to steady himself. 'Upstairs ... in bed ... *dead*!'

Stone the crows, what a Gawd Almighty mess! Arthur stood on the brink of the pond diggings and surveyed the deep, uneven crater. It was like a miniature version of that sand and gravel quarry up the road, the one that the residents were petitioning about. The quarrymen just bulldozed out as much as they could in the quickest possible time, gave no thought to symmetry; Lawrence had done likewise.

Arthur leaned on his shovel and tried to plan his best mode of approach. The banks would need building up where they had fallen in; that could best be done by shovelling up some of the bottom, patching up. It wouldn't be easy – the sand had dried and a lot of it would slide back in. Still, he had to make a start somewhere.

He jumped down into the hole and immediately sank up to the tops of his heavy working boots. He wasn't going to rush, it was far too hot for that. He'd stick at it for an hour or so, then go and take his mid-morning break early. By that time Mrs Prendergast would be up; maybe she'd think of another job. Something in the shade, with a bit of luck.

The sand was showering back as fast as he threw it up. That big hole in the top of the bank would have to be plugged. It looked blinkin' silly like it was; the liner would get all rucked up when it was fitted. What he needed was a good solid clump of damp soil; if necessary, he'd go and dig one from out of the rose beds. At that moment his shovel sank into the soft surface and became embedded in something firm. Ah, that felt just like it, a clod of wet soil beneath the powdery sand, just the job. He took the strain and lifted it out slowly.

His blade had sliced into it, speared and held it. In shape it resembled a badly inflated football. The sand which covered it began to shower away. He shook it to clear it.

And that was when Arthur came face to face with the partially decomposed, decapitated head of Prebendary Edward Wilson.

Chapter Twenty-Nine

Janice had lost all conception of time. Her stark terror had escalated to an hysterical peak; something had snapped inside her. Her collapse brought blissful oblivion.

A long time afterwards she floated up into consciousness. She sat up and stared around her in curiosity. She saw the scaffold with the rope dangling from it but it meant nothing to her. She walked around it, examined it, ran the hemp through her fingers. Her hand rested on the lever; she leaned against it. She leaped away in fright as it moved with smooth precision, opening up a yawning section of the floor only a foot or so from where she stood.

Eventually, she summoned up enough courage to creep hesitantly forward and peer down into the depths of the pit. It was dark and it smelled strongly, but she didn't mind that. She thought it might be a good place to sleep when she was tired.

Then she came upon the small room.

A man was lying on the floor in a patch of congealed blood. She shook him; he was undoubtedly dead. She rolled him over on to his back but his head just *clunked* to one side on the hard floor. He must have fallen and killed himself. She showed no emotion.

The lights were steadily dimming as the old car batteries ran down. It was easier on the eyes without that dazzling brightness; she didn't mind the dark.

Eventually she became aware that she was hungry. She hunted around for food but all she could find was the congealed spaghetti stuck to the wall. She scraped it off with her fingers and ate it. Afterwards she licked the remnants off the brickwork.

She was thirsty but she could not find any water. It wasn't desperate. Yet. Restless now, another basic need plagued her. Her fingers smoothed up the insides of her thighs, found what they were seeking. The movement of her fingertips on the soft flesh brought her pleasure. The feeling intensified as she rubbed. She was moaning softly, jerking and kicking her legs until finally she was spent.

She crawled across to the corpse on the floor. It was a pity that he was dead otherwise they could have mated. The urge was strong in her still in spite of her orgasm. With some difficulty she undressed him, then gazed upon his obese nakedness. She got astride him, became angry because the flaccid flesh would not penetrate her. She pounded his blood-stained face with her fists, raked the flesh with her fingernails, tearing off strips.

Her foot kicked against something on the floor. It was the pocket knife. She picked it up and examined it. She discovered that the blade opened out; she cut her finger accidentally on its sharpness, sucked the blood. The thick warm liquid eased her thirst a little. It was better than nothing.

She was tired now. She stretched out on the floor, using the dead man's body as a pillow. The light had almost gone; it was very restful.

She wondered why she was here but her brain was incapable of reasoning. She was in a lair of some kind, safe from whatever dangers lurked outside. She didn't mind that at all but she wished that she had some food and drink. If there wasn't any here then she would have to explore more fully, find the way out. She didn't relish leaving here — it was such a safe place.

She slept.

When she awoke she had no means of knowing whether it was day or night in the pitch blackness of her prison. But she had her senses of smell and feel; she didn't need to see.

For some time she crawled around the perimeter of the big room, examining every wall and corner by touch, probing for a hidden exit. But there was none. Eventually her circuitous tour brought her back to the small room. Her hand brushed against the knife.

Janice was still thirsty. She was also very hungry. There was a void in her stomach that needed to be filled.

She was starving and suddenly that dominated all her other needs. It began to drive her crazy in the same way that her sexual desires had before she slept.

She picked up the knife.

Chapter Thirty

Jesus God!

Kent thought for a moment that he was going to puke as he looked down into the pool foundations. He had once witnessed a decapitation, but it hadn't been anything like *this*. He was looking at a half-decomposed head, the blade of the shovel wedged firmly under the jaw, holding it upright. The cadaverous skull trailed neck sinews like spaghetti bolognese, liberally laced with tomato ketchup that had dried and solidified. The cranium was completely bald. The eyes were gone; maggots crawled from the empty sockets and the nose holes. The gaping mouth had once housed dentures, but they had fallen out, exposing rotting gums.

Grimacing, complaining: *look what they've done to me*! Seeing with those hollowed cavities, searching you out, fixing you with its dead stare. Accusing.

Kent didn't know whether it was Wilson or Deane. No photograph would bear any comparison – only the pathologist would know. All he knew was that it had to be one or other of them.

Nearby something protruded up out of the sand. He thought he had seen it all but there was more to come. A hand, the flesh peeling and revealing whitened bone, the forefinger rigid and pointing. *Are you the one who did this to me*?

Kent did not doubt that there were more bodies down there. It wasn't his job to dig them up.

A sound like distant castanets distracted him. Arthur's teeth were chattering. He cowered, wide-eyed and pale beneath his gardening grime. Glenn Prendergast stood his distance. Shock had temporarily dried his tears of grief. At least his mother had died in her bed, not down *there.*

'Where's your brother?' Kent spoke without turning his head.

'He ... he's not in the house.'

'What's in *there*?' Pointing towards the hump of the old shelter, a miniature mountain of herbaceous colours, its entrance steps just visible from where they stood.

'I don't know. Lawrence uses it for a photographic studio, a developing room.'

'Is he in there?'

'I don't know.'

Kent strode towards the flight of steps and scrutinised the heavy security door. He descended the steps not expecting to find the door unlocked. His hunch was strong, tautening his stomach muscles and prickling the back of his neck. This was the place, all right. This was where it had all happened. A hidden tomb. a place of madness and mutilation.

'Can you find me a jack hammer?' He addressed Arthur – Glenn was already starting to heave. They would be throwing up in a minute. Kent would save his vomiting for later.

'I think there's one in the truck.' Arthur turned away, stumbling in his haste. 'I'll get it.'

Glenn had backed off. He sat down on a big rockery stone and held his head in his hands. Kent decided he might as well give him something to do.

'Do me a favour, would you? Phone Rykneld Street police station, ask for CID. Tell them Detective Sergeant Kent's here and that I need some back-up. There's one body, possibly more. The murderer could be here, too.'

The *serial killer* if the corpses amounted to three. Kent hoped that Borman might come along. He wanted the DCI to see for himself.

'Thanks.' Arthur was back with the jack hammer, offering it at arm's length. His expression pleaded: *you're not going to make me go in there with you, are you*? Kent put him out of his misery. 'You can go and wait for the police, show them where to come.'

Kent began attacking the lock, decisive blows that split and chipped the heavy woodwork.

'Oi, what's goin' on?' Frank Coleman's face appeared in the gap in the hedge, a soggy smouldering cigarette end between his lips. 'Young Lawrence gone and locked hisself in, has he?'

'You could be right.' Kent concentrated on the lock. The fitting was on the verge of capitulating. A couple more blows should do it.

'Tidy bit o' woodwork, that.' Coleman was still watching. 'Shame to spoil it. Good quality oak.'

'You haven't got a torch by any chance, have you?' The door hung open. Pitch blackness lay beyond. Kent could have gone back to his car for a torch but now that he had breached the defences of this place, he could not leave it unmanned. Likewise, he could have waited for the back-up, but he wasn't going to, because this was *his*. They weren't taking it off him.

'I think there's one in the house.'

'Hurry, please.'

'Who d'you think you're orderin' about, eh?'

'I'm a police officer. Now, hurry!'

The retired undertaker shuffled away. A couple of minutes later he was back, passing a cheap torch through the foliage. 'Want me to come round?

'You can watch from there.' Kent forced the door back and shone his beam inside. His footsteps echoed as he went down the short passage, then turned sharply at right angles.

And stood staring in disbelief at the gallows.

Capital punishment had been abolished when he was a boy, but he recalled a horror comic strip cartoon about an execution. It had been just like this – a dungeon chamber, in almost every detail. The artist might have sketched it from here.

It was the stench that got to Kent first. He recognised the odour of death but there was a foulness that went beyond that: excrementa and the overpowering smell of putrefaction. He found himself gasping for breath. It was as if hands encircled his throat, were squeezing his windpipe.

Perhaps it would have been better to wait for reinforcements. No, he could not delay. Not just because of pride but for Janice Frame's sake. She was probably dead already, her corpse rotting in that pit of death and filth outside. Probably. There was just an outside chance that she was still alive. In here, somewhere. That Prendergast had not killed her yet. It was Kent's duty to make sure; the saving of lives was a priority.

'Prendergast!' Kent's voice echoed eerily, bounced back at him in a waft of decaying evil. 'Are you there, Prendergast?'

Kent stood by the pit and glanced down into the black hole. Those were bloodstains on the floor and walls: somebody had died in there. He glanced upwards as the noose moved, caught in a draught from the open door. As if it hungered for its next victim.

There had been hangings, that much was obvious. The corpses had been buried in the partly filled-in excavation outside. *Serial killers will continue until stopped.*

Which was why Lawrence Prendergast had to be stopped.

'Are you there, Prendergast?'

A host of phantom listeners whispered back, mocked him on the tail end of his echo.

You're too late, Kent. Too late.

His flesh prickled. He thought he heard a movement somewhere and swung his torch beam in an arc. That was when he picked out the open doorway of the small room. It was impossible to see inside from here.

'Mrs Frame. Janice Frame, can you hear me?' Something definitely moved in there. 'Police, Mrs Frame. You're safe.'

Kent wasn't safe; his warning system was screaming at him to get the hell out of here. He wondered how long the back-up would be. He should have brought a weapon except that he didn't have a good enough reason then. He did now.

He dismissed the temptation to go back outside. If Prendergast had the woman in there, he would kill her. He was mad. Kent had to see it through. He shone his beam again, this time looking for a weapon of some kind. There was none.

He moved forward slowly, letting his beam play on the open doorway.

'Police. You'd better come out, Prendergast.'

Something came out but it definitely wasn't Lawrence Prendergast. At first glance Kent doubted whether it was even human: a demented creature in female form, a naked, blood-smeared body. The features were a contorted mask of imbecility and ferociousness, the bloodied lips shrieking their rage from the very pits of hell itself.

Huge in stature, it was stooped, maybe deformed, a demoness that had been disturbed in its dark lair, wielding a knife that had strips of raw meat adhering to its blade. The long dark hair was matted, the eyes wide with maddened fury. Seeing him. Coming for him.

Kent dropped into a half crouch and thrust his torch arm forward, throwing the light directly into those eyes. He saw them squint, dazzled; an arm was thrown up to shield them, the charge slowed.

And in that crucial second he moved in and grabbed the knife wrist. The creature shrieked as he twisted, then loosened her grip on the hilt. He heard the weapon go clattering away, clanging against the far wall. Her sheer strength was unbelievable — and the element of surprise was gone. Her free hand struck him; she was trying to kick him. A jarring blow thudded against his shoulder as he was dragged down. His fingers brushed against a bush of coarse hair. He got a grip, pulled, felt some of them being torn out by the roots. She screamed, writhed and tried to tug herself free. She shrieked again with the pain.

They both fell clumsily. Kent tried to roll but her weight pinned him to the floor. Fingernails raked his face, then she went for his genitals, fighting by instinct, tearing his trousers open.

The torch had been knocked out of his hand and lay on the floor, flooding the far corner with its yellow light, casting shadows and silhouettes for them to see by.

She spreadeagled him, then lay across him, an animal seeking a coital position. Her face was close; he fought to turn away from her stinking breath. Her teeth snapped together and she grunted her frustration. Another inch and she would have torn his throat out.

Now he had her long, raven hair, bunching it, twisting it. She yelled again as her scalp took the strain. His arms came around her, pulling from behind. Her breasts squashed on his shirt front, she flailed him with her arms, kneeling with her legs trapped beneath her. Her mouth frothed; she threatened to drown in her own spittle.

Trying to wear her down, he dared not loose her. He must maintain his hold on her until ...

Where the fuck had the back-up got to?

He could not hold on much longer. He shifted poition, felt his foot in space and knew that they were on the brink of the pit. He tensed, he had to make one final effort. If he failed she would have had his throat out in a trice.

He relaxed, and she took the bait. That was when he straightened up, took her sideways with him felt himself starting to fall. In the same instant he let go, flung himself back, then scrambled to safety over the edge.

He heard her hit the bottom. She didn't even cry out. Then he was running breathlessly, retrieving the torch, shining it down into that rectangular hole. He knelt in case he fainted and toppled in to join her. A sprawled figure, she lay with her head to one side, her legs doubled up beneath her, her bloodied figure not moving. He peered more closely. A barely discernible movement of her chest. She was still alive.

There was no need to close the trapdoor on her.

Kent staggered, rather than walked towards the adjacent open door and shone his beam inside. And this time he could not stop himself from vomiting.

Merciful God, he thought at first that rats had found Lawrence Prendergast, gnawed his corpse and fed ravenously on him. The gashed throat grinned at him, the dulled eyes seeming to stare in surprise at this sudden intrusion of a secret domain.

She'd taken the soft flesh first, sweetbreads and tongue after the throat, used the knife to carve herself slices of belly meat, hacked away in the desperation of starvation once the blade was blunted. In some places the flesh was already decomposing, giving off that stench that had hit Kent when he first came through the door.

Prendergast had been stopped, all right.

Torch beams dazzled Kent but he didn't mind because it spared him further horrors. Leaning up against the door, he let Borman and Finch see for themselves, listened to them retch. Clifford was the only one who actually spewed.

There were other officers, too. Once his eyesight had adjusted Kent recognised a couple from Operational Support. They had come armed but they wouldn't need their guns.

'In there.' Kent pointed towards the pit under the gallows. 'The Frame woman. She's alive but I doubt she'll ever be any use again. She got the bastard at the finish.'

An ambulance was on the way. The crew would pull Janice out, take her away. For her there would be no way back; she was the unluckiest victim of all. The others had escaped in death.

Kent followed them outside. There was no point in remaining down here. Glenn Prendergast and the gardener were in the house. Kent wondered if anybody had put the kettle on.

'He would've got away with it,' Borman said, 'if the girl hadn't got him. As far as he was concerned, that is. He would almost certainly have topped himself because his mother was dead. After she died, he had nothing left to live for. If she'd died a couple of months ago then none of this would ever have happened. Strange, isn't it, how one old woman's living or dying can determine the fate of others? He wasn't clever, just lucky. In the end, his luck ran out.'

An uneasy silence followed. Kent resisted the temptation to fidget with his fingers. The DCI had given a press conference that morning. Their version would be in the early-evening editions.

'You should have waited for the OS unit to arrive.' Now came the reprimand that Kent had been waiting for.

'I couldn't risk the woman, chief.' It came out lame, sounded like an excuse. Because he was tired.

'Except that Prendergast might have escaped.'

'You said he'd've topped himself.'

'With hindsight, I said that. As it transpires, he was just taking revenge on the three people whom he blamed for making him what he was. He could've been a cannibal, another Nilsen or a Dahmer. Instead, he *created* a cannibal.' He paused, then added, 'I've arranged leave and counselling for Clifford ...'

Don't worry about me. I'll be okay.'

'I can't *make* you, Kent. It's entirely up to you.'

After Kent left the station he walked on down to the big recreation park. It was crowded – mostly mothers who had just collected their young children from school and brought them here to use up their energy on the playground. Or to feed the ducks.

For Kent the park had a special meaning. It was as if it cleansed his soul. Simplicity, doing what you wanted to do or just doing nothing, the choice was yours.

He stayed there until the evening sun had dipped behind the tall trees and most of the other people had gone. He had soaked up the atmosphere, now he let it seep back out of him. It was therapeutic, if you knew how to use it.

His thoughts returned to Brenda. He stood up and slipped his jacket back on. She would give him all the counselling he needed, and after that he would be all right.

Then he would be ready to start again.

You have been reading a novel published by Piatkus Books. We hope you have enjoyed it and that you would like to read more of our titles. Please ask for them in your local library or bookshop.

If you would like to be put on our mailing list to receive details of new publications, please send a large stamped addressed envelope (UK only) to:

Piatkus Books: 5 Windmill Street
London W1P 1HF

The sign of a good book